AURACLE

GINA ROSATI

ROARING BROOK PRESS
New York

Published by Roaring Brook Press
Roaring Brook Press is a division of Holtzbrinck Publishing Holdings Limited Partnership
175 Fifth Avenue, New York, New York 10010
macteenbooks.com

Library of Congress Cataloging-in-Publication Data

Rosati, Gina.
Auracle / Gina Rosati.—1st ed.
p. cm.
Summary: A teenaged girl who has the power to astrally project finds her body taken over by a dead classmate, and must find a way to reclaim it if she wants to save herself and her friend who is accused of murder.
ISBN 978-1-59643-710-4
[1. Astral projection—Fiction. 2. Supernatural—Fiction. 3. Best friends—Fiction. 4. Friendship—Fiction. 5. Love—Fiction.] I. Title.
PZ7.R7139Au 2012
[Fic]—dc23

2011032315

Roaring Brook Press books are available for special promotions and premiums.
For details contact: Director of Special Markets, Holtzbrinck Publishers.

First edition 2012
Book design by Roberta Pressel
Printed in the United States of America

1 3 5 7 9 10 8 6 4 2

For Jerry
My husband, my hero, my happily ever after

CHAPTER 1

Rei Ellis whispers to me as the light goes dark.

"Anna, don't go."

I turn to find him staring at me instead of the television screen at the front of the classroom where the film credits are beginning to roll.

"Why?" I whisper back.

"Because," he points his pencil toward our English teacher, Mr. Perrin, who is busy fiddling with the volume knob, "you'll get yourself in trouble."

On the way to the bus stop this morning, Rei told me he'd heard a volcano was erupting in full force on a small, uninhabited island not too far from Hawaii. He seemed to think this was a pretty cool occurrence until I got all excited about it, too.

"I'm sorry," I whisper. I can't help myself, though. This is something I've been waiting for for a long time and it's not like a major eruption happens every day here on Earth.

Three other kids are already napping on their desks, faces down on their pillow arms, so I do the same. I close my eyes and take a deep breath, brush the weight of Rei's glare off my shoulders, and exhale slowly. Inhale. Exhale. The country fiddle music from the movie soundtrack fades gradually, replaced by the thrum of my heartbeat, the rush of blood pulsing past my eardrums.

Slow, deep breaths.

In.

Out.

In.

Out.

This is not quite as simple as popping an ice cube out of a tray. I relax my mind, let it slip into that space between sleep and awake, and my body grows heavy and heavier still. The tingle starts in my toes, creeps up through my legs and past my knees. Once it's climbed the length of my spine and into my neck, my body feels so heavy it seems it will sink right through the desk chair. Now I let go, let the part of me that is matter sink while the part of me that is pure energy rises to the surface like a bubble, up and out of my body . . . free!

I do a little invisible midair spiral of happiness.

Rei has never been out of his body, at least not that he can remember, so he doesn't know just how phenomenal it feels to have this kind of freedom. I've told him it's like when you take off your ski boots after a full day on the mountain and you feel like your feet will float right up into the air, but imagine everything floats, lighter than air, faster than light. Bodies are incredibly useful for things like eating cheesecake and lifting heavy objects, but they're very slow and require lots of maintenance.

Of course, nothing is for nothing. Everything is so much more intense when I'm out of my body—the movie soundtrack is louder, the television screen is brighter, Courtney Merrill's perfume could gag a pig. And everyone is surrounded by their own true colors.

My physical eyes are like sunglasses filtering out the colors, but when I'm out here, the aura that emanates from every living thing is clearly visible to me. People, animals, even plants are each surrounded by this transparent bubble of color. Over the years, I've learned that the colors can tell me quite a bit about a person. Like right now, Rei is surrounded by this lemonade yellow, which looks nice, but it's the same shade of yellow my mom has when she's sold a house to someone and the loan falls through.

Sigh.

For a few seconds I float here, reconsidering . . . stay (and make my best friend happy) or go (and see awesome volcano eruption!). By factoring in the odds of forgiveness, I reach a decision. I absorb a bit of the excess energy floating around me and flick the pencil on Rei's desk, setting it in motion. He grabs it before it moves an inch and writes something in his notebook. *Don't be late!!!*

Like there'll be a clock where I'm going.

It takes me all of a fraction of a second to arrive in the general vicinity of Hawaii, and from here it's impossible to miss the enormous plume of smoke on the distant horizon. Aloha, volcano! I move in slowly and let my overactive senses adjust one at a time.

The air smells like thousands of rotten eggs are baking in the summer sun. I get used to it fast, though, because there is too much to see . . . orange hot lava oozes down over the rocks while clouds of black smoke billow up from the mouth of the crater and red lightning jets randomly from the smoke. The heat is intense, a blistering wind scattering ash over the surrounding ocean, and the constant sound of thunder swallows me.

How cool is this?

I am surrounded by a force that's been silently trapped for

hundreds, maybe even thousands of years. It's like a living thing, this energy, and now that it's broken free, I can feel its fury and frenzy, its exhilaration and ecstasy, random chaos unleashed. I hover high above the mouth of the crater and soak it all up.

I could use a little volcano power right now.

All too soon, I feel that tug, a force that beckons me back from any distance no matter how far—the invisible cord that connects what is ethereal to living flesh. The movie must be over and Rei is probably prodding my sneaker with his, trying to bring me back before the lights come up.

I coast back into the dark classroom so stoked with energy I feel I could light up the room like a thousand-watt bulb. As I pass Mr. Perrin's desk, the stale smell of smoke hits me so hard, I wonder if somehow I brought it back with me from the volcano. I drift back a few feet until I realize it's only Mr. Perrin's beat-up corduroy jacket, which is slung over his desk chair. Silly Mr. Perrin. Teachers shouldn't smoke. Nobody should smoke. I decide to relieve him of this burden.

Inside the brown suede side pocket, I find a crumpled pack of generic cigarettes and matches. Nobody seems to notice as one by one, the cigarettes slip out of his pocket and land quietly in the wastebasket. I move a few crumpled wads of paper around to hide them. There. Someday, he will thank me.

Over by my unconscious body, Rei is anxiously jostling my foot with his. The yellow aura surrounding him has gone neon bright. *Keep your shirt on,* I want to tell him, but he can't hear me. Nobody can hear me when I'm out here, and nobody can see me, either, unless I want them to. I flick his pencil once again before I slide back into my body.

Immediately, I start to stretch, not my physical body, but what's now back inside it. Religion teaches us that each person has a soul, a spirit, a chi. Science teaches us that everything in this universe is either matter or energy. Somewhere in the middle of all that, I'm hurrying to fuse it back together.

Rei's sigh of relief flows over me, tickling my cheek. "Have a nice trip?" he whispers. It will take me a minute to realign this energy with my body well enough to answer him, but he knows this. He's known this about me since we were four years old and my body spat me out during an anaphylactic reaction to a PB&J sandwich.

He's the *only* one who knows.

At one point, Rei thought my ability to astral project was the coolest thing ever. He used to love to hear about all the places I had been; he used to wish out loud he could come with me. And then one day when we were about fourteen, I told him about this unexplainably spectacular . . . *thing* I had found out in deep space. I'm pretty sure it was a supernova. It was this mega-explosion of dust and every imaginable color of light, but the energy that radiated from it was about a million times stronger than the sun. I came back hypercharged, like a poster child for caffeine.

Rei was not impressed.

He had been studying one form of martial arts or another since he was five, so I was not surprised when he developed an interest in the eastern philosophies. Buddha, he told me, did not approve of recreational astral projection. Buddha, I told him, was no fun. Besides, that totally contradicted what he had told me a few weeks earlier. He had said Buddha encouraged his monks to practice astral projection so when they died, they wouldn't become disoriented and automatically reincarnate instead of seeking enlightenment. When I reminded him of this, Rei added that Buddha didn't like his monks to show off.

It goes without saying that Rei thinks I astrally project to show off. So I no longer tell him about most of my trips. And that makes me infinitely sad, but I don't tell him that, either.

I hear backpacks zipping. Mr. Perrin rattles off the key points from the film and a homework assignment. Bits and pieces of disjointed conversations circle around me. When the noise finally dies down, I open one eye and peek over my arm. Rei sits on his desk with his backpack shouldered, watching me patiently.

He greets me with the tiniest of smiles.

"Late night last night, Miss Rogan?" Mr. Perrin's raspy voice comes from somewhere within the room. I consider looking around to see where he is, but my head is not quite working in tandem with my body just yet. "You'd better hurry. Next class starts in two minutes," his voice fades as he leaves the room.

Except for the ticking of the clock, there is absolute silence. I don't move, not because I can't, but because I can't do so with any measure of grace yet. The irony is that I feel like a can of warm soda that's been vigorously shaken. I want to bounce around like popcorn but all I can manage is to count silently to one hundred before I lift my head slowly so I won't see stars.

Rei offers me his hand. "Want some help?"

"No, thanks, I'm good." I push against my desk and stretch, arch my neck and my back until I'm staring at the stained, pockmarked ceiling tiles. "Thanks for waiting for me."

"Sure." Rei glances at the clock. "Take your time. We've got lunch next anyway."

"Okay." Both my feet have fallen asleep while I was gone, and I have to stomp the remaining pins and needles out of them before I dare try standing. Rei is so used to all my little quirks and quagmires that he doesn't even bother to ask.

One, two, three . . . okay, I'm up. I let go of the desk tentatively, one hand at a time.

"So, magical, mystical Auracle girl," he picks up my backpack off the floor and slings it over his own shoulder. "What color am I today?"

Rei bestowed this dorky nickname on me a few years ago when I told him that not only could I see the colors of his aura when I was out of my body, but they also changed according to his mood.

"You are . . . powdered lemonade yellow."

"And is that good?"

"Not really."

"Ha! I didn't think so. And how was your volcano?"

I can't hide my foolish grin. "It was *amazing*! It was . . . what's better than amazing? It was incredible! It was . . ."

As I struggle for just the right adjective, I see that slow, wide smile appear on Rei's face, the one I've known for nearly seventeen years. He reaches over and lightly squeezes the back of my neck, his signature sign of affection for me. "Tell me on the way to lunch."

I am forgiven.

CHAPTER 2

The cafeteria reeks of overcooked broccoli, and even Rei wrinkles his nose. Seating is scarce since we're so late, but Rei's best guy friend, Seth Murphy, is sitting at our usual table. His dust-colored backpack holds a seat for Rei on his left, and his big, grungy sneakers are propped up on the bench across from him, holding my place.

"Want me to go through the line with you?" Rei asks.

"No, thanks. I'm good."

"Yeah?" He rests his hand on top of my head and points out the obvious. "You're still shaking."

"I'm not shaking," I say as I step into line. "I'm converting."

"Converting!" Rei grins down at me. "To what?"

I poke him with my elbow. "You're the one who told me energy can't be destroyed; it can only be converted, so quit laughing at me and go eat. Seth looks lonely."

"He's fine. Do you have lunch money?"

I bounce on my toes and flex my fingers. "Yes, your mom paid me last Saturday."

Rei's parents own a health food store down on Main Street, and Rei's mom, Yumi, also offers yoga classes and Reiki, which is a hands-on healing technique. Yumi has a room set aside where I babysit the little kids while their mothers take yoga classes.

"Yeah, but did *your* mom give you any lunch money?" Rei asks as he hitches my backpack up higher on his shoulder.

"I have lunch money," I assure him. "Go sit. I'll be right there."

I read through today's menu: cream of tomato soup, garden salad, that foul-smelling broccoli comes with mashed potatoes and meatloaf. Nothing exciting. There's always the infamous Byers High Mystery Meat Sub, which is tempting, but Seth will just steal the salami out of it. Even though we're late, the line is still pretty long, which is good. It gives me time to settle into myself a little more. I bounce some more, roll my shoulders, jiggle my arms, and generally annoy the people standing close to me. By the time I help myself to a salad, garlic bread, and a bottle of water, though, I feel good. In fact, I feel great! I hand the lunch lady a five-dollar bill and stuff the change in my back pocket.

I emerge from the cafeteria line with my tray balanced high on one hand like a seasoned waitress, except now I have to sidestep Jason Trent, a senior football jock who reminds me of a Yeti. He stands right smack in the middle of the exit, why, I don't know and I doubt he does either. Of course, just as I walk by him, he decides to move and bumps into me, nearly knocking the tray off my hand. I steady the tray just before it tumbles, but the water falls over the side. I am so pumped with volcano mojo that I manage to hang onto the tray and grab the bottle just before it hits the floor.

Jason glances down and has the audacity to wink at me. What a creep! I let a tiny hiss of steam escape as I stand, then hurry off to Rei and Seth's table.

I put my tray down and sit, one foot curled up underneath me to give me a height advantage.

Rei reaches over and spears a cherry tomato out of my salad with his fork since he knows I don't like them. "*Arigato.*"

"You're welcome. Here, take this one, too."

"Okay. Hey, did I just see Jason Trent wink at you?" Rei sounds amused.

I am not. "I don't know, did you?" I shrug. "He must have had something stuck in his eye."

"Trent is a tool," Seth says as he helps himself to my garlic bread and takes a huge bite out of it before I can object.

"I was going to eat that," I tell him.

Seth sticks out his tongue and makes a big production of licking the entire top of my garlic bread before he offers it back to me. "Here you go."

"You're disgusting."

"Mmm," he takes another bite.

Rei doesn't even bother to referee. Instead, he roots through his backpack and pulls out an orange, then a slightly bruised Granny Smith apple. "I have extra fruit if you want some," he tells me as if this is something new and he doesn't bring extra fruit with him every day. He sets them on the table in front of me.

I reach for the apple, but Rei intercepts my hand with his. Crud. He pushes the sleeve of my black hoodie up slightly and measures his thumb against a bruise on my wrist before he lets go of my hand.

"Where'd that come from?" he asks casually.

"I whacked it on the dishwasher last night." Really. I did. We stare each other down until he's convinced I'm telling the truth.

"You know, if you'd get a little more vitamin C, you wouldn't bruise so easily," he says. "I wish you liked oranges."

"I like clementines better. They're easier to peel."

Rei glances at my chewed up fingernails, then rolls the apple toward me, along with a conceding smile. "Did you at least have juice with breakfast this morning?"

Did I even eat breakfast this morning? My mom was getting ready to leave for an overnight real estate convention, so things were kind of hectic. I think I ate some Froot Loops. Rei pokes his thumb through the rind of his orange, and the sweet citrus scent fills the air.

"I'm working today," Seth announces randomly through a mouthful of the pizza he's now eating.

"So you can't run with me?" Rei doesn't look up from peeling his orange, but I can tell he's disappointed.

"Nah, I need gas money and Remy offered me hours."

Seth works at Remy's Garage up on Main Street after school a few days a week doing stuff like changing oil and tires. It's a good job for Seth, who doesn't care if his hands get dirty and who'd rather tinker with cars than study.

Rei doesn't mind getting his hands dirty, either, as long as they don't stay dirty. And unlike Seth and me, Rei enjoys learning from books. He's a naturally smart guy who is in almost all advanced placement classes and who is consistently ranked in the top three students in our junior class. I don't envy him for that.

It's great that Rei is smart, but the pressure Yumi puts on him to excel is a little over the top, if you ask me. She's always had her heart set on him going to M.I.T. or some Ivy League school, but now that we're juniors, the tension between them is piling up even higher than the stack of college brochures that choke Rei's mailbox each day. Every college wants Rei. He is smart, athletic, community oriented, gets ridiculously high scores on standardized tests, and there are no compromising photos of him on the internet. His parents have saved more than enough cash to cover the cost of his undergraduate and graduate degrees, plus I'm sure he'll be offered all kinds of scholarships. The sky is the limit for his future.

The other two students who vie for those coveted top three ranking spots are Shawna Patel and Taylor Gleason. I like Shawna a lot. She's even more brilliant than, dare I say, Rei, but she's the good kind of brilliant, the kind that doesn't make me feel stupid when she talks to me. Taylor, on the other hand, just never talks to me. Well, once in the girls' room, she asked if she could borrow my lipstick, but I don't even own lipstick and she made it clear she wasn't impressed with my cherry Chapstick.

I haven't quite figured out Taylor. She gets straight A's, she dresses like she's just stepped off a magazine cover, and rumor has it she's a wicked party girl who's faster than Rei's high speed internet. I don't usually pay a lot of attention to rumors, though, because if I did, I'd have to believe that I'm kind of a snob and that Rei and I have been dating since we were in second grade, while the truth is I'm kind of shy and Rei has been not only my neighbor since I was three days old, but he's also my best friend and self-appointed ninja bodyguard.

Anyway, Taylor moved from Long Island to our quiet little town of Byers, Vermont, last summer. By the time school started in September, rumors were already flying that when Taylor was fifteen, she accused some twenty-one-year-old college guy of statutory rape. There are a dozen variations of this rumor, including one that her parents forced her to have an abortion, and there's even a rumor that she started the rumors herself to launch her popularity in a new town, because what cool kid wouldn't want to hang out with the scandalous new girl? Now she's part of a clique of other pretty, shiny girls who like to drive into the city on the weekend to party with the college kids, which leads to even more rumors, most of which I ignore. Except for one rumor I know for certain is true . . . Taylor Gleason is crushing on Seth.

Seth and I have economics right after lunch. We walk Rei to his chemistry class, then take a right and follow the slow-moving river of students to the second floor. Taylor Gleason sits at a desk by the door, surrounded by a haze of musky cologne. While everyone else in the class is dressed in jeans and hoodies, sneakers or hiking boots, Taylor wears a tight, red mini-skirt and a low-cut black tank top that shows off her cleavage. She wears no pantyhose, but her legs are tanning booth bronze, and the heels on her shoes could be classified as lethal weapons.

I take my usual seat near Teri Barnes and Lisa MacNamara. Seth goes off to sit closer to the window, which happens to be as far away from Taylor as possible. He's plugged himself into his iPod, just minding his own business, but I can hear trouble click-clacking her way toward him.

"Hi, Seth," Taylor says in her sultry voice as she puts her books down at the empty desk beside him.

He responds by turning up the volume on his iPod.

She makes a big production of settling in and crossing one leg over the other. Once she's all comfy-cozy, she sways her head dramatically to the left, sending her hair over her shoulder in a long blonde tidal wave. *Swish.* Her ear sparkles with a row of small diamond earrings.

"I like your T-shirt. Is that a skateboard logo?" She reaches over to smooth a fold of fabric with one of her long burgundy fingernails.

Seth flinches away and levels a nuclear glare at her, but this doesn't faze Taylor.

"I've watched some of your wrestling matches. You're amazing. Do you skateboard, too?" *Swish.* The hair goes back over the other shoulder.

Now she has Seth's attention. Amazing or not, I see she's lit a short fuse.

"No," he snaps much louder than necessary. "And quit stalking me!" He focuses his attention back on his iPod, a dark scowl shadowing his face.

Everyone in the class, including Mrs. Watson, heard Seth. Teri and Lisa both look back at me with raised eyebrows and 'O' shaped mouths. I shrug my shoulders in reply. Hey, at least he didn't drop the f-bomb.

Mrs. Watson ahems loudly. "Is there a problem over there, Mr. Murphy?"

"No!"

"Good, then let's begin class."

The hair swishes over Taylor's right shoulder and I glance at her just before she turns to face front.

Surprisingly, she is smiling.

CHAPTER 3

Rei and I met Seth in kindergarten, where we had a rule called Do Not Interrupt the Teacher During Story Time. I have a very vivid memory of Seth sitting criss-cross applesauce on the linoleum floor next to me, his eyes frozen on the teacher and a puddle of light yellow pee growing rapidly around him. We all kept nudging each other as we tried to scoot away, but it wasn't until there was a sizable moat of space surrounding Seth that the teacher finally noticed and hustled him off to the nurse's office to get a change of clothes.

It's always fun to remind Seth of this.

When anyone else made fun of Seth for peeing in his pants, though, Rei morphed into his ninja defender mode. Even in kindergarten, nobody wanted to mess with Rei. That was when the Anna and Rei duo became a trio, and I learned I'd rather share my cookies than my best friend.

Taylor was not a witness to the legendary Pee Incident, and I don't believe she's ever heard him burp the alphabet, either. This explains a lot. I suppose if she judged Seth by looks alone, he would be quite a catch: a six-foot-tall guy with dark, wavy hair and relentless blue eyes that girls whisper longingly about.

Pffft. Rei is just as tall, just as dark, just as handsome, plus Rei is half-Japanese, and his dark chocolate almond eyes are a welcome change in our little ethnically challenged corner of the world. Besides, my father has blue eyes. They are not my favorite.

If Taylor took the time to know Seth, she would realize he's a complicated guy who has Unresolved Anger Issues, according to the school psychologist, or as Seth calls him, That Douchebag. About three years ago, Seth came home from school to find a note from his mother which basically said she met another guy, so goodbye. Seth's reaction was to punch the nearest thing, which was a sliding glass door. This earned him seventeen stitches in his right hand and a required weekly visit to That Douchebag so he could discuss his Anger Issues.

Seth's dad is a decent guy, and Seth has an older brother, Matt, who is now in college. They dealt with this crisis the way any three abandoned men would . . . with the help of ESPN and a steady supply of take-out pizza. Rei and his parents offered all kinds of support to Seth, and I knew I had to do my part and give him more time alone with Rei. Parents are supposed to love us more than anything—more than work, more than booze, more than the Champlain Spring Water delivery guy who never seemed to mind hauling those five-gallon jugs upstairs to Seth's mom's private office over the garage. Seth deals with his rage by channeling all that energy into stuff like wrestling, lifting weights, running with Rei . . . stuff that makes him sweat and forget.

Remy's Garage is within easy walking distance from the school, so while Seth heads off to work, Rei and I ride the bus home together. It's a beautiful spring day, now well into the sixties with a light breeze and puffy white clouds.

"Isn't your mom at that real estate convention in Boston tonight?" Rei asks. Our backpacks are on the bus floor, doubling as footstools, and Rei is slumped next to me in the seat, his knees a full six inches higher than mine.

"Yup. She'll be home tomorrow at around five."

"So did she ask you to make dinner for your father tonight?"

"Yup. And isn't that just a colossal waste of time?"

"Colossal," Rei agrees as he browses through a playlist on his iPod. "So what gourmet meal do you have planned?"

"I'm going all out and making canned soup," I tell him. "Because then he can just drink his damn dinner."

"You're always thinking, kid."

"Always." I am still a little restless from all that volcano energy, so I twist up onto my knees and open the window to let in the breeze.

"So how is he?" Rei asks.

"Who? My father? He's fine." I bounce back onto my seat and resume my slouchy position.

"Fine?" Rei looks so nonchalant, just scrolling through his songs, but I know what he's thinking.

"Don't worry about it."

He doesn't look at me, but he doesn't have to; I know what he's going to say. "So you really banged your wrist on the dishwasher?"

"I really did." That's two. He usually asks me three times before he's satisfied.

I lean against his arm and stretch my neck to see what song he's looking for.

"Hey!" He shields the iPod from me. "Don't look. It's a surprise." He pulls one earbud out of his ear and reaches around me to push it into my ear. "Okay, listen to this intro." He presses play and balances the iPod on my knee. A melody of complicated but beautiful guitar notes drift into my ear as Rei slowly picks at the strings of his air guitar.

"That's nice," I say four beats too soon. The delicate music dies abruptly, and blaring metal guitar music and hoarse, undecipherable words rip through my head. I knew it! I yank the earbud out as Rei wails on the imaginary guitar strings, grinning at me.

"Nice, huh!" he says a little louder than necessary.

I snatch the iPod and spin the volume all the way down. Speed metal, power metal, thrash metal—I can't tell them apart. They all suck as far as I'm concerned, but Rei loves this stuff.

"I feel like my brain exploded and it's leaking out my ears," I inform him.

"It's probably just earwax."

"It is not." I nudge his shin with my knee.

He laughs and shakes his head when I offer him the iPod back. "You can drive."

I flip over to the playlist Rei keeps on his iPod especially for me and choose something quiet and acoustic. Rei strums his air guitar docilely beside me for the rest of the ride home.

My favorite part of Rei's house is the whitewashed porch swing hanging from the farmer's porch. We drop our backpacks and shoes off inside the front door and settle on the swing, listening to music while we wait for Rei's seven-year-old sister to get home. Saya bounces off the bus promptly at three o'clock. Other than the doctor and nurses, I was the fourth person to hold Saya after she was born. Looking down at the tiny miracle in my arms, I laid claim to her as the little sister destiny neglected to send me, so it's no surprise she runs into my arms for the first hug, then scrambles across onto Rei's lap.

Saya makes a face at Rei. "Is Seth coming over today?" I stifle a laugh. I'm not the only one who doesn't like to share Rei with Seth.

"No, he has to work." He says this matter-of-factly, but I hear that little ping of disappointment in his voice again. He stands up and flips Saya onto his left shoulder, prompting a happy little squeal. "Let's go get you a snack."

Saya hops up and down like a sparrow, waiting for Rei to peel a carrot with the green feathery leaves still attached. As soon as he rinses it off, he holds it up and asks, "Are you going to tickle me and Anna with this—do I have to cut the top off?"

"I won't. I promise."

"The eggs in the dish are hard-boiled if you want one," Rei tells me as I look through the fridge, but I don't want an egg. I want sugarsugarsugar. In the freezer, I find homemade ice pops that Yumi made out of green tea, lemon juice, and honey, which will have to do. As soon as Saya finishes crunching through her carrot, we head out to the porch and sit on the swing, sucking on our ice pops. Rei and I kick our bare feet lightly against the wooden floor to keep the swing in motion.

The breeze tickles the wind chimes and a house finch sings along. I close my eyes and listen to the harmony while sweet and sour melts on my tongue and the faint scent of cherry blossoms drifts by.

We swing backward.

We swing forward.

I still feel like I could run a marathon from all the energy I absorbed at the volcano, but it's under control. Saya is fidgety, though, and the swing jostles as she hops off. Even with my eyes shut, I can feel a familiar vibration when Rei slides his hand along the back of the swing to fill the space where Saya was. Every person's energy flows in a vibration that's as unique as their fingerprints. When Rei started meditating a couple of years ago, his vibration changed and grew stronger, calmer, more . . . comforting. I absorb what I can, let it mingle with the volcano energy still simmering within me and tuck it all away for later when I'm home, where I'll need it most.

I open my eyes in time to watch Saya disappear into the house, only to reappear a minute later with a bottle of bubble solution. "I wanna go to the falls," she pouts, and no human with half a soul could resist those blue moon eyes.

Rei and I both roll up our jeans. We head down the wooded trail barefoot, which feels nice on a warm day like today, but is actually pretty stupid because here in Vermont, we're still dealing with mud season. Saya loves the mud. She loves the way it squishes underfoot, the rude noises it makes when she moves her foot just so, the half-hidden worms that try unsuccessfully to avoid her grabby fingers. Rei and I are not nearly as excited to trek through all this mud, but as Rei points out, it's easier to wash mud off bare feet than out of the tread of our sneakers.

As we make our way through the woods, the constant, gentle whisper that lulls us to sleep each night amplifies into the sound of liquid thunder. Byers Falls is not that tall, maybe fifty feet from top to bottom, and maybe seventy-five feet long before the river flattens out again, but it's rocky and it's fast, especially at this time of year with all the spring runoff coming in from the mountains and ski resorts. Yumi and Robert drilled several lectures into our heads before they trusted us at the falls without them. The flat granite ledge at the top is big enough for about ten adults to stand on without crowding each other. Saya knows the rule. She scrambles up onto the ledge and lets Rei hang on tight to her hand.

Years of exploring through the woods and over boulders have given Rei and me the coordination of mountain goats, but we are still careful as we walk to within a few feet of the edge where it's still dry. The water is especially wild today, and the sunlight casts rainbows in the mist. Everything within a foot of the edge is glossy wet.

"Careful!" Rei warns me. I sit down, leaving plenty of space between us for Saya. She has stopped bouncing for once and sits carefully, then hastily unscrews the bubble cap so she can get down to business. She gets a huge kick out of blowing bubbles into the falls and watching them pop in the strong mist. I stretch my legs out in front of me over the ledge, letting the mist wash away the mud from my feet.

"Yuck! Whose idea was it to come down here with bare feet?" I ask. Rei and I both look at Saya, who giggles and blows another round of doomed bubbles.

Rei lies on his back with one arm supporting his head and the other arm wrapped around Saya's waist, staring up at the sky. I lie back, too, and close my eyes.

Life is good. The sunlight is warm; the breeze is cool; Saya's silky black hair is soft against my fingers. Even the icy mist that numbs my feet and the stiffness creeping up my back from the unforgiving ledge beneath us is real and good. As much as I love to astrally project, some things are just better with a body. Despite my date with a can of soup later tonight, I embrace this moment, and I feel happy.

My little nirvana is interrupted by a spastic guitar solo blaring from the pocket of Rei's jeans. "Grab her, would you?" Rei waits for me to reach for Saya, then he retrieves his cell phone and shades his eyes from the sunlight to check the caller ID before he answers it. "Hey." He rolls onto his side and mouths "Seth" to me. "Uh-huh. Okay. I don't know. Hold on." He pulls the phone away from his ear and looks at me hopefully. "Seth got out early. Will you watch Saya so we can go for a quick run?"

"No!" Saya says adamantly.

"Yes," I correct her.

"Thanks!" he whispers to me, and adrenaline is already fueling his smile. "Anna said she'll watch Saya, but we're at the falls right now. I can meet you at my house in about ten minutes."

As soon as he pockets his phone, Rei stands carefully and picks up Saya, putting her down on the other side of him, a safe distance from the falls. He keeps one hand on her shoulder and reaches his other hand down for me, but I'm already halfway up. Oh, what the heck. I let him be a man and pull me the rest of the way.

"Come on, monkey," he swings Saya up onto his shoulders. "This will keep your feet clean." I know the real reason he's giving Saya a shoulder ride is that he's in a hurry and would rather not wait for Saya to examine every rock and bug along the way. He holds on to Saya's ankle with one hand and tweaks a lock of my hair with his free hand.

"*Arigato.*"

Seth's rusty little car is already parked in Rei's driveway by the time we get back.

"Be right back," Rei tells Seth, and we head to the backyard to hose off our muddy feet. Even though Saya's feet are clean, she tags along to play in the water. By the time I've negotiated the hose away from her, Rei has already changed into his running clothes and they are gone.

• • •

While the guys are out running, Saya and I entertain ourselves. First, we leave the green carrot top under a bush for any hungry bunnies that should happen to pass through. Next, I spot Saya on her back kickovers until she gets tired and wants me to demonstrate a round off to a back tuck. And another, and another . . . until finally, and only because I was dizzy from flipping, we play Barbies.

Dolls are one of the few unpleasant things about playing with Saya. Growing up with Rei, I wasn't a big fan of dolls. My mom respected this, but my grandmother insisted on buying me a baby doll for my birthday one year. Rei and I agreed it was creepy looking, so we decided to play funeral and buried it in the woods.

Saya brings four partially dressed Barbies out to the front porch and rations them out, three for her and one for me. My Barbie is having an atrocious hair day. After an interminable time spent chatting with Saya's dolls about clothes, makeup, and which lucky Barbie will be asked to the prom by Ken, I'm relieved to see Rei and Seth turn the corner into the driveway, walking to cool down. They've both stripped off their T-shirts and they're using them to wipe the sweat off their faces and necks. Seth blots his armpits, too, for good measure.

I start to laugh because sometimes Seth just cracks me up, and I look to see if Rei is laughing, too, but now he's walking with his arms swinging down by his sides, his T-shirt dangling from his hand, and I notice for the first time that Rei is all . . . wow!

Really, *really*, wow! When did all this *wow* happen?

It doesn't feel like that long ago when we were just two skinny little kids running through the sprinkler in our underwear, right here in Rei's yard. Now I look out over this same green grass, and

I still feel like the same skinny little Anna, but Rei is now this buff, bronze, glistening *guy*!

How did I miss this?

I knew they started lifting weights in the fall. There's a room over Rei's garage that can only be accessed through Rei's bedroom, so his parents let him turn it into a weight room. I was invited to the premiere weight lifting session, but every time they benched any significant weight, they both had such strained, constipated looks on their faces, I couldn't help laughing. I think I may have taken a few pictures with my phone, too. Needless to say, I was not invited back. All winter long, I saw them wearing mostly jeans and sweatshirts, and not even the gym shorts and T-shirts they wear in P.E. class showed the extent of their progress.

Seth stops to tie his running shoe, but Rei keeps walking across the grass, laughing when he sees the Barbie dolls and the torture I've been put through. Seth stands up and takes a few running steps, and then jumps up to glomp Rei to the ground. Somehow Rei knows; maybe he feels the vibration of Seth's footsteps, because he stops short and braces himself, catching Seth's weight evenly against his back. He wraps his arm up and around Seth's neck and shoulder, leans forward abruptly and flips him over onto the grass. As Seth lands flat on his back, a quiet curse escapes with the rest of the air in his lungs.

Rei bends over him, grinning. "I thought I told you not to do that." He reaches his hand down to help him up, but even from here, I see a mischievous look in Seth's eye. Rei laughs. "You don't want to try that, either."

Seth considers this for a second, then allows himself to be pulled to a stand and swears again, earning him a dirty look. Rei's entire swear vocabulary consists of damn, hell, and a few Japanese words he won't translate for me. He gives Seth a light, open-handed smack to the forehead.

"And watch your mouth in front of the girls."

They stroll toward the front walk, familiar faces superimposed onto the smooth, chiseled bodies of Abercrombie models, although Seth's winter white skin pales in comparison to Rei's golden glow.

That foolish grin is back on my face.

"Excuse me," I call out to them. "Who are you people and what have you done with Rei and Seth?"

Rei raises his eyebrows at me, but I can tell he's pleased I've noticed the outcome of all their hard work.

Saya scrambles up the steps and leans heavily on my shoulders. "Eww! You guys smell stinky!" she complains as the essence of Seth wafts past us on his way inside the house in search of a drink of water.

"Come here, Ironman," I wave Rei over but he just stands there.

"You're sure? I thought I was stinky."

"You are!" Saya insists. "You smell like a boiled fish head!"

"No, that's Seth," I tell her. "Barbie hasn't melted yet, so I think Rei is okay." I wink at him and pat the step next to me. "Sure I'm sure. Park it!"

Rei rolls his eyes, but he sits.

"Wow," I say as I poke at his new and improved bicep. "Very impressive! So that's what you guys have been doing all winter up in your secret lair?"

Rei wipes his upper lip with his damp T-shirt to hide a small grin. "That's what we've been doing."

"Oh, what's that?" I hold Barbie up to my ear and pretend to listen. "Medusa Barbie thinks you're hot. She says she's going to dump Ken for you."

This comment goes completely over Saya's head, but Rei laughs. "Oh boy."

Seth lets the screen door slam loudly behind him and produces a loud, wet burp to further announce his presence. "Oh boy what?" he asks.

"Medusa Barbie's dumping Ken for Rei 'cause he's so ripped."

"Hey, I'm ripped, too!" To prove this point, he strikes a muscle man pose and flexes his pecs, one at a time.

Saya is silly with giggles now.

"Don't worry, Seth," Rei stands and pats him on the shoulder. "I'm sure Medusa Barbie has a friend for you, too."

Now Saya abandons me and tugs at Rei's arms. "Do it! Do it!"

"Careful, I'm all sweaty."

"But I want you to make your chichis go up and down too!" she whines.

I crack up laughing. "Yeah, Rei," I manage to get out, "can you make your chichis go up and down too?"

He pauses and grins oh so slowly at me. "The question isn't *can* I do it, the question is *will* I do it, and the answer is . . . no."

CHAPTER 4

The distance from Rei's house to mine seems much longer than the distance from my house to Rei's. It's seven o'clock, the sun is still bright in the sky, and I take my time meandering home. I stayed and watched Saya while Rei showered and changed, and Rei's parents came home from the store not too long after. Yumi invited me to stay for dinner, but they were having something starring tofu, which is not my favorite.

Besides, I have a date with a can of soup.

The front door creaks slightly when I open it. I smell him before I can see him: that pungent stench of stale alcohol mixed with sweat that seeps from every pore in his body and pollutes the air in my house. I try not to breathe too much. He's slouched on the cracked black vinyl recliner in his usual stained boxers and T-shirt, and the bottle beside him is already half empty. Even though I can't see his colors right now, I know he sits inside a narrow haze of tarnished gray.

There's no indication he heard me or saw me come in; his attention remains fixed on the soft glow of the television. I slip past him unnoticed into the kitchen and root around the cabinet for a can of soup. I would prefer the chicken noodle, but that's a little too chunky for him. I go with the cream of chicken, open the soup can, and dump the contents into a microwavable bowl.

He never once looks at me during the two minutes the microwave hums, but the ding gets his attention. The face that turns to me is blotchy and bloated and tries to focus on me with red-rimmed eyes. " 's 'at for me?" His voice is rusty, and I realize these are probably the first words he's spoken all day.

"Yes."

He turns back to the television and reaches for his glass. "I'm not 'ungry."

No surprise there.

"I'll leave it here in case you change your mind."

No response.

After I pour half the soup into a bowl for me, I grab a can of soda, some saltines, and a spoon, then disappear into my room, locking the door behind me. Fresh air! If I'm lucky, I'll only have to make one trip to the bathroom before I go to bed.

My mom tells me my father wasn't always like this. In my bookcase, between the box where I hide my life savings and a stack of travel brochures I've downloaded, there's an album of all my favorite photos. Tucked in among the many snapshots of me with Rei and his family, there's a picture of a handsome guy with smiling blue eyes, wavy blond hair, and a construction worker's tan, lean body holding a toddler-sized me on his shoulders. This was my father.

According to my mom, he was sweet and funny and a great kisser, which is way too much information. She met him when she started selling real estate. He worked on the subdivision she was hired to sell, and it wasn't long before they got married, moved into this little fixer-upper house, and had me.

Four years later, some scaffolding at work broke, and my father fell more than twenty feet, landing flat on his back. I was too young to remember much, only that my mom shushed me a lot after that, and he would yell, "Shut that kid up!" whenever I cried. The doctors weren't sure if he would ever walk again, but he surprised them all. He can make it from his bed to the toilet to the liquor cabinet to his recliner just fine before the booze kicks in.

As long as I don't provoke him, he's fairly calm. Sometimes he may grab my arm and not realize how tight he squeezes, but he's hit me only once. When I was thirteen, I took a pre-algebra class that was way over my head. I was in my room studying for a test, and he was out in the living room hollering for me to go get him a bottle from the garage. I was stupid. I ignored him, but he just yelled louder until finally, I came storming out of my room. I should have known better than to mouth off to him, especially when my mom wasn't home. I never even saw it coming: he backhanded me across the face so fast, I fell and whacked my forehead against the edge of the kitchen counter.

I knew that crying would only make him madder, so I ran as fast as I could through the front door and down the path to . . . where else? I didn't even have shoes with me. I had no idea how much I was bleeding until I got to Rei's house and saw the look on his face. We had to take an entire roll of paper towels and a plastic trash bag in the car with us on the way to the hospital. It was only because I lied to the doctor and the bruise on my cheek hadn't fully bloomed that nobody called DSS and reported it as child abuse.

Yumi had a very long talk with my mom after that, and my mom told me she made my father promise he would never hit me again.

But grabbing isn't hitting, and this is what I keep trying to explain to Rei. If I showed the bruises on my arm to our school counselor, at best, I would end up with the weekly appointment right after Seth's and at worst, I'd end up in foster care. Either way, it's not worth it. I can handle being grabbed. I can hide the bruises with long sleeves, and in a year, I'm out of school anyway.

Once Rei leaves for college, I'm not sure what I'll do. I'd like to go to college, but it's expensive and I don't even know what I want to major in. I'll probably take a year off, find a full-time job and a couple of roommates to split an apartment so I can save some tuition money. If there's one thing I admire about my mother, it's that she doesn't depend on a man to support her.

I blow on my soup while I wait for my computer to start up. In fairness to my mom, she does make sure I have what I need to survive . . . a computer with high-speed internet, a cell phone, and my iPod. As soon as I log on, my computer chirps at me.

StringRei: ohai
Auracle: ohai
StringRei: did you make his soup?
Auracle: cream of chicken
StringRei: did he eat it?
Auracle: what do you think?
StringRei: i think saya wants you to sleep in her top bunk tonight
Auracle: tell saya i love her, but i'll be fine
StringRei: did you hit yourself on the dishwasher again tonight?
Auracle: no, but the night's still young
StringRei: how's the homework going?

Auracle: i just set my chem book on fire. got any marshmallows?

StringRei: haha—you need help?

The key word here is *need*, and yes, I do need help. Rei talks me through a few chemistry problems that require calculating something about a solution prepared by dissolving this in that, until I excuse myself to go stick a fork in my eye. After chemistry, we chat off and on while I browse the internet for cool places to visit later tonight—Great Barrier Reef, Madagascar, or hmmm . . . I wonder if that enormous ice castle in Sweden has melted yet. Rei knows I still go astral exploring, but I don't share my plans with him because I wouldn't want him to think I'm showing off.

At about ten thirty, I hear my father stagger into the bathroom and throw up, gagging and choking on whatever is coming out of him. I plug in my earbuds and turn up my iPod as loud as I can stand it.

StringRei: i'm working on a new song.

Auracle: cool. acoustic or electric?

StringRei: acoustic

Auracle: nice! what song?

StringRei: it's a surprise.

Auracle: and you know how much i love surprises.

StringRei: :)

Auracle: will you call my cell and wake me up tomorrow ^o^

StringRei: sure. go brush your teeth before you sign off.

Auracle: k, hold on

My father's in pretty much the same position I left him, and the soup is still on the counter untouched. I'll deal with that tomorrow. In the bathroom, I can't pee until I wipe the blood-tinged bile off the toilet seat. I use a new paper towel to clean up the mess that's splattered on the floor and against the wall. After I scrub my hands in the hottest water I can stand and brush my teeth, I tiptoe back into my room, lock the door, and quietly push my desk chair up under the doorknob.

Auracle: thanks. my chair is against the door.
StringRei: what took you so long?
Auracle: had to clean paternal puke off toilet seat, wall, floor.
StringRei: >o<
Auracle: haha
StringRei: my phone is on all night, call if you need me.
Auracle: thanks. i'll be fine.
StringRei: see you tomorrow.
Auracle: kbye
StringRei signed off at 11:14 p.m.

I sign off and shut down my computer. Outside my bedroom door, the television drones on. It will stay on most of the night, until maybe four in the morning when my father will probably vomit again, stumble into bed, and pass out until about noon tomorrow, then get up and open a new bottle for breakfast.

In sixth grade, a police officer came to our class to teach us about the dangers of drugs and alcohol, and that's when I realized my father is an alcoholic. When I shared this epiphany with my mom, she immediately defended him. "It's not his fault," she said. "He's sick."

When I think of sick people, I think of the flu, strep throat, cancer. I don't think of alcoholism.

"That's a lot of crap!" I told my mom one day when I was hiding a particularly big bruise on my upper arm. "He's not sick. He has a choice. He chooses drinking over us."

"Alcoholism is a disease, honey; he can't help it. His father was an alcoholic, too."

"So, what, you're telling me it's genetic? That this is what I have to look forward to?"

"I'm sure this won't happen to you."

"But you can't be certain."

"He was fine before the accident, but he was in a lot of pain after, and the doctors wouldn't give him any more medication. If they had just helped him manage his pain, he wouldn't have had to self-medicate."

I know she still loves him; I get that. And I know she loves me, too. I just hate that she makes all these excuses and never even tries to fix the problem.

"Then just stop *buying* it for him!" I told her. "Then he'll *have* to stop drinking or he'll have to go out and get it himself!" This seemed like a simple and logical plan. She stops buying it, he stops drinking, and we all wake up the next morning as a functional family.

"Anna, honey, it's not that simple. There are withdrawal symptoms. They can be very uncomfortable."

Uncomfortable. Well, we wouldn't want that now, would we.

I lie in bed wondering what new song Rei is learning on his guitar and whether he's wearing a shirt now or . . .

Hello, Anna, interrupts my conscience, *this is Rei you're thinking about: your neighbor and best friend since the beginning of time. Why do you care if he's wearing a shirt? You're not checking him out, are you? Seriously! How would you feel if you thought he was checking YOU out?*

Well, actually, I'd feel kind of flattered.

And *of course* I'm not checking him out, because that would just be . . . awkward. Although how easy would it be to slip out of my body and float over and up through his bedroom window, unseen, unheard . . . uninvited.

I haven't shown up in Rei's bedroom unexpectedly since we were little and privacy wasn't a big deal for us. But after seeing him in all his new, ooo-la-la musculature this afternoon, it's clear to me that he's all grown up now, and the thought of just popping in on him is inexcusable.

But what if I didn't peek in? What if I just stayed outside the window by the weeping willow tree and listened to his song? What would Miss Manners say about that?

Gentle reader, she would tell me, *you are a creeper.*

I feel it starting—the physical sensation that precedes all my trips. The tingle starts down at my toes and climbs up my legs and into my hips. By the time it curls up my spine and I feel myself beginning to detach from my body, I realize I have choices to make, too.

CHAPTER 5

When my cell phone rings the next morning, I answer it with a relatively clear conscience. I did leave my body last night, but I decided to take the high road to Madagascar instead of the low road to Rei's bedroom.

"Baby lemurs are adorable!" I greet him. "I want one!"

"Madagascar?" he guesses, then sighs. "You're incorrigible."

He has no idea.

Since Seth has gas in his car, he drove to school this morning instead of taking the bus with us, so I don't see him until third period, which is our P.E. Adventure class. P.E. is the only class I have with Rei. Seth is also in this class, as well as my friend, Callie Stavros. I love Callie because she's almost as short as I am and in the ten years I've known her, she's never asked why I don't invite her to my house.

Today, we are finally doing the challenge course, which means we get to climb the rock wall to a platform, jump over to the trapeze, swing over to a balance beam that's suspended about twenty feet in the air, walk across it, then jump off and our belayer lowers us down. How fun is that!

I walk to the locker rooms with Seth. By the time I've switched my jeans for a pair of shorts and get to the gym, Rei is having kittens because Callie won't let him hold my rope.

"Rei, we get graded on our ability to maneuver the course *and* belay. If you won't let me hold the rope for Anna, how am I supposed to learn this? It's not like I can hold your weight or Seth's." Callie is busy strapping herself into a harness as she talks.

"Well . . . but . . ." Rei isn't comfortable with this at all. "You know you need both hands on the rope at all times."

"God, Rei," Callie laughs, "don't worry about it!"

Seth snorts. "That'll be the day."

I struggle with my own harness, mostly because the leg loops are too big on me, even when I adjust the straps. Rei comes over and squats down in front of me to make sure I'm putting it on right. "Did you double back your buckle?" he asks as he fiddles with my straps. "Do you want me to hold the rope for you?"

No, I did not double back the buckle and yes, I do want him to hold the rope for me, because I trust him and I know he would never let me fall. But the P.E. teacher assigned Callie as my partner and Rei can't hold my rope forever.

"No, she's right. How are we supposed to learn this if we let you and Seth do all the work? Plus, what's the big deal? You never worried when I did gymnastics."

"I didn't worry as much," he corrects me.

"Are the legs okay on this? They feel kind of big."

"It's as tight as it will go." Rei tugs at the harness leg loops and I am suddenly aware of his hands on my thighs.

"Okay, then, it's good!" I tell him and step back, dangling the carabiner in front of him. "Which doohickey do I attach this to?"

He takes it and clips it on, gives the rope a tug, then gives me a stern look. "You are not Spider-Girl."

"Yes, Anna, you *are* Spider-Girl!" Callie insists. "Now go climb that wall."

Rei clears his throat. "Helmet?"

"Oh, right. Thanks."

It is much more fun to scale the wall if I ignore all the bickering going on below me. Callie good-naturedly blows off all of Rei's suggestions and Seth just laughs at both of them. My only contribution to the conversation is to yell "Slack!" over my shoulder until I finally reach the platform that hangs twenty feet in the air.

Everyone looks smaller than me from up here. I like it.

"You sure you've got her?" I hear Rei ask Callie for the bazillionth time.

"No, I am totally going to drop her on her head," she tells Rei and then she yells up to me, "Let's go, itsy-bitsy Spider-Girl. Jump!"

I decide not to torment Rei with daredevil antics, so I trapeze over to the beam, walk across, and Callie lowers me safely to the ground in a most unadventurous way.

"Was that fun?" Rei asks as soon as my feet touch the ground.

"Yes!" I unclip the carabiner. "It was awesome! I wish I could take rock climbing lessons."

He sighs. "I was afraid of that."

"Ha. Don't worry. I can't afford it."

After Callie, Rei, Seth and the rest of the class have had a chance to maneuver the course, I hang up my harness and we're ready for lunch. "I just need a quick shower," Rei says. "I'll meet you down there."

He hasn't even worked up a sweat during class, but since he doesn't give me any crap about *not* showering, I just nod and head down to the cafeteria. By the time I get through the crowded lunch line, Rei is already sitting at the table, his hair tousled and damp.

There is a familiar buzz in the cafeteria, that collective conversation you hear no matter what day it is. I tune everyone but Rei and Seth out and concentrate instead on dissecting a tomato slice with my trusty spork. As I add another slimy seed to the pile, Rei asks Seth to text him about something later, but then there's one of those long silences that makes you look up just to see if they're both still there.

Seth is frantically searching through his backpack.

"What are you looking for?" I ask.

"My cell phone," Seth says. "I remember putting it in my pocket this morning, but now it's not there."

Rei pulls his own cell phone out of his back pocket. "I'll call you."

"Yeah, but I might have left it on vibrate."

"We may still be able to hear it." Rei presses Seth's speed dial and we listen intently to Seth's backpack, but there are a hundred and fifty noisy kids in this cafeteria with us. To make matters worse, two tables over, Taylor Gleason and her friends are laughing so hard they are choking on their own spit.

Seth shakes his head in frustration. "I don't hear it. Maybe I left it in the car."

Rei snaps the cover onto his lunchbox and bites his apple hard between his front teeth, leaving it there while he jimmies the box back into his crowded backpack.

"Let's go," he says through the apple.

The parking lot for juniors is two lots away from the school. The sky is a deep, cloudless blue, and the sun is so hot, I'm glad we left our hoodies in our lockers. Rei and Seth naturally walk faster than me, and I fall several steps behind.

I never really noticed it before, but Seth is a sagger. It's not so hard-core that his pants are ready to fall off, but they are low enough that I can see he's wearing red and green plaid boxers. Festive. Rei's jeans fit him much better; in fact, they make his tush look kind of . . .

Oops! Rei turns his head back toward me and I look up just in time. He grins at me, hooks my T-shirt sleeve with two fingers, and pulls me up alongside him. "C'mon, pokey."

We search Seth's car, through a jumble of grease-stained napkins, straw wrappers, empty Coke bottles, petrified french fries, and a tattered copy of *Muscle Mustangs and Fast Fords* magazine. No phone. I do find an overdue library book under the passenger seat.

"Hey, I was looking for that!" I hand him the book and he slams the door, shaking his head. "Well, that sucks."

"I'm going to call you again. Maybe we're just missing it." Rei dials, then clicks the switch to speakerphone.

It rings once, twice, then a girl with a singsong voice answers. "Hellooo-ooo."

"Hi!" Rei looks all happy. "Great! You found my friend's phone."

We hear several girls giggling, then silence as they hang up on us. Rei frowns as he snaps his phone shut.

"That's not good. Let's go report it missing at the office."

We head back across the parking lot and into the school. While Seth and Rei go into the office to fill out the paperwork, I wait in the hallway, sizing up every passing girl to see who looks guilty.

Seth comes out and stands beside me, looking hopeless.

"My dad's gonna kill me. That's the third phone I've lost since September."

Rei squeezes Seth's shoulder. "Don't worry, we'll get it back.

Hey, does that phone have a GPS on it?" This question triggers a long techno babble discussion about electronics and satellites and other stuff I have absolutely no interest in.

While they're talking, Taylor Gleason and her posse sashay by in their impossibly high heels, surrounded by an air of perfume and popularity. Except for Taylor, I've gone to school with these girls since kindergarten. They've never been rude or mean to me, but they must have been born cool and I might as well be invisible to them. As they walk down the hall, I watch them and wonder how many dollars these girls must spend on their trendy clothes, shoes, hair, nails, make-up, jewelry, and designer handbags. It must be thousands.

Uh-oh! Taylor's turned to look at me, so I shift my eyes quick over to Seth and Rei and nod like I totally agree with whatever it is they're talking about. When I sneak a glance back at Taylor, I realize she wasn't even looking at me; she was looking at Seth. Her smug little smile tells me exactly who has Seth's phone.

CHAPTER 6

I don't tell Seth I think Taylor stole his phone for the simple reason that I've got zilch for evidence. Besides, even after that long conversation with Rei, Seth is still so grouchy, I head off to economics without him. The first thing I notice when I arrive is Taylor's denim miniskirt is so short, her panties are visible now that she's sitting down. Classy. As soon as Seth walks in, she flashes him that arrogant smile again, which just cements my suspicion that somewhere in that fancy purse she totes around is Seth's phone. I suppose it would be easy enough for her to get her hands on his phone while we were in P.E. class since the school won't allow us to put locks on the lockers, although I've underestimated her level of audacity . . . sneaking into the boys' locker room is really bold.

Seth picks a desk far away from Taylor, and he spends most of the class cleaning car grease from underneath his fingernails and drumming his pencil against his thigh. As soon as the bell rings, Taylor dawdles by the door, waiting for Seth.

"Are you going to . . . ?" she begins, but he hurtles past her and he's gone, swallowed up by the crowd in the hallway, before she can finish the sentence. She swishes her hair over her shoulder and stares after him like a hunter watching her prey escape.

Lisa winks at me once Taylor's gone. "She doesn't seem to be taking the hint."

"Is it that obvious?"

"Totally!" Teri says.

"I don't get it," I say as I shoulder my backpack. "What does a girl like Taylor see in a guy like Seth?"

"He's hot," Lisa blurts out.

"You think so?" I ask.

"Anna," Teri says, "just about every girl in school thinks so, but you."

"Okay, well, maybe he's not bad looking, but I know Seth better than most. Maybe I just see him a little differently than other girls do."

"Maybe," Lisa agrees. "But you know Rei even better."

"Yeah, so?"

"So in case you haven't noticed," Teri winks at me, "Rei's hot, too."

Lisa and Teri head off to their lockers, leaving me to ponder Rei and Seth's hotness factor and the odds that they will someday abandon me in favor of real girlfriends.

It *would* be nice if Seth had a girlfriend. I understand he has trust issues because of his mother, but I hope he realizes not every girl is out to hurt him. And I hope he finds a girl who likes his personality and not just his looks, someone who can deflect all that anger and earn his trust, someone who likes sports and fast cars and is willing to share her mystery meat sub with him. Plus if Seth had a girlfriend, he wouldn't monopolize so much of Rei's time.

It would *not* be nice if Rei had a girlfriend. It's bad enough to be the third wheel when Seth is around, but if Rei started dating someone, where would that leave me? No girl would want me hanging around with them.

I was a little nervous last year when Callie asked Rei to be in the school talent show with her. Callie has an amazing voice. Rei is an amazing guitarist. I babysat for Saya while they practiced over at Rei's house for what seemed like hours. I kept waiting for Callie to declare that she and Rei had perfect harmony, but she never did.

I have so little confidence in my singing voice that I even lip sync the words to "Happy Birthday." I wish I could sing, not so I could be in the talent show, but it would be fun to sing with Rei once in a while. When I finally confessed this to him, he shrugged and squeezed my neck like he does. "We're like yin and yang, Anna," he told me. "I'm the song and you're the dance."

Which made me feel pretty special until I realized it's hard to dance without music.

Rei is waiting for me at my locker.

"So, how do I prove Taylor Gleason has Seth's phone?" I ask him as I swing open the door.

He reaches over my head into my locker and holds my slanting book pile upright so I can fit my economics book in. "Why do you think she has it?"

"Thanks. Because she kept staring at him in the hall and in economics she was smiling this creepy little smile." I turn and demonstrate the creepy little smile for him.

"That is creepy," he agrees.

"And her skirt is so short, I can see her underwear."

"So what you're telling me is you've got nothing."

"Exactly," I yank my Spanish book toward me. "I have absolutely no evidence."

"I have trig with her next."

"Good. Shake her down and get a confession out of her."

"Maybe I'll just try to confirm what you said about her underwear."

I shove his shoulder. "Pervert!"

Rei laughs and absorbs my shove. "I have to be to aikido by four. Want to walk over to the store with me and I'll drive you home?"

"Sure. I'll meet you back here."

"Pink." Rei says forty-five minutes later as he comes up behind me.

"See?" I say without turning around. "Here's where I know you're full of crap. They're black."

"There's Seth. Let's go ask him."

Seth looks pissed! Even from fifteen feet away, I can see his barometer rising. Rei sees it, too.

"Hey, what's up?" Rei asks, all thoughts of Taylor's panties long forgotten. We both follow Seth's glare to a note taped to his locker. The letters on the note have been cut from various magazines and pasted together in a ransom-note style.

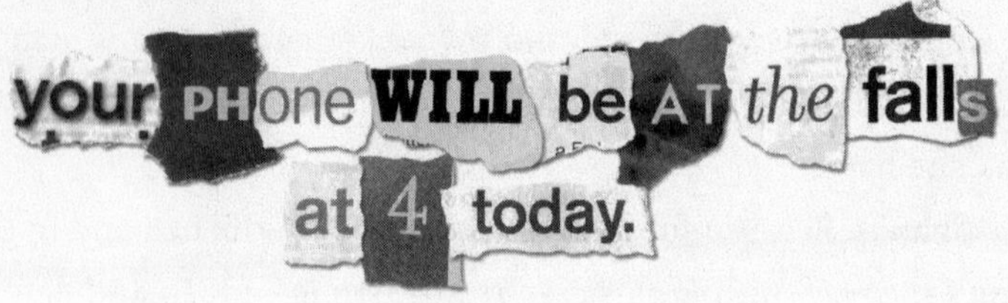
your PHone WILL be AT the falls
at 4 today.

"Wow," I say to Seth, "this must be your lucky day. Guess your dad isn't gonna kill you after all."

Seth scowls at me as he crushes the note in his hands and flings it onto the mountain of trash that already exists in his locker. The entire row of lockers rattles as he slams his door shut.

"What idiot does crap like this?" Seth demands to know.

"I think it's Taylor, but that's just my gut feeling."

"I bet Anna's right," Rei agrees and turns to Seth. "I'll skip aikido today and go to the falls with you."

"That's stupid! I can handle her myself."

"I *want* to go, Seth. I don't care if I miss class." He glances at me to see if I'm going to call him on this most blatant of lies.

"I'll go," I offer. "I think an afternoon at the falls with Taylor and Seth would be very entertaining."

Seth gives me a filthy look. "I can handle her myself, thank you both very much."

We leave school and head to the parking lot together, listening to Seth vent about what a bitch he thinks Taylor is. Rei and I both know Seth's dad won't be *that* upset about the lost phone. What we don't know, though, is how well Seth will control his temper once he's face-to-face with Taylor. We exchange troubled looks behind his back.

"You're sure I can't go with you?" Rei asks as Seth opens his car door.

"Positive! And don't even think about just showing up," he warns us both. Rei and I stand there helplessly as he slams the car door, guns the engine, and peels out of the parking lot.

"Well, this sucks," Rei observes as he watches the dust settle in Seth's wake.

I sigh. "I know, but he's right. He should be able to handle this himself."

Rei looks unconvinced as we head toward Main Street. "I don't know. I keep thinking about that rumor when she first moved up here."

"Which one? There were dozens of rumors."

"Do you know Zack Gillespie?"

It takes me a few seconds to put the name with the face. "The guy with all the freckles from wrestling?"

"Yeah. His brother goes to the same college as the guy she accused of raping her. He says she lied about her age and swore to the guy she was on birth control pills. When she found out she was pregnant, she told her parents she was raped."

"But she wasn't."

"Well, technically, she was. She was fifteen. The legal age in New York is seventeen."

"Oh, right. And how old was he?"

"Twenty-one."

"Oh." I get it now. "So technically, his life is screwed."

"Completely. Her father knew a really good criminal lawyer who made sure this guy got kicked out of school and now he's a registered sex offender."

"Ah! So we can hunt him down on an internet map and there'll be a little black sex offender cloud over his house."

"Exactly."

"Hmm." I mull this over as we approach the intersection of Main Street and take a left, heading toward Rei's parents' store. "You know, I'm having a hard time mustering up any sympathy for either of them."

"I know. Me, too. But that's why guys shy away from her."

"See? And I always thought it was because she wore too much perfume. So you believe Zack?"

Rei thinks for a minute. "Yeah, I do. I'd better skip class and meet Seth at the falls."

"I thought you were testing for your next level soon."

"I am."

"Then you really shouldn't skip. Besides, he'll kill you if you show up."

"So then he kills me. I just don't trust he can control his temper around her."

"Rei," I turn around and walk backward. "Go to class. That's important. I'll go to the falls and make sure they both behave themselves. I have nothing else to do today."

"He'll just get mad if he sees you. I'd rather he's mad at me than you."

"He won't see me."

Rei looks at me for a long minute, then shakes his head. "No, that's not a good idea."

"Why?"

"Because it's the middle of the day, Anna. You can't just . . . no, it's a bad idea."

"Okay, fine." I shrug, turn around, and keep walking. "You go to class. Seth can figure out what to do about his phone. And I'll just go home."

"Now you're mad."

"I'm not. I promise." I stop and hold out my pinkie finger out of habit, and he locks his pinkie finger and his eyes with mine. He's looking for assurances that I'm not mad, and I'm not really, more annoyed. I release his finger and start walking again.

"Rei," I ask gently, because I know how he can get sometimes, "Remember when you used to think my trips were kind of cool?"

"Yeah, and I used to think my Power Rangers underwear were cool, too."

He says this with such a straight face, I crack up laughing. "But they *were* cool, especially when you wore that red cape with them." There, I got a little smile out of him. "You used to think what I did was magical," I remind him.

"It is, Anna. It's cool and you will always be that magical, mystical, Auracle girl who impresses the hell out of me because I can't figure out how you do it."

"Really? I impress you? Wow! That's hard to do," I tease him.

"The point is, the more I learn about physics, the more I realize what you do is also really dangerous."

"How is it dangerous?" I ask. "When I'm out there, I'm all energy. There's nothing to hurt."

Rei's parents' store is about fifty feet away, landmarked by a red awning under the rustic wooden sign that says,

Yumi's Market
Organics ~ Reiki ~ Yoga

He sees it and he takes my hand to stop me. "This is not textbook physics, Anna; this is metaphysics. And yes, there's plenty to hurt," he insists. "You tell me you can move through space at light speed. What if you get sucked into a black hole? Nothing comes out of a black hole."

"God, Rei," I would laugh if he didn't look so serious, "what are the chances of that happening?"

"I don't know, but do you want to take the chance? And what if there was a fire in your house? You'd come back and find yourself cremated. What if your father came in your room while you were gone and you didn't come back in time?" His eyes leave mine for a flash second and travel up to the fine white scar near my hairline.

"I've already told you. If something bothers my body, I feel a tug right here," I point to my belly button. "And I know you hate my father, but . . ."

"I don't hate him. I just don't trust him," he points out.

No, I'm pretty sure he hates him, and there are days when I

hate him, too. But at the end of the day, he's still my father. Even though I barricade my bedroom door, I don't believe he would seriously hurt me on purpose.

Still . . .

Rei brings up logical points. I *know* there are risks when I leave my body, but I don't see how it is any riskier than crossing the street. The cord that tethers me to my body is like an emergency switch, and I trust I'll feel that tug if I'm in any kind of danger.

I don't know if my ability to astrally project at will is a talent or if I'm just a freak, but I consider it a gift. How else would I get to visit so many places, some of which I couldn't get to even if I had a zillion dollars? And I love that rush, that feeling of euphoria that comes with traveling at the speed of light. I've been coming and going for so long, I can't imagine what my life would be like if I were stuck in this body with no means of escape. I'd probably go insane from claustrophobia. This is not something I want to do; it's something I *need* to do, but it's not a bad need . . . not like my father needs to drink. This is different.

Isn't it?

"I'm sorry," I say, because I don't know what else to say. Knowing that Rei doesn't approve of my favorite hobby makes me sad, and I hate that every trip is peppered with guilt. He still has my hand in his, and he squeezes it before he lets go.

"You don't have to apologize for your father."

"I'm not. I'm just . . ." I look up at the signs on the windows that advertise so many good and healthy things within. I know Rei is only looking out for me, trying to protect me, just like he always does. I just feel that sometimes he's trying to protect me from . . . me.

CHAPTER 7

Rei would leap over tall buildings to get me to eat healthy stuff, so my brilliant plan to change the subject is to suggest we get some fruit salad from his parents' store. Yumi is at the cash register ringing up one of her infamous Bento boxes for a girl named Chelsea, who is in my chemistry class. "Hey, you two!" she calls out to us in her singsong voice that's laced with only a trace of an accent.

Yumi's store is a gold mine. Not only is it an easy walk from the high school, but Yumi is a fantastic cook, she's very artistic, and she knows what kids like to eat. We like to eat food that is *kawaii*. Even I will eat raw fish as long as it's cute. Yumi makes these adorable Bento boxes where she shapes rice, chopped vegetables, nori, fish, all kinds of things, into adorable little animal faces. Who wouldn't want to eat a happy panda rice ball?

"That's three dollars and twenty-nine cents," Yumi tells Chelsea, "from five." *Cha-ching!*

Rei immediately heads around the counter and helps himself to a disposable but still environmentally safe bowl, then fills it with fruit salad.

"You want chopsticks or a fork?" he asks me.

"Surprise me," I tell him.

He grins and reaches for the chopsticks.

We have successfully changed the subject. During the ride home, Rei plugs his iPod into the car speakers and we crank up the volume. Yumi does make the best fruit salad. While Rei drives, I chopstick up chunks of pineapple and honeydew and feed them to him because those are his favorites.

"I'll call you tonight," he tells me when he drops me off in my driveway.

"Okay, thanks. Have fun in class."

My father is on his recliner, collecting dust. The bottle is down about six inches, which means that he's still fairly sober by my standards, but I know better than to tickle the dragon. I slip past him, unnoticed, grab a can of soda from the fridge, and lock myself in my bedroom. It's three-thirty. I'm pretty sure the note said she'd meet him at four o'clock.

I didn't tell Rei I *wouldn't* go. There were no promises requested and no promises offered. He just didn't think it was a good idea. Okay, so maybe he said it was a bad idea. But still . . .

I change into a pair of gym shorts and my favorite black T-shirt, the one with the puddle bunny on it, and I pull out the hair tie that holds my ponytail. My door is locked, and I push the desk chair up under the knob. My alarm clock is set just loud enough to remind me that I need to return before my mom gets home from her business trip, but not so loud it would draw my father's attention. The entire conversation with Rei has sucked away the joy that usually accompanies me on my trips. I punch at my pillow to get it just right, and shimmy around until I'm comfortable. There's a water stain on my ceiling that's shaped like a turtle. I stare at it for a while to relax.

Within about ten minutes, the tingle has spread from my bare toes up through my legs and into my back. As soon as I hear a slight buzzing sound, I know I'm ready. I feel myself detaching, releasing, lifting, and I'm free, floating over my body. If anyone ever walked in on me, it looks like I'm peacefully sleeping. Before I leave, I check around my house: the stove is off, and my father is in his usual catatonic state. Rei's just got me paranoid, I remind myself. Everything will be fine. It's time to see what Taylor's up to.

Scientists claim that the fastest thing in the universe is light, which travels at about 186,282 miles per second. I've never clocked myself, but I know I'm faster. All I really have to do is think of a place and I'm there. The waterfalls are still rushing wild with spring runoff, so loud it sounds like a supersonic jet is flying ten feet over my head. Nobody's here except the trees and the bushes, which have stood patiently, year after year, glowing in their own soft blue aura.

I backtrack down both trails until I find Taylor parading down the path in strappy gold sandals with sparkly faux gemstones. Well, at least she's smart enough to leave her high heels at home. In order to avoid the last dregs of mud from ruining her shoes, she walks along the edge of the trail, through long grass intermingled with patches of shiny green leaves. Part of me would like to materialize and tell her to get the hell out of the poison ivy, but it's too late for that now.

I can only see someone's aura when I'm out of my body, so I've never seen Taylor's colors before. I've always pictured her to be a powerful, confident red, like a chili pepper, but instead, she is surrounded by a murky hot dog pink. Other than her aura, she does look very pretty. She's wearing a full skirt in a kaleidoscope of colors that catches the breeze and flutters just below her knees as she walks, and a gauzy black blouse fastened by a dozen silver buttons up the front. Her fingernails are so long they have to be fake, and they're painted with shiny gold polish.

Peeking out from beneath those golden fingernails, I spy Seth's phone.

As soon as she steps onto the ledge, it's apparent she's not here on a sightseeing tour. She ignores the falls, concentrating on where she should sit for maximum exposure. She considers both paths that merge onto the ledge, one from the right and one from the left, and chooses dead center to sit down, a spot that's easily facing both paths. Alternating between several provocative poses, she settles for one where her legs are tucked to the side and she's leaning back on one hand, her hair draped over her shoulder. She tucks the phone under her skirt, out of sight, then slips her sandals off and tosses them to the side, making sure her golden toenails are peeking out from under the skirt.

It sounds like a wild animal is stampeding down the path, crushing dead leaves and snapping twigs under its heavy hooves. Taylor cocks her head, listening, rearranging her face into a wide, innocent smile. I wait to see if it's a bear or a moose, but no, it's only Seth, surrounded by the color of boiled lobster.

"I figured it was you," he snarls.

"Hi . . ."

"Where's my phone?"

". . . Seth. Can we just talk for a minute, please?"

"No! Give me my phone."

"Seth, please . . ." but Seth cuts her off.

"Look! You stole my phone; you left that stupid note on my locker. Well, here I am. Give me my phone!"

"I know it was wrong to take your phone, but I couldn't think of another way to get you to talk to me. Can't you at least give me a chance?"

"A chance for *what?*"

"I just . . ." she squirms where she sits, and the pinkness around her pales. "I want us to get to know each other better."

"I know you well enough," Seth charges up to her and holds out his hand. "Give me my phone. *Now!*"

She stands up slowly and, clutching the phone behind her, takes a step backward. Her eyes are calculating.

Seth makes a grab for her arm, but she scoots back three steps. She is just two steps away from the slippery edge, and the mist from the falls is coating her bare feet. *Get away from the edge, you idiot!* I shout at her even though she can't hear me. If Rei were here, he would be having a heart attack.

"Why don't you like me?" Taylor demands to know.

"Because I don't." Seth is eyeing the distance between them, and I cross my ethereal fingers he's not stupid enough to do what I think he's going to do.

"Are you . . ." A nasty little smile narrows her eyes. "Do you like *any* girls?"

It takes Seth a few seconds to process this question. I'm expecting a big, bad, four-letter reaction from him, but he surprises me with a short, bitter laugh. "You think because I'm not interested in a slut like you I must be gay . . . why doesn't that surprise me?"

Her expression morphs into something sinister and underneath her murky pink aura, a layer of olive green rises up from her skin like a fog. Now I expect *her* to provide the four-letter reaction, but she's so furious that nothing but, "Fffffffffff," fizzles from her mouth. She winds up to hurl Seth's phone into oblivion, but time slips into slow motion.

She swings around too quickly and loses her footing on the slick stone. Her eyes and mouth pop open, arms pinwheel. As her feet slide off the ledge and gravity begins to suck her into the falls, Seth grabs the first part of Taylor he can reach. His right foot steps back hard to balance himself, and I can tell by the tightening of his mouth that he's got her weight secured. The gauzy shirt he's grabbed is not up to task, though, and silver buttons snap off in quick succession. As the last button pops free and her shirt splays wide open, she drops even farther toward the rocks and screams bloody murder. All of her weight dangles from this one wet clump of fraying cloth in Seth's fist. She swings like a pendulum, clawing frantically at Seth's slippery arm. Her acrylic nails leave deep bloody gouges down his arm to his wrist.

"Give me your other hand!"

It looks like she's trying, but her arm seems paralyzed. "I can't!" she whimpers.

Seth goes down on one knee, leaning back to give himself some leverage. He has no problem handling her weight; it's the spray from the mist and the blood that he's fighting against.

"You wanna die? Give me your *hand!*" he yells harshly.

Her bare feet backpedal against the side of the slippery rock, doing nothing more than loosening her grip on Seth's wrist and his grip on her shirt.

"Stop kicking! Give me your other hand!"

But she can't stop kicking. Some feral instinct has taken over and her feet are fighting for her life. Seth reaches out farther with his other hand, careful not to get pulled in himself, but the slippery mist mixed with his blood makes their hands slip-slide against each other, inch by inch.

I wish there was something I could do, but without my body,

I've only ever managed to lift very small things. I try to grab her other hand, just in case I can lift it up high enough for Seth to grab, but she just thrashes right through me.

When their grip breaks, she screams and her eyes bulge wide as gravity sucks her down toward the rushing water. There is a terrible silence when her head hits the first rock. The bright colors of her skirt tumble merrily over flailing arms and legs as her body is flung erratically over the boulders by the rushing water. And then she's gone, swallowed up by the river below.

Time stops. Except for a sudden chilling breeze rustling through Seth's hair, the omnipresent roar of the falls, and the ragged rattle of Seth's breath, everything is static. The only witnesses to Taylor's accident are the birds and the trees.

And me.

I wish I could remember what the symptoms of shock were. Seth's skin has faded to the color of tapioca pudding; his pupils are huge; and his sweat suddenly smells like raw onions. All that boiled red surrounding him is gone, replaced by a shadowy gray. Is that shock?

I wish Rei was here. I'm mentally kicking myself now for talking him out of coming, because I know with all certainty that if Rei had come, none of this would have happened. Rei would have figured out a way to defuse this. He would never have allowed Taylor to stand so close to the edge. He would have picked her up and carried her to a safe place if he had to. Yes, if I hadn't talked Rei out of coming, Taylor would be alive right now and Seth would have his phone tucked safely in his pocket.

Seth stands up shakily and looks downstream. The river elbows off to the right, and the view is obscured by newly sprouted leaves. I feel the familiar tug at my stomach, telling me it's time to get back. The alarm clock must have gone off, but thankfully, the volume is low, so I buy a few extra seconds to look downstream for Taylor's body. About a quarter mile past the bend, I find her body bobbing in a calm, shallow spot by the shore, her skirt caught fast on the branch of a fallen birch tree. I feel that tug again, more insistent this time, but I can't stop staring. Her buttonless shirt undulates to the rhythm of the current, exposing her badly scraped torso. Her hair drifts on the surface like undrained spaghetti, framing a deep purple gouge just above her ear that has been washed clean by the moving water, revealing splinters of crushed skull and what can only be brain matter.

Surprisingly, the rest of her face is unmarked. Her arms and legs are bent at unnatural angles, covered in deep slashes. Three of the acrylic fingernails on her right hand are bent backward, no doubt from clawing onto Seth's arm. All traces of makeup have been washed off her face, and she looks younger, more innocent than the Taylor I had known. I feel an overwhelming sadness for her. Nobody deserves such a brutal ending.

I feel another, more insistent tug, but I just want to check on Seth before I go back.

I wonder how many of her girlfriends knew she was meeting Seth here today. Probably all of them. I zip back to the ledge and find Seth flinging Taylor's sandals into the falls, followed by a long string of swear words that end in one raw sob.

Poor Seth. I've seen him rage, but I've never seen him cry before, not when he was a little kid or even when his mother left. I'm not sure if he's crying because he's genuinely sad that Taylor Gleason is dead or because he can read the graffiti on the rocks and it says, *You are screwed, boy.*

One of the silver buttons from Taylor's shirt catches the

sunlight and winks up at me from a crack in the rock. *Evidence.* I summon up enough energy to flick it into the water. I hate to leave Seth like this, but I really have to get back. The tugging sensation seems to have given up on me, but my mom will be home soon; plus, I need to talk to Rei. I am the only human eyewitness. If Taylor's girlfriends talk to the police, I am the only one who can vouch for Seth's innocence. He tried to save her. He really did.

Seth is no longer crying. He's just sitting there surrounded by a despondent shade of gray. "*Go home, Seth,*" I tell him, even though he can't hear me.

And then I head home to collect myself so I can break this bad news to Rei.

CHAPTER 8

Every religion has its own spin on life after death. The ancient Greeks had the elysian fields. Christians have heaven. Rei says the Buddhists believe souls are reincarnated until they reach a place of enlightenment called nirvana. Some people waste a lot of time worrying whether there's something to look forward to when their bodies die besides eternal sleep.

One thing I know for certain is that each of us possesses a sentient energy that can exist outside our physical bodies. I am living proof, but why should anyone take my word for it . . . even textbook physics says that energy cannot be destroyed.

And the light that's rumored to appear when someone dies? A few years ago, I saw a cylinder of light beaming down from the ceiling in a room I walked past at my great-grandmother's nursing home. Twenty minutes later, the patient was on her way out in a body bag. It's real. But where does the light go? Is there some amazing place for people who are really, really good? Do the nine circles of hell actually exist? Is that light your ride to the greatest party ever or does it just suck up your soul like a vacuum?

Well, that I *don't* know.

I careen into my room and stop short.

Something's wrong.

Something's missing!

It takes me a few seconds of stunned confusion to realize that my bed is empty. The something missing is *me*. I'm not there! I look on the floor, no. I look under the bed, no, *no*, NO!

Pure, raw panic rolls over me like a tsunami.

Where the hell am I?

This is the feeling people must get when they've jumped out of a plane and realize they've forgotten to strap on their parachute; when a scuba diver is deep in the ocean and realizes she's run out of oxygen; when you wake up and realize you've been buried alive!

I can't get back into my body if I can't find it. The cord that normally tethers me seems to be drifting loose, shriveling up as I think. This must be why the tugs I felt back at the waterfall were so insistent: my inner alarm was going off and stupid me was too busy gawking at Taylor's dead body.

Stop, Anna. Calm down and *think!*

I look around the room and realize the chair is no longer wedged under the doorknob. The music from my alarm clock still plays softly. Maybe my mom came home, couldn't wake me up, and called an ambulance. But I felt the tug just minutes ago—there wasn't enough time for that.

Out in the living room, still sunk deep into the recliner, my father faces the television. He looks incapable of moving himself, much less someone else. I hear the toilet flush, and the sound of stumbling around before the bathroom door opens.

And holy *crap!* There I am staggering from the bathroom, animated by some unknown force. What the hell? It's my face, but the expression is something from out of a zombie movie, eyes wild, mouth drooling. Whatever is inside me grasps onto walls and doorjambs for leverage, making its way spasmodically back to my bedroom. It fumbles its way over to the desk and its knees try to bend several times before it finally lowers itself onto the desk chair. It seems completely unaware of me as it reaches for my pink magnifying mirror, clawing at it several times before the fingers actually close around it. When it sees my face reflected in the mirror, it lets out an inhuman moan. It's my voice, but there's something different. The tone is mine, but the inflection is different, but somehow familiar . . .

That *bitch*!!!

That's *Taylor* in there!

But how? Unless she saw me at the falls somehow. She probably died as soon as her head hit that first rock. If she separated from her body then, she could have seen me there, watching the action unfold in all my ethereal glory. But I should have seen her, too . . . if I had been paying attention to something other than watching her body wash downstream.

I can figure that out later. What matters now is to get her the hell out of my body. I float up close and look hard into her eyes. Taylor, through my own dazed eyes, looks right through me. I reach out, tentatively, to slide my hand into my flesh hand.

The reaction is immediate. Taylor yanks my flesh hand away, violently enough to lose her balance. The wobbly desk chair tips, pitching her headfirst against the edge of my desk. The *crack!* is audible, amplified through my own extreme senses. I am going to have one hell of a headache as soon as I get her out of there!

All the sympathy I felt for Taylor at the falls evaporates as I rear back, ready to charge full force back into my body. *Slam!* It feels like

I'm bouncing off a wall. *Slam!* A very solid brick wall. *SLAM! SLAM! SLAM!*

This is getting me nowhere.

She writhes on the floor, whimpering.

I slam her again for good measure, but I bounce off like a racquetball in play. It's too quiet for Taylor to notice, but I hear the front door close.

"Helloooo," Mom calls as she peeks into my room, only to find Taylor struggling on the floor like an overturned beetle. "Anna? Oh, my God, honey, what happened?"

My mom dials 911 with shaky hands. There's nothing wrong with Taylor that an Advil, a little time, and a whole lot of stretching won't cure. The last thing my mom needs after two days at a real estate convention is to come home to all this drama. My father hasn't moved except to reach for the remote and turn up the volume.

I retreat to a corner of the room to wait for the ambulance and try to think over the sound of anxious motherisms.

Why didn't Taylor go into the light? I was so busy watching her body wash downstream, I wasn't looking for a light. Did I miss it? Maybe the sun was too bright and I couldn't see it. If she changes her mind, will the light come back for her?

Or maybe she wasn't invited. What if there *was* no light for her? What if the light doesn't shine for people who steal cell phones and throw them into waterfalls? Where do those people go when they die if there's no light?

Obviously, she goes to *my* house to hijack *my* body.

I have figured out there are a few different dimensions. There is the earthly dimension, right here where we all live. There's an astral dimension, where I consider myself a traveler whenever I leave my body. And there's probably at least one other dimension where the dead go by way of the light, but I'm not dead so I haven't been there.

When I leave my body on purpose and travel in this astral dimension, I remember what I see and do. Every now and then, I see other people floating around in this dimension, but most of them are *not* dead. It's pretty common for people to slip out of their bodies while they dream. They don't have a purpose; they aren't rational. They meet up with other people having other dreams and everything blends together into chaos they will later remember as a very vivid dream, or they don't remember it at all. I've had people at school tell me, "Oh my God, Anna, I had the weirdest dream last night and you were in it," and I say, "Wow, that *is* weird."

Except I remember, too, and it wasn't a dream.

Every once in a while, though, I bump into a dead someone who is rational, but who decided not to go into the light. The dead have auras, too, just not as strong as the living. I don't like to get into conversations with the dead. Especially if their color is off.

Taylor and my mom are at the hospital. They've run diagnostic tests, a CAT scan, and blood tests, but there are no tests to diagnose an extraneous soul possessing one's body. The doctor concludes it's a concussion, which is *oushikuso,* as Rei would say. Taylor is getting better control over my body. Her speech and movements are still slow, but more normal than they were earlier. She is sent home with my mom, some prescription painkillers, and instructions for my mom to wake her up every few hours.

My mom followed the ambulance to the hospital in her own car, so she drives Taylor home. During the ride, I hover in the backseat, listening to my mom's worried questions and Taylor's evasive murmurs. My mom must think Taylor is foggy because of the concussion, but I wonder how she'll manage later. How will she work around the obvious fact that she knows so little about me? I don't think she even knows my last name. Does she expect she can just step right into my life and go from there? I try to picture myself in some of Taylor's outfits and I almost laugh.

Back at home, Mom sits on my bed, stroking my hair and making a huge fuss. Taylor still looks dazed through my eyes. She ignores my mom's attention. She closes her eyes and wants to sleep. My mom covers her up with the blanket and it's not long before I hear light snores. Since when do I snore?

My mom looks so worried. If she even knew half of what's going on, it would freak her out completely! She turns out the light and closes the bedroom door, leaving Taylor and me in relative darkness.

I float over to the bed and watch the dark lump under the covers rise and fall. Now that she's sleeping, maybe her guard is down and I can get past whatever barrier is keeping me out. I reach out with just one finger and tap gently on her cheek. She grimaces, but doesn't wake up. I edge my way around her to the other side of the twin bed and sort of lie down, although I'm really floating about an inch off the mattress. I try to roll into her, but I'm met with a solid wall of flesh who grunts irritably.

I lean very close to her ear. "*Taylor Gleason.*" I know she can't hear me, but I say it anyway. "*GO AWAY!*"

Snore.

I spend the next half hour trying to inch, slide, push, and then force my way back into my own body, but my efforts are for nothing. She is stubbornly impermeable and I am tired. Not physically tired, but I feel like a car running on fumes. There's something about being here in my house, close to my worried mom and my drunken father, that sucks my energy dry. And since I am one hundred percent energy, this is a problem.

A sudden vibration startles me, until I realize it's just my cell phone, still stuffed in the pocket of the jeans I'd traded earlier in favor of the gym shorts Taylor now sleeps in. I don't have to look at the caller ID to know it's Rei. He said he'd call me tonight, and I doubt anyone was home at his house when the ambulance came, so he probably thinks I've just forgotten to charge my phone. The guilt I feel when I think of him drains my spirits even lower.

How can I tell him what's happened this afternoon? Besides the obvious fact that he can't hear me from this dimension, how do I tell him that not only did I ignore his advice, but I'm now trapped outside my body because of my own stubbornness?

Even though I am floating here in my bedroom, I feel a terrible homesickness. What I want, what I *need*, is to be near Rei and all the calm that flows from him.

I drift over by his bedroom window to find it wide open on this warm night. The smooth, sweet sound of acoustic guitar music pulls me closer. Could this be his surprise song? Rei plays by ear, listening to a little piece of a song on his iPod, and then working out the notes and chords on his guitar, playing them over and over until he has it memorized. Sometimes he'll Google the lyrics and sing along, although despite his love for metal music, he realizes his voice is better suited for acoustic. Whatever song he's teaching himself tonight is beautiful and complicated.

I curl myself into a ball, hovering just inside his window, and the music soothes me like a cup of hot sweet tea on a snowy day. A light breeze blows through me, stirring the wind chimes into gentle motion. Rei is lost in his song. He sits cross-legged on the bed wearing a black T-shirt and gray gym shorts, his hair still wet from the shower.

Slowly, I float down off the sill and linger over the swing chair hanging from the ceiling close to Rei's bed, careful not to jar the chair into motion. From here, I can watch his fingers work the strings and chords, listen to his clear, quiet voice. The scent of his citrus soap floats all around him, along with a calm, summer sky blue aura.

I hug my knees to my chest and bury my head in my arms so I will concentrate on the music instead of the complex strands of muscles flexing gently in his arms as he plays. Sitting here with Rei, I feel like a sponge soaking up the energy I badly need. When the music stops, I don't move, I just let myself rest here and recharge. I don't know how much time passes, but I suddenly realize that Rei isn't moving. I peek up to see if he's fallen asleep, and he's not. He's still sitting cross-legged; his guitar still rests on his lap, but his bewildered eyes look directly at me.

"Anna?"

CHAPTER 9

My knee-jerk reaction is to bolt out of Rei's room, so that's just what I do. I hide myself in the tangle of willow branches and listen to him call my name softly, again and again. Finally, he says the one thing that breaks my resolve. "Are you okay?" he asks. "I tried to call you a couple of times and you never picked up."

I float back in through the open window and he relaxes when he sees me.

"There you are," he smiles at me as I hover around the swing chair.

I'm surprised he can see me. Usually, I have to summon up a considerable amount of energy if I want to be seen. Maybe I absorbed enough of Rei's energy tonight just by sitting with him that I materialized without meaning to.

"Are you sleeping?"

What does he mean by that? I must look confused because now he looks positively amused. "I thought so. So you won't remember this conversation tomorrow."

Oh, really! I try not to show the surprise on my face. How does he know this? Have I shown up in his room before and had conversations with Rei that I don't remember?

I shrug a little. Since I have no voice in this dimension, this conversation will be very one-sided. That's a small comfort.

"Is your mom home?" he asks as he resumes his spot on the bed and picks up his guitar.

I nod.

"Did she have a good time?" He strums a few random chords, then adjusts one of the pegs a tiny bit. I wait until he looks up to nod.

"Did you follow Seth and Taylor to the falls today?"

I pause, not exactly sure how to answer this. It's not like I can elaborate, so I nod. He just rolls his eyes.

"I thought so. I tried Seth earlier, but he's not answering his cell and I don't think they even have a house phone anymore. Did she give his cell back to him?"

Um, no. I shake my head, keeping my face as impassive as I possibly can.

"That figures. He must be livid."

Why yes, he is. I nod.

Rei strums one particular string over and over, adjusting the corresponding peg until he gets the sound he wants, then he strums all the strings together. All the lights but his desk lamp are off, and his eyes are half hidden under shadows and dark hair. "So I always wonder what you're dreaming about on the nights you show up here," he muses as the sound of the music fades, "but you can't tell me now and I know you won't remember the next day."

He looks up and smiles that slow, wide smile. "Or can you remember and you just don't want to tell me?"

I have never lied to Rei before tonight. I may not tell

him certain truths that I know would lower his opinion of me, but unless the avoidance of a full disclosure is considered a lie, I haven't deliberately deceived him. Plus, he has been keeping certain truths from me, too. Like the fact that I am one of those people who slips out of their body during a dream and goes gallivanting off to la-la land. And this annoys me almost as much as the fact that I have no freakin' body!

"Want to hear your surprise song? You won't remember any of this, so it will still be a surprise when you hear it later."

It seems there are lots of surprises today. I am starting to realize just how little I know about this dimension, even after a dozen years of wandering in and out of it. How did Taylor get into me? Why can't I get her out? How could Rei see me earlier and all those times he claims I've been here while I'm dreaming? Usually, I have to absorb a considerable amount of energy from around me in order to materialize in front of him. When he does see me, I know I appear solid to him, just as solid as when I'm in my body, but I can't ever remember anyone else seeing me when I'm out here.

When the song is finished, Rei looks up at me, and I smile and silently clap my hands. I love everything he plays on his acoustic guitar, and he knows this. He smiles a sleepy smile, so I know it's time to leave. I wave and point to the window.

"Okay, I'll see you in the morning," he whispers as he parks his guitar on the stand beside his bed. "Sweet dreams."

For one crazy moment, I want to tell him what's happened, that Taylor's dead body is stuck on a branch downstream, that Seth will probably be blamed for her death, that I can't dream because I can't sleep because I'm locked out of my body because Taylor has stolen it. And then I imagine the look that will be on his face, because he'll think this is his fault, and if he had skipped his aikido class, he could have prevented this entire fiasco. I have to get my body back before he finds out what's happened.

I spend the night hovering over my bed while Taylor snores, hoping she'll pop out of my body during a dream so I can get back in. Sometime around one o'clock and then again at four, my mom comes in and shakes Taylor's shoulder, just like the doctor told her to. Taylor wakes up enough to grouch at her, and then my mom leaves us both in the dark again.

I wonder if Rei considered the danger of someone taking possession of my body if I wasn't in it. I never really thought of it before, but it makes sense. If there's an empty shell left lying on the beach, won't a hermit crab move into it? I've encountered spirits in this dimension who are obviously dead and wandering, but I've always shied away from talking to them. Maybe my subconscious was smart enough to realize if a dead soul had known I'd left a perfectly good *living* body lying around unguarded, it would just be an invitation for trouble.

Watching Taylor sleep is like waiting for a pot of water to boil. I need a better plan of action here, and since planning has never been my strength, I consider how Rei would deal with this.

One of Rei's favorite quotes is from Sun Tzu's *The Art of War*: "Know your enemy and know yourself and you can fight a hundred battles without disaster." It's a principle of aikido, too, to get inside your enemy's mind and find out what makes them tick.

In principle, that should work, but know myself? I can't even get *into* myself right now. But maybe I can learn a little more about Taylor. Really, all I know about her is from what I've seen at school. I've heard she lived in a big house on Main Street, which makes me wonder how she'll handle slumming in my crappy little house.

What will she think when she wakes up in the morning and has to deal with my hungover father? I wait until first morning light to head over to Main Street and cruise up and down until I find a mailbox with block letters spelling *Gleason* stuck to it. I don't bother with such formalities as ringing the doorbell. I just slip right through the wall and find myself in a lavish master bathroom that's bigger than my bedroom.

The girl was loaded. I mean, you can't even compare apples to oranges; this is more like watermelons and raisins. I drift through a wall into an opulent master bedroom where the king-sized bed is still made, and then another bedroom that has the sterile feel of a guest room. One of the bedrooms is decorated in a sporty boy motif, with a tween-aged boy asleep in the bed. The last room looks like a picture out of a magazine, and the furniture in here easily costs more than all of the furniture in my house combined. Her computer is state-of-the-art, and she has a flat-screen television attached to one wall. On another wall, there's a floor-to-ceiling bulletin board hosting a rainbow of award ribbons and dozens of photographs. I take a minute to check out all the glamorous shots of Taylor. Nope, she is not going to like living in Anna Rogan's bony little body.

Three doors lead out of Taylor's room. It's pitch-black through one door, so it's probably a closet; one door leads to the hallway; and the last one leads into her own full bathroom. She has her own bathroom? She *had* her own bathroom . . . with cushy two-ply toilet paper and everything. Again I wonder: what did a two-ply girl like Taylor see in a one-ply guy like Seth?

And how will this upper-class girl deal with my lower-class life? Maybe after she's had to clean my father's puke off the toilet seat a few times, she'll leave my body of her own free will.

Or maybe she'll find my life is better than no life at all.

The smell of coffee wafts up the stairs. I follow it downstairs to the kitchen where Taylor's parents pace around two silent cell phones which sit on a granite countertop. Their auras are a strange mix of anger, sorrow, and hope. If I could appear right here and tell them what's happened to their daughter, would I? Or would I let them hang on to that little thread of hope just a bit longer?

It's a ridiculous question because I can't let these people see me in my astral state, and Taylor is so obviously dead, but still . . .

I would leave them with hope.

CHAPTER 10

I leave the Gleasons to the misery that awaits them and return home through a gray gloom.

Today would have been a good day to stay in bed and listen to the heavy rain hammer at the roof. Through the bedroom wall, I hear my mother's alarm clock start to squawk. She will hit the snooze bar once, then she'll get up and usually she'll wake me as soon as she's showered. I can't imagine she'll make Taylor go to school after the night she's had. I move out to the living room for the sole reason that I'm sick of listening to Taylor snore. It's not much brighter out here, except for a small light on over the kitchen sink. The recliner is empty, but not inviting. There's a greasy indentation where my father's head usually rests, and an overall flakiness dusts the black vinyl. Last night's empty bottle and glass wait on the end table for my mom to pick them up, making way for today's bottle and glass.

It will be interesting to see Taylor's reaction when she meets my father. Best case scenario is she's completely disgusted and would rather be dead than to live with the guy. Worst case? She shows him attitude and he shows her the back of his hand, promise or no promise.

My mom's alarm clock starts bleating again. She shuffles out in her bare feet, opens my bedroom door without knocking, and peeks at the lump on the bed. She sighs as she pulls the door closed behind her, then goes to the phone and calls school to tell them I won't be in. Next, she calls her office and tells them she'll be working from home today. Finally, she calls Rei's cell phone and leaves a message.

"Rei, honey, it's Lydie. Don't wait for Anna this morning. She's not feeling well, so I'm keeping her home. Stay dry."

This is the same message she leaves him whenever I have serious cramps, and Rei broke the code on that a long time ago, so he shouldn't worry. Much. My mom goes to start coffee, so I head back into my bedroom. God! I sound like a chainsaw! I ram into Taylor, just in case anything's changed overnight. It hasn't. I bounce off and drift toward the wall. She opens one eye and snarls at me, then pulls the covers over her head.

Keeping my distance, I check on Rei. If he saw me, he'd probably think I'm still dreaming since I'm home sick, but still, I'd rather he didn't see me. I'm glad my mom didn't tell him I whacked my head, because he'll just blame my father. There's an overgrown blue spruce tree near his driveway which offers good camouflage should I erroneously appear again. After a while, he steps onto his front porch, looks toward my house, then turns his phone on and discovers the message that's waiting for him. No, he doesn't look too concerned. He snaps the phone shut and pulls up the hood of his sweatshirt before he steps off the porch and into the downpour.

I wonder if Seth will be on the bus. He should still have plenty of gas in his car, but I feel this nasty medley of guilt, fear, and curiosity when I think of Seth. I was so freaked out to find Taylor in my body that I admit it: I forgot about Seth until just now. I wonder where he is.

I don't expect he'll be on the bus, but I check it anyway and find his usual seat empty. I check Seth's house, but he's not there either. I swoop over the school parking lot, but I don't see his car.

Taylor's parents must have talked to her friends by now, and at least one of them must have known about her plans to meet Seth at the falls. Seth knows the police will come looking for him. He might not be very academically inclined, but he's not stupid.

Once I've touched someone a few times, I can memorize the unique rhythm of their energy pattern. It's like hearing the drumbeat from a song, and wherever they go, they leave a slow fading echo. Even though Seth seemed chronically sweaty to me, we've high-fived a few times, and I arm wrestled him for three-quarters of a second once before he slammed my arm against the tabletop, much harder than necessary, and whooped like he had just scored the winning touchdown at the Super Bowl. That was enough touching for me, but I know his energy pattern well enough to find him.

I follow the echo of his vibration and find him walking down a road so filled with muddy ruts and potholes that only the very brave or very foolish would dare drive on it. It's quiet except for the steady hiss of raindrops and an occasional hardy soul in a pickup truck sloshing through the puddles. Seth looks like a hunchback, wearing a bulging backpack under an army green rain poncho. He looks exhausted, and his aura is as muddy as the road around him.

I wonder where he's heading. He's about fifteen miles from the Canadian border, so I'm going to assume he's parked his car close to the border to fool the authorities into believing he snuck into Canada. Somehow, I doubt the police are that stupid. It just seems odd he's traveling on foot now, and that he carries no tent, no sleeping bag. I wonder if he has a plan, because I sure haven't come up with one yet.

School won't get out for a long while, so I decide to check the evidence. Taylor's body is still stuck fast by her skirt, bobbing up and down in the current. She's bloated from waterlog and her skin has turned a mottled gray. Something has been gnawing or pecking at the soft arch of her foot and a good sized chunk is missing. If she hadn't stolen my body, I would be overcome with emotion at the sight of this girl right now, but as the situation stands, crows have to eat, too.

Back at my house, Taylor is still sleeping. I slam into her, just in case, and she wakes up in a grizzly mood. She sits up, bleary-eyed, and swears viciously. For a minute, she seems discombobulated, but then reality hits and she buries her head under my pillow, groaning. "Why didn't I just die when I had the chance?"

Good question. I slam her again.

"Go away, Anna," she looks straight at me and hisses. "You're not getting back in here, so quit trying."

I slam her again, but all the energy I soaked up from Rei last night is fading fast now that I'm back here. She rolls over and looks at the clock. "Your house is a dump," she sneers.

Then leave, I tell her.

"What? I can't hear you. Are you talking to me?" she taunts.

PLEASE GO *AWAY*! I mouth the words slowly, deliberately, and, as much as it pains me, politely.

"*What?* Are you telling me to go away?"

Hey, it's worth a shot. I nod.

"Finders keepers, Anna. I'm not going anywhere. *You* go away." She pulls the pillow back over her head.

I don't have the energy to take another whack at her.

If only frustration were a positive emotion, I'd be running on a full tank now. How ironic that I can wander around the White House, I can whiz through the vaults of Fort Knox, but I cannot get back into my own body. What do I do now? This is an enormous mess of my own doing, and I don't know how to fix it.

Rei is at lunch, and he doesn't look happy. I'm sure he's figured out by now that Seth is absent. He sits alone at our table and works on homework, oblivious to the rumors that are spreading through school about Taylor and Seth. When he dials my phone, he gets my voice mail. He must be lonely, because he leaves a long message for me. "Hi Anna, it's me. How're you feeling? Seth's not in school today either, so I was wondering if you had any idea where he is. Call me as soon as you get this? Please? I'll come see you when I get home from school anyway."

An empty police cruiser is parked outside the school in the fire lane. I find two police officers in the principal's office, asking him about Taylor and Seth. The principal looks concerned, but not surprised. Unlike Rei, he has heard the gossip. The shorter, balder police officer produces a notebook from his jacket pocket, and shows a page to the principal. There are names scribbled on it—all the names of Taylor's girlfriends. The principal jots down the list of names on a separate sheet of yellow lined paper, pushes a button, and a secretary appears at the door.

"Yes, Mr. Bowers."

He hands her the list. "Please ask these students to report to my office."

I follow the secretary back to the cafeteria, where Taylor's friends are huddled together at their usual table by the window.

None of them looks surprised when the secretary approaches them. They give each other knowing looks and get up quietly, following the secretary out into the hallway.

They sit in a row in the front office, leaning over to whisper to each other as they wait. They all have the same story, as if they've collectively rehearsed it. Taylor had plans to meet Seth at the falls at four o'clock yesterday, and they haven't heard from her since. She doesn't answer her cell phone. Her mom called each of them last night looking for her, but they don't know where she is. Did she have a prior relationship with Seth Murphy? She really liked him, but he was mean to her. How was he mean? He ignored her, gave her dirty looks. He moved his seat if she sat too close to him. Sometimes he yelled at her. They conveniently leave out the part about how she stole his cell phone and used it to coerce him into meeting her. Cori Schneider impatiently cracks her gum throughout the entire questioning.

By one o'clock, the rain has stopped and the sun is out, drying up the muck. At three, Rei surprises me by pulling into his driveway in his parents' car. Saya must have gone to a friend's house, because as soon as Rei drops off his backpack, he's punching my house phone number into his cell. My mom answers. "Sure, come on over, honey. She could use some company."

I skulk around behind plants, doors, anything that will hide me, just in case. I feel like a snake. Back at my house, my mom is hustling Taylor to get ready for company. Taylor's eyes narrow, but she gets up slowly and goes into the bathroom to splash some water on her face and brush her hair and teeth. She regards my toothbrush with total revulsion, as if she's going to catch some horrible disease from using it. Leaning on the counter, she stares at my reflection in the mirror.

"Girl, you need one hell of a makeover." Wearing the same

gym shorts and T-shirt Rei saw me in last night, she goes outside and sits on the damp front steps. I see Rei coming down the path between our yards.

"Hi!" he calls out before he even reaches the sparse clumps of grass we call a front lawn.

"Hi," she responds suspiciously.

"How are you feeling?"

"My head is killing me," she replies as if this is obvious and he's an idiot.

"I thought you had cramps." He's reached the steps and his face is all worried now. "What's wrong with your head?"

"Didn't she tell you I have a concussion?"

"No! How'd that happen?"

"I fell off that piece of shit desk chair and hit my head on the side of the desk."

Disapproval of Taylor's language trumps worry for a split second before he asks, "Where? Show me."

Taylor moves her hand up and through her hair, first to the spot where she smashed her head against the rock yesterday, then over to the other side where she whacked my head against the desk. She points. "Right here. See?"

Rei reaches out and touches it gently. "Here?"

"Ouch!"

Rei pulls his hand back. "Sorry. I was trying to be careful. It hurts that much?"

"Yes!" she confirms, swishing her hair behind her shoulder. It definitely does not have the same satisfying effect when she does it with my hair.

"And the doctor says it's a concussion? What did he say to do about it?"

"Rest. They gave me some prescription strength ibuprofen,

which is doing nothing. She," Taylor jerks her head toward the house and winces, "kept waking me up all night long."

"You should have my mom take a look at it."

"Why? Is she a doctor or something?"

"Wow! You must've hit your head a lot harder than I thought." Rei sits sideways on the next step down, but he's still taller than me.

"I *did* hit it really hard. I can't remember a lot of stuff." Taylor drops her head in her hands and combs her fingers through her hair. "Ow!"

"Well, stop touching it, then. Here, let me see your pupils." He puts his hands on either side of her face to hold her steady and looks into Taylor's eyes, studying them for a minute. He frowns slightly. "Same size, that's a good thing. Is the light bothering you?"

"No. Are you a doctor now, too?"

Rei shakes his head without smiling and talks in that detached tone people use when they are saying one thing and thinking something else. "Sometimes people land on their head in aikido. You learn what to look for." He stares into her eyes for a few seconds more, his eyebrows creasing together.

She leans forward and looks right back into Rei's eyes. "Hello? What are you looking for in there?"

Rei blinks and drops his hands onto his lap. "I don't know. So you really fell off your desk chair?"

"Um, yeah. Did you ever see that chair? It's ready to fall apart."

"Yeah, I know. Your mom's been meaning to buy you a new one for a while."

"Oh."

"So what do you mean, you don't remember stuff. What don't you remember?"

"Hmm . . . Oh, my full name—isn't Anna short for something?"

Rei's jaw practically unhinges. "You don't even remember your own name?"

"I remember Anna Rogan."

"Annaliese Grace Rogan."

"Oh." She nods thoughtfully. "That's pretty. Where's my driver's license?"

Rei grins. "You don't *have* a driver's license."

"You're kidding."

"Sorry. Your mom never got around to teaching you how to drive. My dad said he'd teach you this summer."

Taylor rolls her eyes and leans back on her hands. "No license. This is really going to suck! How am I supposed to get to school?"

"You take the bus with me."

"The bus." She shudders. "Great. And what's the deal with the guy in there?"

"Your father?"

She shrugs. "I guess."

Rei suddenly looks uncomfortable and he lowers his voice. "Anna, your dad's been an alcoholic for years. You don't remember that?"

She shakes her head. "What about my mother?"

"She's not home a lot, but she's fine. Remember? She sells real estate."

"So is he a mean drunk or a mellow drunk?"

Rei bites his lips together and hesitates before slowly shrugging his shoulders. "You get along best with him when you stay out of his way."

"What do you mean by that?" *Swish.*

"I mean this," Rei reaches up and traces his index finger along the scar on my forehead, "happened one time when you didn't stay out of his way. He hit you and you fell against the counter. It only happened once, and he promised he wouldn't do it again. Anna, does your mom know how much stuff you don't remember?"

Taylor shrugs. "They figure it's temporary."

"But what if it's not? This isn't little stuff you're forgetting; this is some major stuff! You remember me, right?"

"Pretty much. Aren't you, like, my boyfriend or something?"

Rei grins at this. "Wow! Um, well, I'm a boy and I'm your friend, but you never considered me a boyfriend. You've always thought of me more like a brother."

"I have?"

I have?

"You have."

I don't remember that.

"What are we, then, just like neighbors?"

Rei is still smiling. Obviously the concept of us dating is extremely amusing to him. "And we've been friends forever." He stops smiling and groans. "This isn't funny."

"No," she agrees as she hugs her knees to her chest. "Not at all."

"So Seth never showed up at school today either, and I doubt he got his phone back. I wonder where he went."

Taylor freezes for a second, then turns slowly toward Rei. "You mean after he killed Taylor Gleason?"

Rei stares. "What are you talking about?"

"I saw him kill her." Taylor sits straight up, and her voice is serrated. "I went to the waterfall, and I saw your friend Seth push Taylor right off the ledge into the waterfall. He just threw her off. She's dead now. Did you know that?" She's staring daggers at Rei now.

Rei's mouth is hanging open. "*What?* Anna, you're not making any sense. Seth would never . . ."

"Never what . . . commit first-degree murder? I saw the whole thing." She's talking more to herself now than to Rei. "I need to call the police! I need to talk to my parents. I'm an eyewitness."

"Anna! Listen to yourself," Rei puts one hand on her shoulder and turns her to face him. "You told me yourself your memory is all messed up. No offense, but you can't even remember your own name."

Her aura turns the color of dirty bricks as she slaps his hand away.

"*This* I remember!"

CHAPTER 11

Rei's voice is carefully controlled when he says goodbye to my mom, but he sprints the entire way home, trying to stomp the anger out through his feet. He kicks off his sneakers before disappearing into his house, and the front door closes with a little more force than usual. I'm not used to seeing Rei angry, especially at me.

I really wanted to fix this myself. Maybe it's my own stubbornness or maybe it's because I'm the cause of this mess, but I did not want Rei to have to worry about this. Now I know that not only is Taylor planning to blame her accidental death on Seth, but she's using me as the star witness. If I can get my body back, I can exonerate Seth, but how do I get her out? I tried to force my way back in. I even asked her politely to leave, but it's done me no good. It's time to swallow my pride, admit I screwed up, and ask for help.

The garage door grinds open, and Rei comes out, wearing only a pair of torn, faded blue jeans and dirt-caked work boots, a shovel slung over his bare shoulder. He walks right by me, so I must be invisible to him at the moment, which is a good thing because I'm kinda sorta staring right now. Off to the side in the front yard there's a small crabapple tree that Yumi got for Mother's Day waiting to be planted.

I suppose I could materialize now and try to tell Rei what's happening, but he looks kind of busy at the moment. He starts to dig, stepping all of his weight on the shovel until it sinks through the thick turf. The grass is very much alive, and the thick clumps of sod won't let go of the earth without an angry hiss. The sound of ripping grass seems to calm him, though, and by the time he's cleared a sizable circle of grass, he's breathing slower and his expression is neutral. He pays no attention to me, so I must still be invisible to him. I float near the porch swing and watch him scoop shovelful after shovelful of dirt and rocks into a pile on a tarp, prying loose the bigger rocks with the tip of the shovel and throwing them overhand into the woods between our houses. It takes him a good five minutes to wrestle one particularly large rock out, and he heaves that into the woods with a satisfied look on his face. By the time he's planted the tree and replaced the soil, he's streaked with sweat and soil, and . . . okay! So maybe I *am* checking him out. A little.

He shoulders the shovel and the rolled hose, then heads back to the garage with his usual calm face restored until he passes the porch. He stops cold and looks directly at me. Uh-oh. He looks mad again.

"Anna!" he says sharply.

My first reaction is to dart into the spruce tree so fast, it appears I've vanished into thin air. Rei continues to talk to the swing in the same steely tone. "I know you're there." He waits a few seconds for me to materialize, and when I don't, he lowers his voice. "I don't know what you think happened, but I would appreciate it if you would think this through before you talk to anyone about

Seth." He stares at the swing expectantly. "Do you have any idea where he is?"

His colors are wavering between red and green, like Christmas but not at all joyful. It's the aura of conflict, of someone who is trying really hard to keep an open mind and make sense of this. I glide out of the spruce and settle on the steps to the left of him. I latch onto the small bit of positive energy that's radiating from him and recharge from that. He catches sight of me in his peripheral vision and jumps slightly.

"Don't DO that!"

Of course I know where Seth is, but I don't know how to tell him. Through the years, Rei and I have learned to silently communicate a lot to each other through our eyes and gestures. Little things, like *hey, do you have an extra pencil* or *I'm freezing; can I wear your hoodie?* are easy to figure out. But even if I didn't suck at charades, how would I communicate *he's on a back road about fifteen miles south of the Canadian border?*

Rei sits down next to me and rests his elbows on his knees, his chin on his fists. His eyes are assessing me again, trying to fit together the pieces of my puzzle. "Are you really going to the police?"

I shake my head.

He relaxes a little. "Then why did you say you would?"

I shake my head again.

"Yes, you did. I heard you. Oh, right, you don't remember, do you?" His tone is uncharacteristically condescending.

I shake my head, and point to my house. I mouth the word *that's*.

Rei rolls his eyes. He sucks even worse than I do at charades. "Great. Now I have to guess what you're trying to say, right?"

Right.

He watches carefully as I mouth the word again. "This," he guesses.

I shake my head and try again.

"Uh, that."

Close enough. I nod. I mouth the word *not* and shake my head.

"Not?" he guesses. Good, he's doing better than usual.

I nod again, and point to my chest, mouthing the word *me*.

"Me," he says softly. " 'That's not me.' That's not you? Well, then, who is it?" He looks more confused than ever. Over at my house, the front door opens. Taylor comes out barefoot and walks slowly up the driveway toward the mailbox. She doesn't look over, but Rei sees her, and he knows I can't be here and there at the same time.

I mouth the word very slowly. "*Taylor*."

CHAPTER 12

"So what you're telling me is that's *Taylor* inside *your* body," he says quietly.

I nod. Taylor's still at the mailbox, pulling out a wad of catalogs and bills, but she's too far away to hear him. I scoot to the side so if she looks over, she can't see me.

"Why isn't she inside her own body?"

I run my index finger across my throat.

"She's really dead?" he whispers.

I nod.

Rei lets out a slow deep breath and rubs his temples with his dirt-caked hands. "That's bad. She said Seth pushed her."

I shake my head hard.

"No, I didn't think so. Do you know how to find Seth?"

I nod.

"Okay, good. Let's go inside before she sees us," he says. Once he's inside, he looks at his grungy hands apologetically. "I need five minutes to shower."

I wait downstairs and imagine every possible reaction Rei

might have when he realizes all that's happened. He's so good at hiding his emotions from the world, but how can he not be feeling, disbelief, anger, fear, and worst of all disappointment.

As soon as Rei is all clean and dressed in shorts and a T-shirt, he calls me upstairs, motioning for me to follow him to his room. The sight of the swing chair sparks his memory.

"So last night," he says, "you weren't here because you were dreaming, were you?"

I shake my head.

"And by that time, Taylor was already dead, wasn't she?"

I nod.

"So, why didn't you *tell* me?"

I didn't tell him because I wanted to get my body back first, because I didn't want him to worry, because I am so profoundly embarrassed that I am locked out of my *body*, of all things. And the number one reason I didn't tell him? Because while I'm stuck in this dimension, I have no voice, no words, no way to tell him all the complicated details of this debacle.

I must look very contrite because Rei's voice softens. "I'm sorry," he says as he sits on his bed, "you must have been pretty shocked to come home and find someone else in your body."

I open my eyes wide to show him "shocked" doesn't even begin to cover it.

"So have you tried to get her out?"

Big emphatic nod.

"So . . . what's the problem? It's your body. Can't you just pull her out?"

I shake my head. This lack of a voice is starting to drive me nuts. I look around for something I can use to communicate with him besides head shakes and nods. Rei's room is always immaculate, which sucks because a little dust would be handy to write in. There's a pencil on the desk, but even though I can pick it up, it flops around when I try to write, producing nothing more than a few illegible squiggles. I let it fall back onto the desk and look around in desperation.

"It's okay, Anna," he consoles me, "we'll figure this out. So you can lift the pencil, but you can't control it. . . ."

Rei turns the power strip on with his foot, and while he waits for the computer to power up, he gives me menial tasks to perform. Can I move that book? No, I can't. Can I move this piece of paper? Yes, I can. He seems to be looking for a magical weight limit I can lift metaphysically, and I hate to burst his bubble, but I don't think it's consistent. I can manipulate these objects around him just because I'm fueling off his energy. Rei seems to vibrate at a much higher frequency than most people I know, probably because of all the meditation he does in his secret lair. At my house, my parents and Taylor have such a negative effect on me, it's like draining juice through a straw. I don't think I could lift that pen at my house.

The computer is up, and Rei selects the word processing icon. The screen comes up as a blank document. "Can you type?"

He starts wheeling his chair back to give me access to the keyboard, but then he stops and looks at me curiously. "Can you just move right through me?"

Who knows? I reach my hand toward his to see if he feels solid like Taylor, or if he's like an inanimate object I can slide right through if I choose to. He reaches out to meet me halfway, and when our hands touch, he feels solid and secure, like an anchor to keep me from drifting away.

"That is so cool! It's like you're vibrating." I watch him stare in childlike fascination at my hand resting in his. As his fingers curl naturally around mine, they sink right through my hand into a loose fist. "That's weird." He sounds disappointed. "But you can't put your hand through mine."

I shake my head.

"Weird. So," Rei leans back in his chair, "back to the big question. Can you type?"

I stoke myself up on Rei's energy before I move my fingers helter-skelter on the keyboard . . . *lkdjg oerufj*

Yes, I can type.

"Good! That'll make things easier. Now start at the beginning and tell me everything that happened from the time I dropped you off yesterday afternoon."

I tap into quite a bit of Rei's energy in order to type the entire story, but he doesn't seem to miss it. He leans forward, reading as I type, interrupting me with questions. When I'm done, he sits back with that worried look on his face.

"I should have been there with him. At least I could vouch he's innocent."

If I can just get back into my body, I can vouch for him.

"Yeah, well, that's the next topic up for discussion. How do you get her out?"

I have no idea. I keep trying to push her out, but as you can see, I can't travel through people. If I can't get into her, I can't push her out.

"Well, how'd she get in there, then?"

It must be because I wasn't in there. Maybe she saw me at the falls with Seth and figured she could sneak in while I wasn't there.

Rei is quiet, thinking. "So you're in some other dimension?" he finally asks.

I think so. It's the same place I always go.

"And Taylor has taken possession of your body."

I nod solemnly. *I don't think you should tell her you know she isn't me.*

"No, you're right, I won't."

I don't know how she thinks she can pull this off. Do people with concussions really have such drastic memory issues? She didn't even know my full name.

"They can. And she knows your name now. I told her."

I have a feeling she'll be pestering you.

"That's okay. You know," he says quietly, "I thought there was something odd about you. Your eyes. They just looked . . . unfamiliar."

I wonder if my mother will notice a difference in my eyes, too, or if Rei is the one person in this world who knows me best.

Rei presses the spot between his eyebrows hard for a minute, and the red and green layers surrounding him seem to roll into each other and become an indigo blue.

"Okay, so let's look at this logically. If she hadn't come into you, what would she have done?"

She should have gone into the light, but I didn't see one. I don't know if I wasn't paying attention or if the sun was too bright. Or maybe there just wasn't a light for her.

"Okay, so for whatever reason, she didn't go into the light. So she's a spirit that's taken possession of a living body."

Now that he puts it that way, it sounds so sinister. I nod.

"So can you search 'spirit possession'? See what the internet has to say."

I type in the magic words, hit the enter key, and voilà . . . nine million hits.

I make a *wow* face at him, and he smiles for the first time in a while. Not a big smile, but enough to charge me up for a few more minutes.

"So why don't I look these over and see what I come up with while you go find Seth."

I flip back to the word processing screen. *What do you want me to do with him once I find him?* Surely he doesn't want Seth to see me.

"Just find him; make sure he's safe. Let me know where he is."

Okay, I'll be right back.

Seth is a little farther south now. I trace him to a wooded area not more than twenty miles away, and he's still moving at a steady pace. I would love to know where he's going. What he's doing for food and water. What thoughts are swimming around behind that blank expression on his face. As bad as he might think this is, he cannot imagine how bad it could get unless I get back into my body.

I bounce back to Rei's bedroom before he's finished reading the first article on spirit possession. As soon as he sees me, he pushes his chair back so I can use the keyboard.

He's fine. He's walking through some woods between St. Albans and Milton.

"So he's not too far away. Let's go get him."

It takes me all of a second and a half to determine this is a dangerous idea for Rei.

What are you going to do with him once you find him?

"I'll talk him into going to the police and they'll straighten this whole thing out," he says. "You said it yourself: he didn't do anything wrong."

It doesn't matter what I say—nobody can hear me. The police will be listening to the Anna Rogan who tells them Seth pushed Taylor.

"Well, the law says he's innocent until proven guilty."

The school already has him coded with behavior issues. And all of Taylor's friends have told the police Seth was there with her, and they didn't exactly portray Seth in a very positive manner.

"How do you know that?"

I went to the school today. I heard them talk to the police.

"Okay," Rei sits back and spins his desk chair in little quarter circles while he digests this latest bit of bad news. "How can I help Seth, then? I can't just leave him out there."

He seems to have something planned. Let him do what he's doing. He's done plenty of camping; he knows how to fend for himself. If he doesn't get in touch with you by tomorrow afternoon, I'll bring you to him.

"Fair enough," he turns back to the computer with his poker face in place, but his aura tells me differently. He's not happy with this compromise, and his blues give way to layers of dismay.

The air feels heavier, like a wave of negativity has rolled into the room. I'm sure it's Rei's energy reacting to my reluctance to lead him to Seth until I hear a car door slam, then another. I fly to the window just as the doorbell rings.

CHAPTER 13

I give Rei a warning look while the sound of the doorbell echoes through the house.

As soon as he sees who is here, he mutters one of those Japanese words he won't translate for me.

"Wait here," he tells me.

Not a chance. I hover at the top of the stairs, out of sight. The police look in expectantly when Rei opens the door.

"Can I help you?"

"Are you Rye Ellis?" asks the same short, bald police officer I saw at school.

"Rei Ellis," he corrects them.

"Okay, Rei. I'm Officer Daigle; this is Officer Mooney. We'd like to ask you a few questions about Seth Murphy."

Even if Taylor called the police right after Rei left, they wouldn't be here asking questions so soon, unless . . .

I zip over to the river where I last saw Taylor's body bobbing in the current. The birch branch now cuts freely through the water, and the mud along the shore has been trampled and stamped with dozens of heavy boot prints.

They know.

There's very little Rei can tell the police about Seth. He mentions Seth's stolen phone, the note on his locker, the fact that he hasn't heard from him since yesterday afternoon. The police ask Rei about me, so I'm going to take a wild guess here that Taylor wasted no time after Rei left to make that call. Rei mentions my concussion and memory issues. Twice. They don't leave until the short, bald police officer hands Rei a business card and asks him to call if he hears from Seth.

Rei crumples the card slowly in his hand as he watches the cruiser back out of his driveway and head over to my house, then he takes the stairs two at a time. "Anna!" He stops short before he plows right through me. "Sorry. Hey, the police are on their way to question Taylor. Can you go listen to what she says?"

Me? Eavesdrop on a private conversation? Sure, why not.

Twenty minutes later, I'm back, furious at Taylor and even more anxious for Seth. Rei stands at his bedroom window watching the police car leave my driveway when his keyboard clatters into motion.

She described everything Taylor was wearing, how all the buttons were ripped off her shirt and her fingernails were all bent back. Nobody would know that unless they were there or they had seen the body. Which they found, by the way—I checked.

Rei sits on the edge of the bed and leans over to read the computer monitor.

"Wait a second. You told me before that when Seth grabbed her, her shirt ripped. You meant all the buttons were ripped off?" I can tell by his expression that his attempt to visualize this is having staggering results. "Wow. That's really . . . bad."

It was a really flimsy shirt, but still, it does look really incriminating.

"Well, yeah, I guess it would."

If I can just get her out of my body, they'd have no witness.

"You know," Rei says with a trace of bitterness, "it would be nice if your father could just tell the police you were home in your room the entire time."

Yes, it would, but Rei knows as well as I do that my father's brain has all the mental retention power of a sewer drain.

"Okay, so we've got to get you back in your body. We were Googling spirit possession. Let's get back to that."

Rei sits in the chair and I read over his shoulder.

"I read one while you were gone that said we just need to convince her she's dead and her loved ones are waiting for her on the other side of the light."

Nothing is ever that easy. This light, this highway to heaven is an obscure thing to me. If Taylor qualifies for the light, if we could figure out how to summon the light, could we convince her to cross over to the other side? Ha! I can just imagine the conversation now:

Rei: "Taylor, I'm sorry to break this sad news to you, but due to a tragic accident, you are dead. On the brighter side, your loved ones are waiting for you on the other side of the light!"

Taylor: "Piss off."

I give him a thumbs down and point to the next result.

Rei opens it up and we both read. "So this site wants me to enter my credit card number, and for one hundred euros, they'll perform a long distance spiritual release exercise on your body." He smirks. "Is anyone really that stupid?"

Sadly, yes.

He clicks over to another link. "This one says some people can be partially possessed. Maybe your mom could negotiate a time share with her." I go through the motion of smacking his shoulder and he goes through the motion of pretending he felt it, but he won't meet my eyes as he toggles over to the next screen. Down at the bottom of the page, one heading catches my attention. I point to it.

"That one?" Rei clicks.

Yes, that's the one. I hover close to Rei so I can read.

SMUDGING: In order to clear negative energy, the Native Americans tie white sage twigs (salvia apiana) *into bundles which are then lit and allowed to smolder. The pungent smoke is waved through the air to cover all areas that are thought to harbor negative energy. Traditionally, an abalone shell is used to catch falling embers.*

Rei looks very unconvinced as he reads through the article, but I'm excited. Taylor is nothing if not negative energy, and maybe if she gets a few whiffs of white sage smoke, it will break her grasp on my body and I can push my way back in.

"This doesn't look like the same sage my parents sell at the store," Rei finally says. "Where would we even get this stuff?"

I wave him away from the keyboard and search for new age shops around the greater Burlington area. The closest one is over by the waterfront.

"The Hallowed Eave. Discover the magick of your true spiritual self. " Rei's shoulders wilt as he reads this. "Books, jewelry, aromatherapy, tarot . . . ritual tools? Cauldrons? *Voodoo?*" He looks positively distressed now. "Really? You're sure about this?"

I nod emphatically. If nothing else, it will give us something to do besides sit here and worry.

"Okay," he sighs. "Let's get this over with."

Down an alley off a side road that's several streets away from the waterfront, we spy a violet colored storefront with a tangerine roof. Four dragon-faced gargoyles jut out from beneath the wide eaves, alternating with a dozen or more neon windsocks. There's a brightly painted, bohemian-looking sign that welcomes us to The Hallowed Eave. Rei looks less than enchanted.

A bell tinkles when we open the door and the cloying smell of incense nearly bowls us over. I know my senses are more sensitive when I'm out of my body, but one look at Rei tells me I'm not the only one who thinks this stuff stinks.

"I hope that's not what white sage smells like," Rei mutters.

There's an odd blend of dark and light energy sparring in here, almost as if the displays of witchcraft and voodoo merchandise want to overthrow the angel and fairy wares. Scattered around the shop are rustic baskets filled with gemstones—quartz, amethyst, and other pretty rocks I can't name, but there is a powerful buzz generating from them. I am sloughing off their energy as fast as I absorb it in an effort not to materialize in front of anyone. In the middle of all this chaos, Rei's energy is idling quietly as he gets his bearings in this strange shop.

"Merry meet, brother!" The middle-aged woman behind the counter reminds me of a cardinal with her poufy red hair, conical nose, and heavy eyeliner surrounding sharp little eyes that look Rei up and down over the rim of her psychedelic reading glasses. She hops off the stool and flits toward him. "Can I help you find . . . oh!" She takes her glasses off and lets the beaded chain catch them. Her fingers twitch at her sides, and I'm only slightly horrified by how long her fingernails are. "Oh, my! You have a lovely aura," she coos at him. "Are you here for a psychic reading?"

Rei does not have a lovely aura, at least not at this moment, unless she's partial to the color of Dijon mustard. "Um, no. I'm looking for white sage," he says cautiously. "It comes in a bundle."

"Why, yes," the woman winks at him. "It certainly does. Follow me, dear." She leads Rei through a cluttered maze of bookshelves and clothing racks, past glass display cases featuring crystal balls, a collection of ornately carved daggers under a sign that advertises Ritual Knives, and a creepy assortment of voodoo dolls, complete with their own lethal-looking hat pins. "Here 'tis," she chirps. "Would you like the abalone shell, too, dear? It's very handy for collecting the ash and it's only $9.99 more."

"No, thanks. I'm good."

"All right, then." Rei follows bird-lady to the register at the front of the store.

Three minutes later, Rei is sprinting to the car, having survived the bizarreities of The Hallowed Eave. Once he's in the car, he tucks the magical sage bundle under the seat.

"Did you see the ritual knives? What do people *do* with those?" he asks me as we head up the highway ramp. "And you must have loved the voodoo dolls."

Later that night in Rei's bedroom, we try to figure out the best way to fire up the sage bundle and smoke Taylor out. "My mom will kill me if I light this in the house," he says as he sniffs the sage bundle for the zillionth time. "It doesn't smell like sage," he says, also for the zillionth time. I have no idea. If someone wants to know what vanilla smells like, I'm their girl. Even blindfolded, I can identify garlic, cinnamon, even rosemary. But sage?

Rei is on the computer, Googling "what does white sage smell like" and he doesn't like what he finds. "If I burn this in the house, not only will she kill me, she will bury my dead body under the front porch for the worms to eat," he says flatly. "It smells like marijuana when you burn it."

Marijuana. Rei can be so formal.

I'd heard that Taylor and her friends used to go to Burlington and drink with the college kids, but I don't know if the party extended to drugs outside of alcohol. Did she smoke? I don't know. I wasn't privy to the conversations she had with her girlfriends.

Why don't we see if she'll smoke it?

Rei squints at the computer screen, not because he can't see what I've typed, but because he doesn't like it. "How do you know what smoking this stuff will do to you? Those are your lungs, too. And you never know what that stuff would do to your brain." Rei hides the sage in his bottom desk drawer, under a pile of college brochures. "I'll figure it out in the morning." He stretches out on his bed, flat on his back, and folds his hands under his head. He closes his eyes and I drift up and hover next to his bed. He looks tired. I've been feeding off his energy a lot today, and I can see the toll it's taking on him.

"Hi," he smiles without opening his eyes. "I can feel you there." He opens his eyes and rolls over onto his side, bunching the pillow up under his head. "Did you know that?"

No, I didn't. I shake my head.

"Yeah, I can feel you near me," he repeats with a trace of melancholy in his voice, "but I can't touch you." He reaches out and runs his fingers back and forth through my arm like I'm the flame on a candle, and it tickles when he does this. "I wish I knew how all this works. You're energy, I know that, but I wonder what kind."

Probably nuclear, I tease.

"Well, you are kind of glowing," he teases back. "Let me see your hand." I hold my left hand out, palm up, and let him inspect it. "I think maybe you're some kind of energy that humans haven't identified yet," he finally says.

Who knows? I usually need to pull energy from around me in order for you to see me, and I need a lot of it if I want to move stuff. Are you tired right now?

"Yeah, but it's getting late."

Still, I'm getting some of my energy from you. Does the room feel cooler than normal?

"Yeah, it feels good, though."

Because I'm also pulling heat from the room in order to have enough energy to type.

"I still don't understand how you can type." He runs his fingers through my arm a few more times. "How do you do it?"

I don't know. How does the wind move things? That's not solid, but it can rip a building apart.

"So what would happen if I wasn't around to pull energy from and you were someplace cold, like the South Pole? Then what would you do?"

Pull from the sun.

"What about at night?"

It doesn't matter. Stars give off a lot of energy and it's all just floating around in space. And the energy that comes from nebulas or supernovas is pretty powerful. It's like drinking a couple of Red Bulls. If I concentrate really hard, I can tap into that.

Rei's smile is sleepy and sweet. "When have you ever had a couple of Red Bulls?"

When you weren't around to yell at me.

He smirks. "That's what I thought." He rolls onto his back and stares up at the ceiling. "It must be cool to see a supernova."

Want to see one? I can show you. Not that I seriously expect him to consider it, but how much fun would it be to show Rei around the universe!

He turns his head to read the computer screen and shakes his head. "Ha. Nice try, though."

Are you afraid someone will hijack you, too?

"Maybe. But like I said before, think about how fast you're moving out there. What would happen if you got sucked into a black hole? There's a lot of stuff in space that scientists have no clue about. What if something *can* destroy energy, and we just haven't discovered it?"

You worry too much!

"And you don't worry nearly enough," he says. He closes his eyes and within minutes, the rhythm of his breath becomes deep and predictable.

For all the macho muscles he's built, I still see the little boy in Rei when he sleeps. His face relaxes. His lips part slightly, but he doesn't snore. He's never snored, *ever,* and I can say this without exaggeration because I have known Rei *forever.* We napped together as babies; we were potty trained together; we held hands as we boarded the bus on our first day of kindergarten. And this is why I feel so guilty now.

For years, I thought it was unfortunate that Rei's top lip is slightly fuller than his bottom lip, only because it was perpetually chapped. But Rei's all grown up now, and those lips aren't chapped anymore; in fact, they look *really* tempting.

I rest my hand on his chest to feel it rise and fall, feel his energy hum along in harmony with his heartbeat, and it hits me for the first time: Rei has always been my ninja protector, but he's not invincible. I know it's late, but how much energy have I pulled from him today? I can't keep doing this to him.

Yumi offers a type of hands-on healing called Reiki in her store. Literally, the word *Reiki* means unseen energy or life force, and it's something Yumi went to classes to learn back when she was pregnant with Rei, which accounts for his full name—Robert Reiki Ellis. I used to wonder where she got this unseen energy, if she got it from the same places I find mine, but it's not something I could just go up and ask about, not unless I wanted her to know my secrets.

I don't know Yumi's source of energy, but I wonder if I can use my energy the same way she uses hers. One of the laws of physics states that energy always travels from order to chaos. Well, if I'm not a bundle of chaos, I don't know who is. I sit very still with my eyes closed, and I concentrate on that profusion of energy that exists within the universe. Like a magnet, I draw this power from the edges of creation, through all dimensions beyond me, pulling it toward me and through me, until I feel myself tingling. I float my hands over Rei and let the energy seep into him, little by little, until intuition tells me *enough!* I smooth his hair off his face and let him sleep in peace.

CHAPTER 14

Before she dresses for work the next morning, my mom wakes up Taylor and decides she's okay to go to school. Taylor allows herself to be kissed on the cheek, and as soon as the bedroom door closes, she gets up and starts searching through my closet for something to wear.

"This is fugly, this sucks, absolutely hideous, wouldn't be caught *dead* wearing this!" she bitches as she pulls one thing after another out of my closet and flings it over her shoulder. By the time she's done, there's a considerable pile of clothes on the floor and still nothing she deems worthy to wear. She settles on a pair of jeans and a shirt my mom bought me a year ago that still has the sales tag on it because I thought it was a little on the sleazy side. Once she tries it on, I realize I was right.

She roots through all my drawers looking for makeup and finds nothing but cherry Chapstick, so she waits for my mom to leave before sneaking into her room to use her stuff. The light is better and the mirror is bigger in my mom's bedroom, so she puts on foundation, blush, purple eye shadow, a thick rim of black eyeliner all around my eyes, a few layers of mascara, and a heavy layer of dark reddish lipstick. She blots her lips and makes a kissy face in the mirror.

Who the hell *is* that? I don't recognize my face anymore. She stands there surveying herself, then grabs a hairbrush and with a disdainful look, begins to brush. I don't have that long, blonde Rapunzel look Taylor is used to. My hair is straight, tree bark brown, and I keep it long enough to put up in a ponytail. I tolerate the inconvenience of side bangs only because they hide the scar on my forehead. She has no choice but to make the best of it this morning.

Once she's ready, she looks uncertain. She glances at the clock, then at the phone, and then she stares out the window for a few seconds. My cell phone is on the bookcase, so she picks it up and flips through all five of my speed dial numbers. Rei's number is on top. I watch her press '1' and we both wait for Rei to answer.

"So yesterday when we were talking on my front steps, you said I take the bus with you," Taylor says by way of a greeting.

My hearing is sharp enough in this dimension that Rei's voice is loud and clear right through the phone.

"Good. You remembered that," Rei says. "You meet me at the top of my driveway every morning at seven, which means I will see you in . . . six minutes. Did you take anything out of your backpack?"

"No. Why?" Taylor kicks through the piles of clothes she tossed, looking for what I can only assume is my backpack.

"Because you keep your epi in your backpack, but you probably don't remember that."

"An epi? Am I allergic to something?"

"Peanuts. But you don't eat tree nuts, either."

Taylor groans. "Peanuts? You're kidding me, right?"

"No, I'm not kidding," Rei's voice is crisp. "And I'll see you in five minutes."

That's long enough. I fly over to Rei's and find him still in his room. Damn! His computer is off and we don't have time to boot it up.

"Good morning," he says with a wry smile. "Nice of you to drop by."

I wave and I point to the bottom desk drawer.

"What . . . the sage?"

I nod emphatically.

"Yeah, I haven't figured it out yet."

I roll my eyes in exasperation and point to the clock.

"Yeah, I know, four minutes. I have to go."

That wasn't what I meant!

I bounce back home to find Taylor mumbling little obscenities about me and my allergies, as if this is somehow my fault. She digs around the bottom of my closet until she finds a pair of seldom used clogs, and she unearths my black hoodie and backpack from the pile of castoffs on my bedroom floor. She doesn't bother locking the front door behind her.

Rei waits for her at the top of his driveway, one earbud stuck in his ear. When he sees Taylor, he whistles softly. "Whoa. I guess you forgot you don't wear makeup."

"I do now," she said shortly. "Does the bus pick us up right here?" She attempts her epic hair *swish*, which fails since my hair is not so swishable. It makes me laugh.

Rei shakes his head and grins down at her, clearly amused, as well. "Nope. It's up here."

She follows him toward the bus stop, and I follow along from a safe distance. Along the way, Taylor quizzes Rei about her schedule and asks more questions about things she 'can't remember.' I realize now why I never wore those clogs. They are not compatible with mud.

On the bus, Rei offers an earbud to Taylor, probably to keep her quiet. She frowns when she hears the music, and from my safe vantage point, I can barely hear her ask to see his iPod. Rei hands it over. She spins through his music, frowning.

"Don't you have anything good?"

Rei sucks in his cheeks. "Define good."

"You know, *good*. Don't you have anything, like, current? Some decent pop or R&B?"

Rei laughs, probably because she used the words *decent* and *pop* in the same sentence. "There's a lot of current stuff on there, but most of it is from indie bands you probably don't remember." He holds out his hand for the iPod, and when she hands it over, he surfs for something. "Here, try this."

She sits back with a look that clearly tells him she is settling for this music. Rei turns toward the window and rubs the center of his forehead just above his eyebrows.

For the rest of the school day, Rei coaches Taylor on where to be at what time, tells her which locker is mine, takes the package of cookies out of her hands in the lunch line and reminds her she's allergic to peanuts.

"So? These are chocolate chip, not peanut butter."

Rei flips the package over. "Read the ingredients."

She huffs at him. "Flour," she says sarcastically, "sugar . . ." she's quiet as she scans the ingredient list. "Processed on shared equipment with peanuts and tree nuts," she reads. "You're shitting me, right?"

"Wrong." Rei puts them back on the rack. "And in case you forgot, you hardly ever swear."

"Yeah, okay, good. So what happens if I eat them?"

"Bad things. Just don't eat them. And make sure you keep your epi with you *all the time*. Okay? When we get back to the table, I'll show you how to use it."

Rei is helping Taylor find her spiral notebook for Spanish class, when Callie comes striding up.

"Hey, I've been looking for you two."

"What's up?" Rei greets her.

"I just wanted to see how Anna's feeling," she says, and then she addresses Taylor, who is still poking around in my locker. "You okay?"

"No, I have a concussion," Taylor finds a sharp pencil on the floor of my locker and finally turns around.

Callie gasps. "Wow, Anna! Why are you covered in makeup? You look like a . . ."

"Hey, Callie," Rei jumps in, "Anna's having some trouble remembering things because of her concussion, and one of them is that she doesn't wear makeup."

"Really? A concussion? Oh, you poor thing! Well, that explains the outfit, then. Nice sternum, by the way."

Taylor makes a face like she's going to defend my lack of cleavage, but then Callie asks the worst possible question.

"So what's going on with Seth? I hear all these rumors about him and Taylor Gleason."

"Seth killed Taylor Gleason in cold blood," Taylor cranks up the volume of her voice. "I was there, and I saw him throw Taylor right off the ledge. He's a murderer."

Everyone in the hallway has now stopped to listen. Callie looks confused. "What do you mean, you were there?"

"I was there," Taylor repeats. "The police are looking for him, and when they find him, I am an eyewitness."

Callie looks at Rei for some kind of confirmation, but Rei just reaches into my locker, grabs my Spanish textbook, and thrusts it into Taylor's hands. "You have Spanish in room 137," he says coldly. "Meet me back here after."

"I'm not . . ." Taylor begins.

"Go!" Rei orders in a voice that seems to jump-start all the eaves-droppers on their way again. Taylor huffs and stomps off toward Spanish.

"So what's really going on?" Callie asks. "I heard that Taylor's dead, but I can't believe Seth had anything to do with it. And what's up with Anna? She's acting *really* weird!"

"She is," Rei agrees. "But don't worry about it," he slams my locker door. "As soon as Anna's memory comes back, everything will be fine."

"Well, the good news is Spanish is a Latin-based language, so this shouldn't be too difficult," Taylor greets Rei after class.

"That's good. Because Spanish is one of your best subjects," Rei points out.

Of course it is. I love Spain. I spend enough time there when I'm out of my body that I'm practically fluent in Spanish.

As the day drags on, I notice Taylor's eyes are lingering on Rei for longer and longer periods of time when she thinks he's not looking. During the bus ride home, Taylor gradually scoots closer to Rei until their hips are touching. By the time they get to their bus stop, Rei is hanging halfway off the seat in an effort to leave some space between them.

On the walk home, she turns to Rei. "So I really said you were like a brother to me?"

I swear I don't remember saying that!

"Yup," Rei answers without looking at her. He looks tired again. I think Taylor sucked even more energy out of him today than I did yesterday.

"You don't seem like a brother now," she says coyly.

Something between amusement and annoyance is simmering in his eyes. "No?"

"No, in fact, I think since we know each other so well, maybe we should, you know, go out sometime."

He still won't look at her. "What if I still think of you like a sister?"

"Trust me," Taylor tells him in a silky voice, "I'm *nothing* like your sister."

They've reached the top of Rei's driveway now, and as far as I know, Saya is expected home at three o'clock. I'm curious if Rei has given any thought to the bundle of sage that's hidden in his desk drawer. In my opinion, it would be tough to light that thing with Saya around. How would we explain that? I suppose we'll have to talk about it tonight.

"So, it's settled," Taylor turns the corner and starts walking down Rei's driveway. "I'm coming over."

CHAPTER 15

Rei is a badass poker player. I know it goes against the moral, upstanding reputation he's so well known for, but the reason Rei consistently wins all of Seth's pennies is because he's a master at hiding emotions. After nearly seventeen years with him, though, I can read the subtle changes in Rei's poker face that Seth cannot. The reason Rei consistently wins all of my pennies is because I can't remember the difference between a flush, a straight, and a full house.

When I'm out of my body, though, I have the added advantage of seeing Rei's aura. Right now, he's sick of Taylor and wants nothing more than to go for a long, hard run, but on the other hand, he wants her out of my body.

"You're welcome to come over," he tells her in a vanilla cream puff voice, "but I have some stuff I have to do."

"Like what kind of stuff?"

"Well, I have to babysit Saya. And I have to start dinner, stuff like that."

"I can help you."

"Do you remember how to cook?" I materialize behind Taylor's back just long enough to give Rei a snide look, which he ignores. Taylor has no way of knowing I'm a really good slicer/dicer, my tuna salad rocks, and I make awesome zucchini-carrot muffins. Just don't ask me to cook meat unless the fire department is nearby.

She must have picked up the double-edged sarcasm in his voice, because she asks, "Could I cook before?"

"Some things," Rei admits as he follows her down the driveway.

Something is wrong. Rei's meticulously clean porch has somehow become smudged by a path of muddy footprints that lead directly to the front door. I look for the obvious explanation, but I see no packages waiting by the door, and the footprints don't turn around and head back the other way. Rei's colors deepen and there's a subtle shift in his expression, a slight tension in his shoulders.

"Why don't you wait here just in case the bus comes to drop off Saya," he tells Taylor calmly, gesturing toward the swing. "I'll go get something for us to drink."

I follow him in through the door, and the footprints stop abruptly on the mat just inside the door. I do one fast loop around the downstairs to see if anyone is there, but Rei heads directly upstairs, taking the steps two at a time. I reach the landing at the same time he does, just in time to catch the bedroom door opening wide on its own accord and a deep voice calls Rei's name.

Rei's hand flashes out like a bolt of lightning, silencing the voice, and he body slams the intruder into his room and kicks the door shut behind him. It takes me a second to process exactly where the danger is.

It's downstairs sitting on the porch.

"Shhh!" Rei whispers. "There's someone here. You need to be quiet!"

Seth doesn't seem all that surprised by Rei's reaction. "Who's here? Anna?" he whispers back.

"Yeah, but I don't want her to know you're here."

Seth shrugs. "Rei, I need to talk to you!" he whispers urgently. "I think the cops might be looking for me!"

"The police *are* looking for you, you idiot!"

"*Shit!*" Seth moves to punch the wall, but Rei's hand intercepts his fist. "I knew it! You know for sure they're looking for me?"

"They were here yesterday asking me questions."

"Here? Asking *you* questions? Like what?"

"Like we don't have time to talk about it right now." Rei shepherds Seth over to the door of his weight room and opens it wide. "Wait in here until I get rid of her. And don't abuse my walls!"

Now Seth is surprised. "Get *rid* of her . . . what, are you two mad at each other?"

Rei glances toward his bedroom door. "It's a long story. She can't know you're here."

"I didn't push Taylor. You know that, right?"

"I know you didn't, and we'll figure this out when I get back. Here," Rei pulls his iPod out of his jeans pocket and hands it to Seth without bothering to untangle the earbud cord. "I have Saya home today, too, so this may take a while, but I need you to *stay* in here and stay *quiet*."

Seth shrugs. "Okay, I get it. Hey, hope you don't mind, I borrowed some of your clothes."

I hear the bus growling up the street, and from the look on his face, so does Rei. "Fine, whatever, just stay in here until I come and get you, okay? We'll talk later." The bus is pulling up in front of his house.

Rei gives Seth one last look before he closes the door quietly behind him.

And of course *I'm* not allowed in the weight room, which will make it nearly impossible for me to spy on Seth.

In one fast fluid motion, Rei leans down the stairs while he slides his hands halfway down the railings, then he locks his elbows and swings himself to the floor below. He bolts out the door just as Saya jumps off the bus.

"I thought you were getting drinks," Taylor chides him.

"Sorry, I heard the bus. I'll get them in a minute."

Saya is like a single ray of sunshine on an otherwise dreary day. She runs down the driveway and doesn't slow down until she hops onto Taylor's lap, catching her by surprise.

"Oh! Well aren't you an energetic little thing! Look at those eyes!" The first thing anyone *ever* notices about Saya is the color of her eyes, which are blue like her daddy's. "Aren't they gorgeous!" Then Taylor makes her first mistake at the Ellis home. "Your eyes are the color of forget-me-nots."

No, they are definitely the color of morning glories, but I learned a long time ago not to engage Saya in a conversation about eye color.

Saya giggles and looks into Taylor's stolen eyes. "*Your* eyes are the color of overcooked asparagus." That's pretty mild. Over the past two years, my eyes have been every unappealing shade of green from algae to zucchini.

Taylor's jaw drops, and she looks owlishly at Rei to gauge his reaction. He's had a minute to calm himself down, and he's sitting with his back against the porch column, his legs stretched out along the top step. He drops his chin to hide a smile.

"Well, isn't she charming," Taylor says sarcastically.

"I wouldn't feel too bad if I were you," Rei assures her. "Saya, what color are *my* eyes?"

"Your eyes are the color of elephant poop!" Saya giggles

uncontrollably. The names of the animals will change, but as far as Saya is concerned, Rei's eyes are always the color of poop. Yumi forbade Rei and me from playing this game with Saya a long time ago, so she's pretty thrilled she's getting away with it now.

"See, there you go. Isn't overcooked asparagus a whole lot better than elephant poop?"

"Charming." Taylor repeats and brushes Saya firmly off her lap. Saya bounces from Taylor over to Rei, and climbs on him like a monkey, stepping on his legs and tugging at his arms.

"I'm hungry. And I wanna go to the falls," she pleads.

"Hey, that's a great . . ."

"No!" Taylor cuts him off.

"Please?" Saya gives Taylor the look no one can resist.

"I thought your brother had work to do," she says icily.

Rei lifts Saya off his lap, stands up, and heads inside. "Are you hungry, too?" he asks Taylor.

"Hungry for what, exactly?" Taylor asks in a smoky voice as she follows Rei.

Rei opens the fridge and scouts around. A devious little grin appears on his face. "How about an orange?" he asks.

"Sure, I love oranges. They smell like your body wash."

That comment wipes the smile right off Rei's face. "It's not body wash, it's soap," he informs her. "Here, catch." He tosses the orange over his shoulder, and I'm surprised she catches it.

"Thanks."

He pulls a bunch of carrots out of the refrigerator as Taylor struggles to peel the orange with my blunt nails.

"Need some help with that?" he finally offers.

"Thanks." She hands the orange to Rei. "So, how long have I been a nail-biter?"

"When we were four, your father broke a few of his vertebrae." Rei strips the orange down in seconds and hands it back to her. "That's when you started."

This revelation doesn't inspire any comment from Taylor besides, "Well, I'm cured now, so I guess this concussion wasn't such a bad thing after all." She winks and pops a section of orange into her mouth.

Rei mumbles something about carrots and pulls a paring knife out of the wooden block that sits on the counter. As soon as he cuts the green tops off the carrots, Saya swipes one. "Tickle, tickle!" she waves it under Taylor's chin.

Taylor stares at her impassively. "Why don't you go watch TV or something."

"Hey, you're right!" Saya hollers at Rei. "Anna doesn't even remember the TV rule."

"You have TV rules? You poor, unfortunate children," Taylor sucks orange juice off her fingers. "Where's your bathroom? I need to freshen up."

"Down the hall, first door on the left."

Rei has three carrots peeled before Taylor wanders back.

"You're out of bathroom tissue." She smiles as if this is a very classy thing to say.

"What's bathroom tissue?" Saya asks.

"Toilet paper," he tells her impatiently. "Hold on. I'll get you some."

But Taylor is already halfway up the stairs. "I'll just use your upstairs bathroom. No *problemo*."

The towel in Rei's hand falls onto the floor as he charges after her. "*Wait!*"

"Can't I have a little privacy?" she asks from the top step. "Or are you one of those guys who like to listen outside the bathroom door?" She grins wickedly at him.

"Okay, fine," he says as he pivots on the step he's on and heads back down.

Rei is definitely not one of *those* guys, but it's my body, so . . . oh, ew! I just realized she's seen me naked. I barge right in on her. Well, she's not here to pee, that's for sure! She opens every cabinet door, every drawer, even peeks behind the shower curtain, and besides finding the orange glycerin soap Rei faithfully showers with, she learns that Rei and Saya use cinnamon-flavored toothpaste and Rei is almost out of razor blades.

Rei paces at the bottom of the stairs, waiting for Taylor, trying hard not to appear as though he's *listening*. . . .

Somehow, he doesn't hear her as she slips out of the bathroom noiselessly and walks the few steps to Rei's bedroom door. The knob turns easily and the door pushes open with no complaint.

Rei's room is, as always, neat and clean. Rei is a minimalist. There are no piles of papers cluttering his desk, no dirty clothes strewn around his floor, no empty cups stacking up. His bed is made, his bureau is bare except for several trophies he's earned in karate, even his hardwood floor is free of dust. The look on her face says it all. Boring!

I don't want to risk scaring Saya by materializing in front of her, but Rei needs to get up here fast. I try to knock over one of the trophies on his bureau to get his attention, but they are heavy suckers, and I can't budge them.

She opens the first door she sees. Rei's closet.

Crap! I weigh the lesser of two evils and waste no time getting downstairs. Saya is busy searching through her backpack, thankfully, so I surge into view and point up. Rei understands immediately and takes the stairs three at a time. He opens the bedroom door just in time to see Taylor close his closet door and turn toward the door leading into the weight room.

"Anna!"

Taylor smiles at Rei, ignoring the fury in his voice. "Hi! I like your room. Cool swing chair! What's in here?" She reaches for the knob to the weight room as he steps on and over his bed and lands beside her.

"That," he pries her hand off the doorknob, "is off-limits."

He puts his arm around her shoulder, which seems to make her happy, and herds her away from the door and out of the room. "And you know it's off-limits. At least you *knew*. That's my weight room, and you were banned from going in there after you gave me grief when I first started lifting weights. You've been really good about staying out of there for the past year, so do me a favor and stay good."

"Where's the fun in that?" Taylor pouts.

When they reach the foot of the stairs, Rei puts both hands on Taylor's shoulders and leans down to look her in the eyes. "I need to finish making dinner. If you're bored . . ."

"Who, me? I never get tired of watching men work." She winks at him and takes a seat at the counter beside Saya, who is whizzing through a math worksheet.

Rei glances at the clock and gets a package wrapped in white paper out of the freezer.

"What are you making?"

"Smoked fish."

Smoked fish? The Ellis family never eats smoked fish. They always poach it or broil it or sometimes they don't even bother to cook it and Yumi makes sushi. And Yumi always brings home fresh fish from the store, so why is Rei tapping into their emergency stash of frozen fish? That's there in case of a blizzard or other natural disaster.

Rei unwraps the fish and sticks it in the microwave to defrost.

"Saya, why don't you go watch the Disney Channel in Mom and Dad's room."

Saya is dumbstruck. "But I'm not done with my homework."

"That's okay, I'll help you with it later," Rei promises.

"But won't Mommy be mad?" she asks.

"Not at you," Rei replies. This is good enough for Saya. She skips off down the hall, and I hear the door to her parents' room click shut just before the microwave dings.

Rei opens the cupboard door and roots around until he finds an old saucepan we use occasionally to melt suet for the birds. "Be right back," he tells Taylor. "Stay put."

I materialize in front of his bedroom door and draw a question mark in the air with my finger.

"Shhh," he warns me. Like I'm making any noise. I follow him into his bedroom where he retrieves the sage bundle from his bottom desk drawer.

"What is that?" Taylor asks when Rei returns with the peculiar bundle.

"This is what we use to smoke the fish." He reaches up onto the top shelf and pulls down an old metal tea canister where Yumi keeps the birthday candles and packs of matches. It takes him three strikes to light the match, but when it ignites, there's a subtle shift of energy in the room.

"*That's* how you smoke fish?" Taylor asks skeptically.

"There are a lot of ways to smoke a fish," Rei replies without looking at her. I'm not sure if he's trying to be mysterious about this or if he's concentrating on not burning the house down. He holds the match to the end of the tied bundle, then blows the flame out gently. The smoke wastes no time filling the room.

Wow! It really does smell like marijuana. Not that I've ever smoked, but I've been to dozens of concerts, astrally of course.

"What is that stuff? Oh, my God! It smells like a doobie!" Taylor looks pleased with Rei's choice of ingredients and she leans in to inhale the smoke. I wait for the sage smoke to work its magic and for Taylor to come tumbling out of me so I can move back in and get on with my life. "Rei, you rock! I've eaten magic brownies before, but smoked fish? Brilliant! And all this time I thought you were so straight." She giggles in a way that clues me in that this is not working exactly as we had planned.

Rei coughs and waves the smoldering bundle, surrounding her in a cloud of heavy smoke, and she sucks in the smoke and holds her breath. "Although," she exhales after a long while and laughs, "isn't the fish the one who's supposed to be smoking this?"

She amuses herself much more than she amuses me, but while she's busy with her fit of giggles, I try to work myself back into her. I feel my way around her stealthily, because if she knows I'm here, she might know Rei is on to her, and that would be bad. Rei tries stamping the sage bundle out in the saucepan, but the smoke is persistent.

The television is suddenly louder and I hear little feet running down the hall. "Rei?" Saya sounds scared. "Something's on fire!" I try to picture how this would look to a seven-year-old. Taylor is laughing so hard she's crying; Rei is at the sink, rendering our eight-dollar miracle into a bundle of wet twigs; smoke pirouettes gracefully around the room, and everything stinks.

"Uh-oh," Saya says. "Mommy's going to be mad at you!"

CHAPTER 16

Saya is a smart little kid, but Rei is smarter. As soon as he sends a rather giddy Taylor on her way home, he opens all the windows to air out the house, gives Saya a can of orange scented nonaerosol air freshener and permission to spray as much as she wants, then he bribes her with the emergency stash of sugary Bazooka bubble gum I keep in his room to guard this secret and go watch television again.

"And don't get it stuck in your hair!" Rei calls after her.

As soon as Saya is settled, Rei heads upstairs to talk to Seth.

I am not actually in Rei's weight room. I am hovering just outside the window, so technically this is not breaking the rules.

Seth is lying on the floor with his feet up on the futon, listening to Rei's iPod when Rei comes through the door. Seth pulls the earbuds out and breaks into a wide grin. "Hey!" His exuberance reminds me of a puppy.

"Shhh! Anna's gone, but Saya's downstairs watching television. I don't want her to know you're here, either."

"What'd the cops say?"

"They want to know where you are. Why did you take off?

You did nothing wrong, but now that you left, they think you had something to do with it."

Seth sits up and leans his back against the futon. "It wouldn't have mattered. Just the way everything happened, I'm as good as screwed."

Seth's version of the story is exactly the same as mine, which is *nothing* like Taylor's version. "And when I tried to pull her back up over the ledge, this is what she did to me."

He must have wrapped his wrist with gauze from Rei's medicine cabinet shortly after he got here, but he unwraps it now, and Rei winces. "Seth, that's *really* infected! You need a doctor to check that out!"

"No way."

Even from my spot outside the window, I can see green pus leaking out of the long ragged gashes.

"Wait here." Rei returns with his hands full of stuff—hydrogen peroxide, antibiotic ointment, cotton balls, more gauze, and tape.

"Son of a *bitch* that burns!" Seth complains as the peroxide fizzles against his wrist.

Once Seth's wrist is wrapped in fresh gauze and he's eaten a sandwich and some fruit, Rei tries to talk some sense into him.

"Just tell the police what really happened."

Seth shakes his head. "They won't believe me. I'm that psycho kid who punched a glass door, remember? I bet Taylor's friends already told the cops she was supposed to meet me."

"Well, what are you going to do? If my parents find you, they'll make you go to the police."

"Do your parents know yet?"

"They didn't as of this morning, but you know how people talk at the store."

Yes, we all know how gossip spreads around this little town.

"I left my car at the border so they'd think I crossed over into Canada. I figured if I walked back here and you let me borrow your bike, I could go see what Matt thinks I should do."

I'm trying to remember exactly where Seth's brother, Matt, goes to college. Somewhere in upstate New York. That's a long bike ride!

"Seth, why run if you're not guilty?"

"Because I can't prove I'm *not* guilty!" Seth slams his fist against the futon cushion. "I have no witnesses, and when I grabbed her, her shirt ripped open. Like, *wide* open. That doesn't look good. And you know what the really sad part of this is?"

Rei shakes his head. I'm sure it's all sad as far as he's concerned.

"If I didn't try to catch her, if I just stood there and let her fall, I wouldn't have this problem. Her shirt wouldn't have ripped and she wouldn't have trashed my wrist." Seth leans back and stares at the ceiling. "This is what I get for trying to be a nice guy."

"What are you going to do, run for your entire life?"

Seth shrugs. "It's better than going to jail. Maybe I'll change my name. Maybe I'll end up in Canada. Who knows?"

"Somehow I think that's easier said than done, Seth. You need money to get a new identity. You need to know someone to get forged documents." Rei stands up. "I'm going to check on Saya and finish making dinner. Think about it. I'll be back in an hour or so."

But it's Rei who is deep in thought as he seasons the fish and puts a pot of water on the stove for rice. While he waits for it to boil, he goes out to the garage and pokes around until he locates a pup tent and some seldom used camping supplies from his long ago Boy Scout days. He pulls the tent down and stares at it for a minute, then sticks it back on the shelf and goes inside.

• • •

The house smells like an orange grove burned to the ground, but Yumi seems too thrilled that dinner is made to comment. While Rei and his family eat, I go upstairs and start searching online for more options now that our sage idea has literally gone up in smoke. It doesn't take long before the door opens quietly and Rei comes in. I pull enough energy to surge into view and wave to him.

"Hi," he whispers. "Seth is in the next room, you know."

I know.

"He won't turn himself in," Rei frets.

Maybe you should just call the police.

"No!" he snaps. "This has to be his decision! I just have to figure out what to say to make him realize it's the right thing to do."

I am obviously walking on thin ice here, but I have to say it anyway.

Be careful. If you get caught helping him, you'll get in trouble, too. I don't dare type in what *kind* of trouble, because who wants to see the words *accessory to murder* all lit up on the computer screen?

"I'm not worried about that," he scowls at me. "I'm worried about Seth."

There is nothing I can say that will console Rei right now. His aura clings to him in a thin, dense band, shades of yellow that have gone muddy brown. "I'm going to talk to him some more. Can you hang out downstairs and keep an eye on my mom? If she's looking for me, come up and do something to get my attention. Just don't let Seth see you and don't let my mom see Seth."

Okay.

Robert and Saya come up at eight thirty to get Saya settled in bed, but they're singing so loud on their way up the stairs, Rei comes out before I have to go in. Yumi and Robert head off to bed shortly after, giving Seth the freedom to finally use the bathroom. As soon as Seth is safely back in the weight room, Rei brings him more food and water. He is in there for at least another hour, talking so quietly even I can't hear them. It's eleven o'clock before he opens the door.

"Get some sleep," he whispers to Seth. "We'll talk more in the morning."

He returns from brushing his teeth to find my message on his computer screen.

Any progress? I materialize beside his desk as he's reading it.

Rei shakes his head. He rolls into bed and covers his eyes with his hands. "I need some sleep, too, Anna," he whispers. "I can't even see straight."

By the blue glare of the computer screen, I watch Rei slowly relax for the first time today. From the first phone call with Taylor this morning to Seth's surprise appearance, I realize Rei has not had one peaceful moment all day. No wonder he's exhausted. I focus on the vast sources of energy far beyond us and absorb what I can, until his hands slip away from his face and land softly on the pillow beside his head.

I reach out and touch my fingertip to his, gently, to see if the vibration of my touch wakes him. When he doesn't move at all, I trace my finger down the length of his, releasing a trickle of energy into him. I try to ignore how soft his skin feels to me since every little sensation is magnified when I'm out here, because I'm doing this for Rei, not for my own selfish pleasure. I trace all his fingers, one by one, replacing his tired colors with indigo, then I inch my way up his arm until I reach his shoulder, skim my fingers over his collarbone, his Adam's apple, up to the fine stubble on his chin. It's not his head I'm concerned about today. I take my time, releasing a steady stream of energy until I reach the center of his chest.

Yumi can recite volumes of information about Reiki and how it works with a person's chakras, but I can't keep all that straight. All I know right now is this is where Rei needs me most. I swirl my hand around until I've created a tiny vortex of energy around Rei, and as he gradually absorbs it, I'm relieved to see the indigo unfurl around him.

I can't manage to lift the comforter over him because it's too heavy, but I feel better knowing my best friend sleeps with a clear aura. I know I had promised not to go into Rei's weight room, but I want to make sure Seth is sleeping, too.

In the darkness of the weight room, I locate Seth by his erratic vibration and the wet dog smell that clings to him. He's snoring, not so loud that Yumi or Robert could hear him from the floor below, but loud enough that I know he's asleep. He appears to be half on, half off the futon, which makes sense since he's so tall.

There's nothing else for me to do here tonight, and I don't have enough juice to go check on Taylor. I need a mini vacation . . . somewhere sunny.

Some people read the Bible; some read the Koran. I read *The Little Prince* by Antoine de Saint-Exupéry. It's a lot less violent, plus there's a talking fennec, which is an adorable desert fox with ginormous ears that lives in the Sahara where it happens to be very sunny. In the story, it's the fennec who shares his wise secret with the Little Prince in exchange for being tamed.

I've been to the Sahara before. I've played with a family of fennecs and I know their vibrations well enough to find them now. Fennecs mate for life—another reason to love them.

Rei tries hard to tame Seth and me. I know he feels responsible for us. I know we disappoint him. I know we make his life a living hell sometimes, but I know Rei and I will always be friends. I just don't know if Seth and I are ready to be tamed.

I cruise back into Rei's room early the next morning, pumped up on Sahara sunshine and baby fennec bliss, only to find Rei pacing in front of the open door of his weight room.

Even before he blurts it out, I know.

"Seth is gone!"

CHAPTER 17

Rei blames himself for Seth's escape, but since he needs to sleep and I don't, my guilt-o-meter can't stand the expression on Rei's face.

Don't worry! I'll find him!

I find Seth riding Rei's mountain bike on a back road in New York. I can only guess he's on his way to talk to his brother. Part of me wants to materialize in the middle of the road just to scare the crap out of him because it would serve him right for sneaking out and stealing Rei's bike. I will say this much for him: he's fast. He must have left when it was still dark in order to have made it this far. I go back to break the bad news to Rei.

He stole your bike. He's already in New York.

Rei just closes his eyes and sighs. "Then he's going to talk to Matt."

Rei is so organized. He flips through the contacts on his cell phone and calls Seth's brother. It's barely past six o'clock on Saturday morning, so it's no surprise Rei gets Matt's voice mail. "Matt, it's Rei Ellis. Call me as soon as you get this. It's important!"

He hangs up and turns to me with that authoritative look of his. "Let's go get him."

And do what? When Matt calls you back, tell Matt what's going on and let HIM try to talk some sense into him. Maybe he'll have more luck than you.

"But I have to do something!" he argues.

Just wait for Matt to call you back. Then you can decide together what to do.

I don't see Rei's mad face very often, and I'm glad for that. I hold my own during the staring contest that follows until I notice his colors cool down and I know he finally agrees. "Fine." His stomach rumbles as he stuffs his cell phone in his pocket. "So do you ever get hungry over there?"

Now he's going to worry about my diet? *I can't eat over here.*

"Yeah, I figured. That must suck."

It does suck. Everything sucks. *I miss cheesecake.*

Rei nods sympathetically. "Do you miss oatmeal, too?" Now he's teasing me. He knows I hate anything that looks predigested.

Are you trying to tell me you're hungry?

"Sorry. I wasn't sure what the deal was with food in that dimension. I didn't want to eat in front of you if it would bother you."

You need to eat. Don't worry about me.

"Don't worry about you? Oh, okay. I won't breathe, either." He reaches for the back of my neck, then stops and lets his hand drop to his side. He sighs. "I guess I'll go take a shower."

I notice he takes his cell phone into the bathroom with him.

Fifteen minutes later, he's sitting at the kitchen table, barefoot, wearing jeans and a faded gray T-shirt. The newspaper is spread out in front of him, and he's stirring cinnamon into a bowl of oatmeal.

"Yum," he holds up a big gloppy spoonful and sticks it into his mouth. "Mmmm."

I open my mouth and pretend to stick my finger down my throat.

The usual high school crowd doesn't come into the store on Saturday, so Robert and Yumi take the opportunity to sleep in until seven. Miraculously, Saya is still asleep, too. Rei turns each page, commenting on this and that, until he comes to the obituaries, and he pushes the paper toward me so we can both see it.

Taylor Ann Gleason ~ Beloved Daughter

We both take a minute to read to ourselves all the wonderful things it says about Taylor.

"There are two viewings. Tonight from six to eight is for anyone local, and tomorrow night is for their Long Island people. The funeral is Monday morning. Should we be going to any of this?"

Without the computer, I'm essentially mute. I nod.

"Since we're not going after Seth, we should focus on what to do about Taylor. That sage stuff obviously didn't work. Any more ideas?"

I shake my head. I want to tell him I plan to spend the morning on his computer looking for more ideas, but I can't do that without a voice.

"Well, think about it. I have to work today. Will you keep an eye on Seth for me?"

Of course. I nod.

I ping-pong back and forth from Rei's house to Seth, who is steadily progressing toward Matt's college. Rei and his family leave for the store, and it doesn't occur to me until I hear Rei tell Yumi that Anna doesn't feel well, so he'll babysit the kids at the store while

Yumi teaches yoga class this morning. Kids love Rei. He's like a human jungle gym, and since we've been taking care of Saya since she was born, babysitting comes naturally to both of us. Still, it's adorable to watch him wrangle a dozen little kids, all under the age of five. I stay and watch the shenanigans until class is over and Rei goes off to the back room to do some real work.

I know I'm supposed to be figuring out what to do about Taylor, but I've been avoiding the computer because I know what I'm going to find . . .

Exorcism.

I never saw the original movie, *The Exorcist*, but I've heard plenty of rumors. Rotating heads. Puking pea soup. Flagrant disregard for religious artifacts. The list goes on. I really don't want to go there.

So I decide to check up on Taylor instead. I find my mom and Taylor bonding at the mall. They look happy. My mom is chattering away, laughing, and Taylor responds to her in an easy, comfortable way. I keep hearing the word *lavender, lavender.* I really hope they're talking about the flower or the fragrance, because I despise the color lavender. In fact, any shade of purple depresses me. Watching Taylor and my mom depresses me, too.

I love my mom and I know she loves me, but aside from a short stature, celery-colored eyes, and an insatiable sweet tooth, we have little in common. She loves shopping at discount stores for designer clothes, trendy jewelry, and knock-off perfume. I like blue jeans, Rei's hand-me-down hoodies, and unscented antiperspirant. Ever since seventh grade, school picture day has started with an argument at my house. "I will not buy another school photo of you wearing that same old black hoodie with your hair just *hanging* there!" is her usual battle cry. "Can't you at least put on some blush? A little mascara?" she begs.

I respect that my mother works hard to support me and my deadbeat father. What I don't get is why she lets him get away with being such a lush. Why she expects me to change, but not him.

They click-clack over the tile floor, mom in her heels and Taylor in my clogs, heading over to Nadia's Nail Boutique. My nail biting has been a thorn in my mother's side for many years, and she just can't contain her excitement that I'm finally interested in acrylic nails. The chemical stench from Nadia's is overpowering to me. Before I leave, I hear Taylor ask the girl in the white coat for the extra long nail tips.

Delightful.

In the back room of the store, Rei breaks down cardboard boxes and stacks them. He's plugged into his iPod, and his attention is equally focused between the music and the boxes. He jumps a mile when I appear.

"Anna!" He yanks out one earbud and looks around for his parents, but they're in the front taking care of customers—I already checked. "Could you please give me a little warning?" I point to the pocket holding his cell phone.

"You want my phone?"

I nod.

"Why?" he asks as he pulls it out and holds it in my direction with a confused look.

Guess what, I text curtly.

"Oh . . . okay, what?"

I'm getting acrylic nails. Extra long.

Rei grins. "Oh, boy!"

I glare at him. *My mom likes shopping with Taylor better than me.*

"No, she doesn't," he says reassuringly, but we both know it's true. "Taylor just likes all that trendy stuff your mom likes. Just hope they keep the receipts."

Texting is hard. Even with Rei and his super Zenergy right here, texting requires too damn much effort. I hover over a neat stack of empty boxes and fume.

"So I finally talked to Matt. I told him to call me as soon as Seth shows up." Rei motions to the stack of boxes. "I need to finish up a few things, and then I'm heading home. You're not going to the viewing dressed like that, are you?"

I summon up all the energy I can muster and send the stack of empty boxes tumbling down around him. He laughs, which annoys me even more. "Okay, I deserved that. Hey, can you check on Seth and meet me back at my house in about an hour?"

I nod and let myself dissolve in front of him. I've been checking up on Seth all day, anyway. He's robotically pedaling along in his bubble of gray, like he's surrounded by his own personal rain cloud. Ahead of him, the road curves and rises, and the pavement is scarred with frost heaves from the long, hard winter.

A week ago, Seth had a pretty good idea about where he was going in life. I don't think he expected anything too fancy: maybe go to tech school, get a job working with cars, hopefully deal with the fact that his mom abandoned him, and realize that not all women are selfish and hurtful. Now he has no idea if he'll make it around the next bend without getting arrested. And maybe Seth is right: if he didn't try to save Taylor, things would probably be a lot different right now. Maybe he would still be a suspect, but there would be no evidence against him. Except Taylor would still be claiming to be Annaliese Rogan, the only eyewitness.

It all comes down to me.

This does nothing to improve my mood. I'm not a big fan of

responsibility and I hate to see people suffer. As soon as Rei gets home, we exchange a wave and he immediately heads for the shower. I leave Rei a message on the computer to read when he comes back, because I don't want my bad mood diluted by the cheerful scent of his citrus soap.

I'm going to check on Taylor and her stupid new nails. I'll see you tonight.

Taylor stands in front of my dresser, brushing blush onto her cheeks in front of my pink magnifying mirror. She's sporting a sparkly diamond nose stud that wasn't there earlier, so it must be with my mom's blessing. What was that woman thinking? Just for my own childish pleasure, I knock her mascara off the dresser. She bends to pick it up, clasping it carefully between her ruby red, extra long nail tips, and sets it back on the dresser. I knock it off again. She looks around suspiciously.

"So you're still around, eh?" She picks up the mascara and clutches it in her hand. "I thought by now you would have found something better to do." She opens the mascara and looks into the mirror, opening her eyes wide to sweep the wand across her eyelashes. *My* eyelashes. "Your mom is *such* a sweetie. Did you see all the amazing stuff she bought me? I didn't even have to use any of your money stash. Which I found, by the way."

Great . . . I'd managed to save close to five hundred dollars by babysitting the kids at Yumi's store over the past two years, and now that money's at the mercy of Taylor Gleason.

Sweep, sweep. I nudge her arm, and she pokes herself in the eye with the wand. "Ouch! You little . . . !" She grabs a tissue from the bookshelf to blot the big black tears. "You can scratch someone's cornea doing that, you know."

Yeah, MY cornea. I flick her blush compact onto the floor, and take great satisfaction in the crunching noise I hear when the powder cake inside shatters.

"Stop it!" she hisses. I roll the eyeliner, a bottle of foundation, the blush brush, eye shadow, and a small bottle of cologne, one by one, onto the floor. The cologne hits her in the head while she's leaning over to pick up the other stuff.

"STOP IT!" she orders again.

There's nothing left on the dresser to dump, anyway.

There's a knock at my bedroom door and my mom pops her head in, smiling expectantly.

"Did you just call me, honey?" she asks.

"No, mom, I was just talking to myself," Taylor says sweetly.

As soon as the door shuts, she glares around the room. "Go away, Anna," she says in a cold, quiet voice. "You don't live here anymore. In fact, you don't *live* anymore, period."

CHAPTER 18

McGregor & Sons is the only funeral home in Byers. Separated from Main Street by a wide circular driveway and two adjoining parking lots, it's a huge white Queen Anne-style house with black shutters and a deep wraparound porch, complete with rocking chairs and ashtrays shaped like genie bottles. Mr. and Mrs. McGregor and their two sons, who are still in elementary school and apparently doomed to follow in their father's footsteps, live on the top floor. There's an ornate three-car garage that sits separately from the house, and in back of that, out of view, I discover . . . the embalming room.

I dare myself to go inside.

It smells vile in here, a mixture of potent chemicals and the underlying odor of forgotten meat, which I pick up despite the room's sterile appearance. No dead bodies, though. Not here on this skinny table. Nope, not in the freezer, either.

Inside the main house it is eerily quiet now, except for the hum of a computer in an office adjoining the vast viewing room that takes up virtually the entire bottom floor.

Oh, *here* is the dead body. The last time I saw Taylor's body, it was stuck fast to a birch branch, nibbled on by hungry critters, bloated with river water and stone cold blue. I can only assume the undertaker is a magician, because here she lies in her high-collared, long-sleeved blue dress, looking as though she died peacefully in her sleep instead of being brutally beaten against dozens of boulders.

She looks as though she's made of wax. After seeing three dead grandparents, I know this is pretty common. I also know if you stare at her stomach long enough, it will look as though she's breathing. It's very creepy. Taylor wears the requisite thick layer of beige face powder that undertakers rely on, and you can see little particles of powder clinging to her nose hairs. Other than that, her makeup is much more understated than it ever was when she was alive. There's a subtle sweep of light pink blush across her cheeks and a natural looking lipstick has replaced her usual burgundy lip gloss. No eyeliner. Her acrylic nails have been replaced and painted pale pink, and her hands are neatly folded across her stomach, a pink rose resting between them. The undertaker has taken care to position her so the deep gash by her ear, which is now filled with some kind of beige putty, is not visible from the side the mourners will approach from, and for added insurance, he has tilted her head slightly to the side. She looks tragically beautiful, lying here so absolutely, hopelessly dead.

But I know better. I plunk myself down on the coffin and sit cross-legged beside a spray of spicy-smelling stargazer lilies and wait for the first mourners to arrive. Since Taylor thinks I'm the one who's no longer alive, I should be up here, too.

At five thirty, Taylor's parents and little brother arrive, proving that the aura of grief has many colors. Her brother looks to be about eleven and miserably uncomfortable in his navy suit, starched white shirt, tie, and stiff brown dress shoes. He keeps glancing at Taylor's body as if it's going to come alive and eat him. Taylor's father has zombie eyes. He kneels before her body, professing his love and promising to find the little bastard who did this to her and make him pay. I can't see Taylor's mother's eyes through all her tears. They drip all over the satin lining of her daughter's coffin as she leans over and kisses Taylor's lifeless cheek. I sigh. And here I am, apparently not alive either, and my mom couldn't be happier.

At six o'clock sharp, the funeral director opens the door and a steady stream of mourners files into the room. Taylor's girlfriends are toward the front of the crowd, and it appears they've consulted each other about what the well-dressed teenager should wear to a viewing—black, black, and more black. They sob and lean on one another for support as they wait for their turn to kneel on the prie-dieu in front of the coffin. I wave to each of them, welcome them by name, and let them know they can take those black sunglasses off anytime now.

As they make their way through the receiving line, I watch the girls cry with Taylor's mother, shake hands with Taylor's father, and kiss Taylor's little brother on the cheek, leaving a bouquet of lipstick marks. I find it odd he doesn't object until I notice him sneaking peeks down their low-cut shirts as they bend to kiss him. After they've all passed through, the girls find a cluster of comfortable armchairs which they pull into a tight little circle. They huddle together like a coven of witches and the whispering begins.

Teri and Lisa show up together, looking apprehensive. Teri has apparently never seen a dead body before, and she's afraid to approach the coffin. Lisa looks relieved and they go off to find friends to talk to. Callie comes in shortly after, looking very appropriate in black slacks and a teal blue blouse that looks nice with her olive complexion. After she pays her respects at the coffin and expresses her condolences to Taylor's family, she goes to talk with the rest of the swim team.

It seems just about every student and teacher from Byers/ Westover High is here. From my perch on top of the flowers, I study their expressions as they kneel in front of the coffin and pretend to pray for Taylor's soul. It's pretty obvious what they are really doing: they're examining her, looking for the rumored gash in her skull where her brain peeks through.

"It's on this side," I tell everyone and point, but of course, nobody can hear me or see me. For a fleeting second, I consider surging into view, just for fun and to see what people would say, but then I decide this is a stupid idea. What would it prove? I have a feeling Taylor will bring enough attention to my life.

Rei comes in at about six thirty, wearing beige-colored chinos and a crisp-looking white polo shirt. His hair is damp and combed neatly back away from his face, which makes his eyes look even darker and more intense as he scans the room. He sees Callie and they exchange a wave, but then he sees a group of Seth's wrestling buddies and chooses to join them instead of approaching the coffin or Taylor's family. I don't blame him. The receiving line is out the door now, and the viewing room, foyer, and front porch are packed with at least two hundred people, congregated in small, closed circles whispering hushed conversations.

Gee, I wonder what everyone is saying!

I take a break from my place of honor and drift around, eavesdropping. Even though people are trying to keep their voices respectfully low, I have to zoom in pretty close to filter out all the chatter. I think I make people uncomfortable. Some of them shiver a little when I get close. Some stop talking for a few seconds and look around suspiciously. Some just take a step back. I try not to take it personally. Funeral homes are supposed to be creepy.

Most of the conversations center around rumors the students and faculty have heard about Seth and Taylor, although I do hear several people defend Seth. They are all careful to keep Rei and Taylor's parents in sight so they can stop talking if necessary, but Rei hasn't moved from his group, and he manages to keep their conversation centered on wrestling.

At about seven o'clock, I notice Taylor is just standing in the doorway, like Cinderella arriving at the ball. Rei catches and holds sight of her out of the corner of his eye as she makes her way to the coffin. She stops about eight feet away and bursts into deep, dramatic sobs.

All conversation stops, and everyone stares at Annaliese Rogan, who is making a colossal fool of herself in front of the entire school.

Both Rei and Callie excuse themselves and hurry over to Taylor's side.

"Anna?" Callie asks tentatively. "You okay?"

"I've got this, Callie," Rei tells her. He takes Taylor's arm and leads her away. It's obvious to me he is trying to save some last shred of dignity for me, bless his heart. His voice is low and persuasive as he brings her out into the foyer. "You don't have to do this. Do you want me to take you home?"

Taylor shakes her head, sobbing.

Rei pulls a few tissues from one of the many tissue boxes parked around the room and tries to hand them to her. "Come on, let me take you home. Please?"

She shakes her head. "No! I want to see my . . . *Taylor's* parents." She finally takes the tissues out of Rei's hands and scrubs her black tears away. "I'll be right back," she sniffles and heads to the ladies room.

Rei sits alone on the couch, waiting, drumming his fingers on his knee.

When Taylor finally comes out, the black tear streaks are gone and her face is calmer. "I'm going in now," she tells him in a stiff voice. "If you still want to drive me home after, you can."

"I'll come with you," Rei offers.

"Suit yourself." She swishes her hair behind her shoulder, walks in slowly, and kneels on the prie-dieu. The effort it takes to control herself is clearly visible on her face, and in spite of everything, I do feel sad for her. It's bad enough watching myself walk around, but I can't imagine seeing myself lying dead in a coffin, like she is seeing herself now.

She reaches out tentatively to touch her own dead hand, but then changes her mind. Several shuddering breaths later, she stands and approaches her parents.

"Mr. Gleason? I'm Annaliese Rogan." She offers her hand, and my name sparks some obvious recognition.

"You're the girl who witnessed Taylor's murder!" he declares, still holding on to her hand.

"Yes, I did," her voice cracks. All of the conversation in the room fades to a murmur, and it sounds as if someone has just handed Taylor a microphone. "And as soon as they find that monster, Seth Murphy, I'll be there to testify against him so he can't hurt anyone else!"

Rei's face shows no emotion, but his aura looks like raw steak. Taylor doesn't seem to notice everyone is eavesdropping. "I am *sooo* sorry." Tears spill down her cheeks, and Taylor's mother gives her a hug.

"Thank you, Annaliese," she murmurs. Taylor clings to her mother and sobs. Her little brother looks at her as though she's sprouted antlers.

After several awkward seconds, Rei steps forward and takes Taylor by the arm. "Okay, Anna," he says in a tight voice, "there are other people waiting."

"So let them wait," Taylor is indignant, but it's so crowded that once Rei moves to the side, someone else steps up to talk to Taylor's mother. Rei makes his way with Taylor to the door leading to the front porch. "Why did you pull me away?" she demands to know.

"Because you were making a scene," Rei responds without looking at her. "And I know you think Seth had something to do with this, but you need to keep your opinions to yourself. He's innocent until proven guilty."

"Bullshit! He's guilty." Taylor insists as they reach the exit. It's several degrees cooler outside and Rei's colors fade to orange. Briefly. Taylor yanks her arm from Rei's grip. "And stop holding on to my arm so tight. What is wrong with you? One minute you're all nice, and the next, you treat me like crap."

"I'm not treating you like crap. I'm just sick of hearing you accuse Seth of something he didn't do," Rei shoots back.

"Look, Rei, you need to make up your mind. Either you're on my side, or you're on his side. Decide."

Wasn't she just crying two minutes ago? Now she looks ready to punch Rei in the face. Rei must know that either way, he will lose something in this argument. "I'm not choosing one friend over another. But," his voice softens, sweetens, "you and I have been friends for a long time. We don't want to throw that away."

"I'm not interested in being *just* your friend." Taylor wears four-inch heels and she uses that extra height to her advantage. "If you want to be friends with me, Rei, then you need to *be* with me."

Rei folds his arms in front of his chest. "We already talked about this."

"And we can talk about it some more when you drive me home." She grabs the brass door handle and pulls hard. "I'll be out in a few."

Rei leans against the railing, standing as far upwind from the smokers as possible. After he calls my mom to tell her he'll drive me home, he closes his eyes, and his breathing becomes slow and deep.

I watch Taylor work her way through the crowd. Even though I never spent much time looking in the mirror, I know what I look like, and this isn't it. She's trimmed my hair, plucked my eyebrows, covered my face with makeup, dressed me up in a low-cut shirt and black miniskirt and she walks with a certain swagger I'm certain I never had before. It looks like she's stuffing my bra, too.

Her old friends are still sitting in their little snake pit, hissing to each other. By this time, they've all pushed their sunglasses up onto their heads and kicked off their high heels. The look of collective surprise is priceless when Annaliese Rogan confidently infiltrates their circle and sits on the padded arm of Vienna Beaulati's chair.

"Hi. I'm not sure if you know me," Taylor says smoothly. "I'm Annaliese, and I just want to tell you all how sorry I am to hear about your friend, Taylor."

It's like someone pushed a button: all their eyes and mouths go *pop* at the same time. If they know anything about me, it's probably that I'm one of the shyest girls at school, more shadow than substance. As soon as the initial shock wears off, they are trying to figure out not just who I am, but what I am.

"Weren't you on the gymnastics team in ninth grade?" asks

Olivia Farrell. Yes, for all of six weeks. I picked up a lot of tumbling skills just by hanging around with Rei and Seth during their ninja-wannabe days in fifth and sixth grade, and by the time we got to high school, I was pretty decent. Rei sweet-talked me into trying out for the girls' team by spewing some crap about how it would be good for me, that it would get me out of my shell. God gave some of us shells for a reason—ask any snail. I did it to make him happy, but more to prove to him that I could. Unfortunately, most of the competitions were at least an hour away, and I hated mooching rides off my teammates almost as much as I hated performing in those claustrophobic gyms in front of hundreds of people. Taylor didn't even live here then, so how would she know that? She ignores the question.

"Didn't you come in third in the state ski finals this year?" asks Mandy Paxton. It doesn't surprise me she remembers this since her brother is also on the high school ski team. Every Christmas since I was six, Yumi and Robert have bought me a season pass to Smuggler's Notch so I can ski with them. Rei and I used to be two of those obnoxious little kamikaze kids without poles who weave in and out between the civilized skiers like they were gates on our own personal slalom course. There are not many civilized skiers on the slopes we choose now. Rei flows like molten lava down the mountain, but I move like lightning, my knees and hips seemingly engineered to bounce over icy moguls. Skiing is about as close to astral projection as you can get with a body in tow—the speed, the height—it's all second nature to me. The crowds are not as concentrated on a giant slalom course as they are in a gymnasium, and the ceiling is unlimited. I can tune out everything except gravity and that path I carve between the gates. I was positioned to place this year with one race to go, but Rei had already finished fourth in the boys' division, and I didn't want to go to regionals without him. Rei didn't know I blew the next race on purpose. Taylor just doesn't have a clue. She ignores that question, too.

"Aren't you the only eye witness who saw Seth Murphy push Taylor into the falls?" Cori Schneider asks boldly. Every head in the circle swivels toward me. Ah, *now* I am someone of interest. Taylor nods emphatically.

Friendship is a funny thing. For all the years these girls have ignored me, they're happy to accept this new and improved Anna Rogan into their group, as long as she provides them with some juicy gossip. Here is an eyewitness to the most shocking crime to ever happen in Byers. That's as good a hook as any. Vienna scoots over in the chair to make enough room for Taylor to squeeze in.

Rei snaps into focus twenty minutes later when the girls emerge as a group onto the porch. Pushing away from the railing, he walks up behind Taylor.

"Anna? Are you ready?"

She whips around to face him. "Cori's driving me home now."

"What?" It's understandable that he's confused since he was Zen-ing out on the porch while Taylor was in there bonding with her old friends.

"Chill, Rei. I'm an awesome driver," Cori grins. "You should take a ride with me sometime."

"Thanks, I'm good." Rei sticks his hand in his pocket and pulls out his keys. "Okay, then I'll see you later."

The group is giggling around Taylor now, and the general consensus is that Rei is cute. Kids at school just assume Rei and I are a couple since we're always together, but the girls want details.

Taylor winks and smiles salaciously. Lots more giggles.

Rei walks fast to his parents' SUV, jingling the keys hard against his thigh. Before he gets in the car, he calls my mom to let her know the change in driving plans. Once he shuts the door, he closes his eyes and rubs that spot in the middle of his forehead. I pull from deep within space to get the energy I need to surge into view, but he doesn't notice me. I reach over toward his forehead and let some of my energy trickle into him.

He opens his eyes and looks over at me.

"Hi." His voice is worn thin. He closes his eyes again and leans his head back against the headrest. "Well, that really sucked."

I hover over the seat, feeling helpless as I watch him brood.

"Okay," he tells me without opening his eyes, "this is where we stand tonight. We already know Taylor has a vendetta against Seth, and she's willing to perjure herself to get Seth convicted of killing her."

Well, not really. She's willing to perjure *me*, but I have no voice without the computer, so I let Rei finish.

"She's reestablished contact with her parents," Rei continues, "your mom actually seems to *like* her, and tonight she's rallied her old friends around her again. She doesn't have any interest in staying friends with me unless I want to *date* her, which I don't, but I need some way to keep tabs on her." He opens his eyes and looks at me, curled up over the passenger seat.

He sighs and his voice softens. "I'm sorry, I'm just frustrated."

I nod and mouth the words, *It's okay* to him.

"Well," he says hopefully, "at least my headache's gone now."

He starts the car and turns back to me with a short, ironic laugh. "I guess I don't have to remind you to buckle your seat belt."

I guess not.

CHAPTER 19

Rei's cell phone rings just as he pulls into his driveway.

"Hello." As he shifts the car into park, his face lights up. "SETH! Where . . ." and just as quickly, all goes dark. He jabs at the steering wheel with his index finger as he listens, then he leans his head back against the headrest and closes his eyes. "Okay. Find somewhere safe to wait. I should get there in about two hours. Call me back then and let me know exactly where you are." He listens again, rubbing that spot on his forehead. "Just sit tight, okay? Bye." His hand makes a fist so tight when he closes the phone, for a second I wonder if the phone may shatter.

"The cops were staking out Matt's dorm when Seth got there, so he made a run for it," he tells me. "He got away, but they confiscated my bike. He thinks they pulled Matt in for questioning. Now I have to figure out what to tell my mother."

I point to his bedroom window and pretend to type, indicating I need to talk to him. He nods, pulls the keys out of the ignition, and opens the car door with all the enthusiasm of a convict heading to the electric chair.

Yumi and Robert are sitting on the sofa, each with a different section of the newspaper.

"Rei?" Yumi calls out from behind the front page. "Why didn't you tell me Seth was involved with this girl who died?"

The red aura surrounding Rei flares brighter. "Where does it say he's involved with her? What are you reading?" Rei's been reading the newspaper every morning, and there's been no mention of Seth's name.

Yumi folds the paper closed and looks at him over her reading glasses. "I didn't read it. I heard some talk in the store today, and Seth's father called tonight and asked if we've heard from him."

"Well, you shouldn't believe everything you hear at the store," Rei snaps and starts up the stairs.

"Hold on, I'm not finished with you." Yumi puts the paper on the end table and gets up. "Come here and sit." She pulls a chair away from the table for him on her way to the kitchen. Rei inflates his lungs to full capacity and turns around slowly, his poker face in place. By the time he gets to the kitchen, Yumi is already at the sink, filling up the teakettle. "Have you talked with him? Do you know where he is?" She takes three cups out of the cupboard and sets them on the counter and reaches for the glass canister that holds the teabags. Rei takes one cup and returns it to the cupboard.

"He just called me. He was heading to Matt's college and the police were there, so he took off. I want to go see if Matt and I can talk Seth into turning himself in." He looks Yumi straight in the eye. "So can I take the car?"

Yumi's eyebrows arch up a good inch. "Absolutely not!" she retorts. "*What* are you thinking?"

"I'm thinking my best friend is in trouble. I'm thinking Matt and I can find him and talk some sense into him. And I'm thinking it would be really nice if you didn't give me a hard time about this."

And here I was thinking *I* am his best friend!

Yumi is a full twelve inches shorter than Rei, but one narrow look from her is usually all it takes for Rei or Saya to back down. Tonight, Rei stands firm. "Look, you've been really good to Seth since his mother left. Please don't let him down now. Please Mom," he begs. "He's in trouble for no good reason. This girl stole his phone and wouldn't give it back unless he met her at the falls, and she fell in by accident. What did you hear—that he pushed her?"

Yumi nods, frowning.

"Well, he didn't. He's scared. There's all this incriminating evidence against him, but he *didn't* push her. Let me go get Matt and talk him into turning himself in."

"Rei, you do *not* want to get involved with this," Yumi implores him. "This is between Seth and the police."

"Dad," Rei turns toward Robert. "Can I borrow the car?"

"Oh, no you don't!" Yumi sputters.

Robert lifts the newspaper up in front of his face. "Sorry. Talk to your mother."

This could go on all night. I head upstairs and pull enough energy to turn on the computer. Rei's voice is low and persuasive; Yumi's voice is high-pitched and defensive; and Robert is silent. By the time Rei comes upstairs, I've already typed a message.

I can find him once we get to New York.

Rei looks about ready to burst into flames. He yanks a duffel bag off his closet shelf, shoves a change of clothes into the bag, and goes off in search of stuff from the bathroom. Once he's packed, he reads my message and nods once, deletes the message, and shuts the computer down.

At the bottom of the stairs, he stops and looks Yumi straight in the eyes. "I'm taking the car," he says calmly. "If you want to call the police and report it stolen, then do it. I have my phone, and I should be back early tomorrow." Rei opens the screen door and steps out into the night.

Now it's Yumi who looks ready to explode. "Robert Reiki Ellis! You get back here this *instant!*"

Rei keeps on walking across the yard through the darkness, opens the car door, and tosses his duffel bag into the back. "Bye, Mom. I love you," he calls just before he shuts the door. I slide in through the passenger door and watch him back out of the driveway.

During the first half hour, I swear he looks in the rearview mirror at least a hundred times. By the time we cross over the bridge at Chimney Point, I think he realizes Yumi didn't call the police, but he doesn't turn on music, and he doesn't speak, except when he stops to gas up the car and ask the man at the register for the key to the restroom.

He's getting tired. Before he leaves the convenience store, he gets himself a cup of black coffee, and he makes a face when he sips it.

It started to rain while Rei was inside, the type of heavy, sheeting rain that comes down sideways. Rei makes a run for the car and I'm waiting for him when he gets in.

"Coffee sucks," he informs me.

I agree. Unless it has a generous amount of cream and five packs of sugar, I really have no use for it.

"We should be there in another hour or so, although this rain might slow us down." He frowns out the window. "Like Seth needs this on top of everything else. Can you check on him for me?"

I nod and I'm gone before he can turn the key in the ignition.

• • •

I've lost Seth. Seriously, I can't find him. I focused on that staccato rhythm I've memorized as Seth's energy pattern and followed it to a set of electrical power lines running up and down a weedy hill on an open slice of land between two pine forests. From here, his signal jumbles with other signals into an indistinguishable static which blends in with the faint buzz of power surging through the thick wires and the hiss of the light drizzle still falling here.

As soon as I get back to the car, there's a thin layer of fog building on the windshield. I could use the fog to write with and tell him the truth, or I could just placate Rei and try again before we get there.

"Is he okay?"

I nod without looking at him. Sometimes I really hate myself.

Rei turns the radio on now, and the classic rock station Robert loves has been reduced to static. Rei fiddles with the knobs until something halfway decent comes on, but he turns the volume down low so he can hear his cell phone if it rings.

"Three more exits," Rei's mood is getting lighter. "He should be calling anytime." I motion to him that I'm leaving and wave.

Once again, his signal ends at the power lines, but at least it's stopped raining. I look to my left and right, into the pitch-blackness of the forest on this starless, moonless night, and try to imagine being in there all alone with something as vulnerable as a human body. Even without a body, I get that prickly feeling of fear just thinking about what might lurk in those woods. I skirt the perimeter of the forest, and find something even more frightening than a black bear or a full-grown bull moose.

A police car cruises slowly down the adjoining road, and the officer in the passenger side shines a floodlight into the woods.

• • •

Rei pulls the car in through the campus gates and parks in the first parking lot he sees. He pushes a button on his speed dial and waits.

"Matt!" he says finally. "It's Rei Ellis." He presses the phone closer to his ear and talks louder. "REI ELLIS. YEAH! HEY, HAVE YOU HEARD FROM SETH?" I hear a party in Rei's phone. There's a long pause while Rei watches the beads of drizzle gather into streams of water that trickle down the windshield. "NO, oh, okay, that's better. No, I'm on campus right now. What dorm are you in?" Rei cranes his neck, looking around until he locates whatever it is he's looking for. "Okay, I see it. I'll meet you by the door."

Matt looks like Seth, only with shorter hair and that persistent five o'clock shadow that some girls find ruggedly sexy. I think it looks like he forgot to shave.

"Rei!" Matt throws his arm around his shoulder and gives him an affectionate squeeze. "I haven't seen you in forever. Good to see you, kid!"

"Hey, you too, Matt."

"Sorry about the noise. It gets a little crazy here on Saturday night. Come on up."

"Have you heard from Seth?" Rei asks on their way up the stairs before the music amplifies out of control and makes conversation impossible.

"No, I've been waiting for him to call since I heard from you." Matt stops halfway up. "What the hell is going on with him? My dad called me earlier this week and told me Seth left him a note saying he was in some kind of trouble so he was heading to Canada. Then my dad called to tell me they found his car at the border. All week, there've been cops trolling the campus, and not the campus security. Some of them were plainclothes cops in unmarked cars, but I didn't put two and two together until you called this morning. Then they pulled me in and asked me a million questions about Seth." Matt starts up the stairs again, slowly. "So what the hell happened to that girl? They seriously think Seth pushed her into the falls?"

"I guess so. He didn't, though."

"That's unfrickin' believable!" Matt looks even more like Seth when he scowls. As they make their way down the hallway, the smell of beer and its aftermath becomes increasingly potent. The party is in full swing when Matt and Rei walk through the door and the room is covered in wall-to-wall people. Someone is blasting loud music, techno mostly, or as Rei calls it, the bastard child of disco. Some people are dancing. Others are standing around shouting at each other in order to be heard over the music, or swilling beer from plastic cups, or making out in the dark corners of the room. Rei shakes his head no when someone offers him a beer.

"I'll see if I can find a bottle of water for you," Matt shouts and disappears into the crowd.

Rei looks around impatiently, and I figure nobody will notice if I surge into view in front of him.

"Anna!" He sounds somewhere between relieved and shocked to see me. "What are you doing? Someone might see you!"

I shrug. Half of these people look too tanked to know the difference between a real person and me. He looks around to see if anyone is looking at us funny, but nobody cares.

"Where's Seth?"

I point to his phone, which he has been holding tight to for the past several minutes, waiting for Seth to call him.

He's in some woods near power lines. It'll be hard to find him in the dark.

The energy in this room is classic chaos, and it's easy to suck up enough to type effortlessly on his phone.

"I thought you knew where he was," Rei challenges me.

I roll my eyes. *I know the general vicinity, but the power lines make it hard to pinpoint exactly where he is. And once I find him, I have to bring you there in the dark. Not impossible, but not safe.*

"I'll worry about safe. You worry about finding him. Let's go."

Matt makes his way back across the room with a bottle of water for Rei, so I shake off the extra energy and disappear. Matt motions for Rei to follow him to the quieter hallway.

"Sorry that took so long. I had to go back to my room. Hey, I didn't know you brought Anna with you."

"Anna?" Rei looks like he's been caught cheating on a quiz. "I didn't bring Anna."

"Oh. I thought I saw her standing in there with you." He shrugs. "It must have been someone who looks like her."

"Yeah, I guess. You know, I was thinking I'd go look around, see if I can find him."

"I'll go with you," Matt offers.

"You don't have to," Rei says quickly. "I was just going to drive around town while I wait for his call. How late will you be up tonight?"

"Who can sleep with all this noise? Things don't usually settle down until around five."

Ha! Rei's going to love college. Five o'clock in the morning is when he usually gets up to work out and meditate.

Rei nods. "I'll be back long before then. I'll call you when I find him. I'm sure I'll need you to help me talk him into turning himself in."

I materialize beside him as he's walking through the parking lot.

"So, other people *can* see you."

I shrug and nod. But just because someone *can* see me doesn't mean they will *admit* they saw me.

"So you should be careful. Matt thought I brought you with me."

I shrug again. Matt didn't push it, so I'm not worried about it.

"Did you find his exact location yet?" he presses.

I point to his phone. *Not yet. And I already told you, I don't want to take you in the woods when it's dark.*

"Why? Isn't Seth in the woods when it's dark?"

I nod. I get the feeling Rei's going to get all macho about this.

"So what's the difference? If Seth is in there, it's no more dangerous for me."

There he goes. Frustration fuels me as I type. *You can't see to walk. If you fall and break your ankle, I can't get you out of there.*

"I have my phone."

If the power lines are interfering with Seth's vibration, they may interfere with your phone signal, too. The phone does you no good if there's no reception.

Rei ends up driving around, and I leave the car a few times to see if I can pick up Seth's energy pattern. It stays consistent, leading me back to the power lines, time and time again.

"Then just take me to the general location and I'll find him myself," Rei insists.

That's not happening. He could be anywhere within a square mile of where I lose his vibration. *You need sleep. I'll wake you up when I find him.*

"Anna, what if he's not hiding in the woods? What if you can't find him because he's *dead?*"

CHAPTER 20

It took me over an hour to convince Rei that Seth couldn't possibly be dead, and that he was only thinking these bad things because he was exhausted. Even his aura is a tired shade of beige. Matt offered Rei his roommate's bed for the night but since the sheets looked like they hadn't been washed since school started last September, Rei made a diplomatic excuse and spent the night in the car. It's now after five o'clock in the morning, and he looks painfully uncomfortable, but his internal alarm clock hasn't kicked in yet to wake him up. Good. I need more time anyway.

The static by the power lines is still buzzing, but not nearly as strong as it was last night. Maybe because it's daylight now and not as much electricity is needed. I don't know and I don't care. I allow myself the luxury of hope.

The forest extends about a mile on either side of the power lines. Light filters through the tall pines casting soft shadows and morning brings birdsong and the scuttlings of squirrels and chipmunks as they start their day. Every tree, every bush, every blade of grass and patch of moss is alive, surrounded by shades of soft, serene blue. It's the aura of peace, like everything in nature is attuned to each other in perfect harmony.

Even me. Even though I am without a body, without a plan, I allow myself this one perfect moment to be without a care, to feel like I'm part of something bigger than bodies and plans, something eternal and omnipresent and hopeful. Something positive. The trees nod their branches even though there is no wind.

And then the blues shimmer into silver and from somewhere above me, the colors gather together into this brilliant beam of light that reaches down to me.

My first reaction is to bolt, but I'm too mesmerized. Is this the light? THE light? The same one I saw in the nursing home, the one that comes for the dead? Why is it here, then, in the forest? Is it here for me? Is this some sort of cosmic hint that because I have no body, I am now invited to the big heavenly party?

I don't have time for a party. I need to find Seth.

I feel like I'm spitting in the face of God. "Thank you," I tell the light because there is obviously some divine connection here and I don't want to seem ungrateful, "but I need to find Seth before I can go anywhere."

The light seems to have no hard feelings. It shimmers with tiny shards of color, like glitter is swirling around inside it, and disappears in an upward motion as if vacuumed up into the sky. The stillness that follows is absolute, except for one lone vibration. . . .

That convoluted buzz I know as Seth is as clear as an arrow pointing me in the direction I need to go, and I know this is no coincidence. I whisper more thanks and follow the vibration to this massive pine tree that had fallen, roots and all, what must be years ago. Seth is sleeping on the muddy ground, almost completely hidden under a blanket of brittle brown pine needles. He's soaked to the skin, filthy, and he smells like boiled cabbage, but he's very much alive.

CHAPTER 21

Yesssss! I do my little invisible midair spiral of happiness! I am so freakin' happy I finally found Seth and I can't wait to tell Rei! I get a fix on Rei's calm, steady vibration, which I know so well, and swoop down to it, realizing too late that Rei is wet and soapy and . . . oh God!!

I hear him mutter a Japanese swear followed by my name as I retreat into the hallway. I didn't see any of his boy parts, I swear, but Rei doesn't know that. All he knows is Hurricane Anna blew into the shower while he was in there wearing nothing but bubbles. Rawr! I should have known better. I mean, this is Rei we're talking about—a nuclear warhead could be heading straight for Vermont and he'd want a quick shower before it hits. I wait outside the room marked SHOWER, and the hallway is quiet now that almost everyone is asleep after their wild night.

I know Rei must be annoyed, but honestly, I didn't see anything lower than his chest. Besides, he knows I wouldn't intentionally peek in on him while he's showering. I imagine how I would feel if the situation was reversed . . . mortified, for sure. He's a guy, though.

Don't guys all shower together? And it's not like Rei and I haven't seen each other naked. The first time I tasted honey was at Rei's house and we made such a sticky mess that Yumi stuck us in the tub together and hosed us off. Okay, so we couldn't have been more than three years old at the time. Obviously, a lot has changed since then.

The door opens and out walks Rei, clean but very flustered.

"Next time, knock first!" he growls quietly at me. I mouth my most sincere apologies to him and motion for him to follow me into the shower room, where I hope there are no more naked people and the mirrors will still have a layer of fog on them. By the time Rei walks through the door, I've already written on the mirror.

I found him!

Matt catches Rei on the way out of the shower room. He looks like he's pulled an all-nighter; his eyes are bloodshot and his five o'clock shadow has morphed into something a little more grizzly.

"Hey, how 'bout some breakfast?"

Rei looks like he's about to say no, but then he changes his mind. "That sounds great. Do you mind if I get something to go, though? I want to get an early start."

Rei carries his duffel bag over his shoulder as they make their way through the quiet cafeteria line with their trays. Matt eats just like Seth, and his tray is piled with sausage patties, scrambled eggs, some white toast smeared with margarine that refuses to melt, and a foam cup filled with black coffee and four packets of sugar. Rei has his usual: fiber, potassium, vitamin C, and plenty of it.

Matt surveys Rei's tray. "Stocking up?"

"I thought I'd bring some food with me just in case I find him."

Matt nods thoughtfully. "Good thinking, kid. You mean to tell me Seth will actually eat a banana for you?"

"He will if he's hungry enough."

As soon as they've paid for their food, Rei shoves the cartons of orange juice, bananas, and granola bars into his duffel bag.

"I'll call you if I find him," Rei promises as he swings his duffel bag up onto his shoulder again.

"Yeah. Hopefully he'll listen to you. I just don't get it," Matt shakes his head. "Why the hell did he run if he didn't do anything wrong?"

"I don't know. He got scared, I guess. You know Seth."

"Yeah!" Matt grins. "Can you believe it, though? He outran the cops! On *foot*! He's pretty damn fast, isn't he?" he says proudly.

Rei grins back. "Yeah, he is. We run together a couple of times a week and he can run circles around me."

I sincerely doubt that.

"Leave it to Seth to get screwed like this. Who was this girl, anyway? Anyone I know?"

"No, her name was Taylor. She'd been chasing after him for a while."

"Oh, man," Matt laughs. "It must be tough to be such a stud that all the chicks are after you."

"I wouldn't know."

Oh, please! Even from here, I notice a few sleepy coeds in their tank tops and low-riding sleep pants peeking over their fat-free yogurts and bowls of Kashi to check out Rei and Matt.

After breakfast, Rei jogs out to the car to find me waiting for him. Once he backs the car up, I start pointing, right, left, left, straight, until we reach a greasy spoon-style restaurant on a plot of land bordering the forest. Rei pulls the car into the parking lot. After he fills his pockets with food for Seth, I lead him the rest of the way on foot.

He's in a hurry. "I thought you could travel at the speed of sound," he prods me. "Why are you moving so slowly today?"

The speed of *sound?* Oh, please. Mach 1 is for amateurs. He grins at the look I give him, but I pick up the pace for him anyway, ignoring the wicked urge I have to make him sweat to keep up with me. He's every bit as fast as Seth, even while picking his way over jutting roots and fallen branches, but a twisted ankle would not be in anyone's best interest right now. As soon as we reach Seth's hideout, I point and hover over Seth, who has obviously heard the footsteps and pressed himself as far under the canopy of pine needles as possible.

Rei steps up onto the fallen trunk and walks down the length of it, looking around. "Seth?"

"Rei?" Seth's head pops up and his eyes bug out with relief. "How the HELL did you find me here?" He's on his feet in a second and there's that awkward moment where guys hug, then realize they are hugging and step away from each other with that embarrassed look on their faces. Oh, good. Now Rei is wet and muddy, too, but he seems too happy to have found Seth to care. Rei pulls a banana out of his pocket.

"Food! Yes! I haven't had anything to eat since yesterday morning."

It's like Seth is a sword swallower, the way he shoves that banana down his throat. Rei hands him a carton of orange juice and fishes the granola bars out of his pocket. Seth stuffs an entire granola bar into his mouth.

"Did the cops see you come in here?" Seth asks with his mouth full.

"No, but Seth . . ."

"Every time I tried to come out to call you, I'd see a cop!"

"Seth, I am begging you. You've got to turn yourself in."

Seth's expression immediately turns defensive. "Rei, we've been through this. It's not gonna happen. If I turn myself in, what'll that do for me? Just get me to jail a whole lot faster."

"Come on," Rei implores him. "You look like you've been through hell."

He smells like he's been through much worse than that.

"Look, I'm parked at a restaurant about a half mile away. They have bacon and eggs . . . and hash browns," he bribes. "We'll get something to go and we can sit in the car and talk about it."

Seth looks reluctantly at Rei, but we all know that granola bars and a banana don't even qualify as an appetizer to Seth. "Fine. But those better be some damned good hash browns. And if I see any cops, I am out of there!"

CHAPTER 22

It almost feels normal, just three friends hiking through the woods. Except I have no body. And the police in two states are looking for Seth.

I am relieved and grateful that I found Seth first. After last night's confusion with the static from the power lines, I doubted whether I'd ever find him. But then this morning, everything was so peaceful just before the light appeared. I'm still trying to figure out just what happened, why it appeared . . . was it something I did? Or is this a divine message telling me things are hopeless here and it's time to cross over into heaven or wherever the light takes us?

But I can't cross over. If I don't get my body back, Taylor will testify against Seth and he will end up in jail for the rest of his life. I can't just give up. I don't *want* to give up. This is my life, my time, and even though I feel bad that Taylor's life was cut short, I'm not ready to give up my life without a fight. Plus Rei would never give up on a friend. Even now, he keeps hinting, unsuccessfully, that Seth should talk to the police. It's funny how deep their voices have become, something else I never paid much attention to until recently.

As we move through the forest, I almost miss the metallic buzz of another voice that belongs to neither Rei nor Seth.

What is that weird voice, anyway? It sounds like a radio or something. We are almost to the parking lot, so I speed ahead and stop short.

CRAP!

There, surrounding Rei's SUV with the bright green Vermont license plate, are not one, but three police cruisers. Six cops and a voracious-looking German shepherd are sniffing around the car and the outskirts of the woods. I fly back to Rei and I don't care who sees me when I materialize with a desperate look on my face, pointing like a lunatic for them to go back into the woods.

"What the . . . ?" Seth yelps, but Rei understands immediately.

"Go back!" Rei grabs Seth's arm to turn him around, but Seth is spellbound.

"Hey, where'd Anna . . ."

"Just go! Run! I'll come back for you!"

"But . . ."

But now it's too late. The dog starts barking, guttural and fierce. The voices in the parking lot rally in excitement. They light their torches. They take up their pitchforks. They release the hound from hell.

And Seth finally realizes what's going on.

To his credit, Seth is fast, but the dog is faster. Rei is almost to the parking lot when the dog bolts past him. I spin around and reach Seth just as the dog leaps up and knocks Seth to the ground, clamping its jaws around Seth's right forearm just inches from where Taylor shredded his wrist.

"*Bad dog! Let go!*" I shriek. I don't know if it can hear me, but it growls a warning and tightens its grip, so I shut up fast. Seth yells for the dog to let go, too, but he wisely doesn't try to wrestle his arm away.

Four cops have chased the dog into the woods, each of them with their right hand clamped onto the butt of their guns. A guy with hair so blond it appears he has no eyebrows gives the dog a command in a language that sounds like real German. The dog's aura reflects its disappointment as it drops Seth's arm and slinks over behind the cop. Seth is curled in a ball on the ground, panting and rubbing his arm, which is covered in dog drool but thankfully not pierced by fangs. The other three cops stand there with their guns aimed at Seth's head, their index fingers quivering on the triggers.

"Casey, get him cuffed! Now!" one of the cops shouts, and another one slaps the cuffs onto Seth with no regard for the bandage on his wrist. Casey ignores Seth's gasp of pain as he and the third cop yank Seth to his feet.

"Seth Murphy, you are under arrest."

"I didn't kill her!" Seth insists. "It was an accident!"

"You have the right to remain silent. . . ."

I get back to the parking lot just in time to see a tall, heavy-set police officer push Rei's head against the roof of the police car and cuff his wrists behind his back while a shorter, even heavier officer kicks his feet apart so he can frisk him. Officer Short finds nothing but two empty granola bar wrappers, Rei's keys, and his wallet. He drops the wrappers on the ground, pockets the keys, and searches through his wallet, removing Rei's driver's license. Funny, I thought littering was illegal. Officer Tall puts his hand on top of Rei's head and pushes him down into the backseat of the cruiser, all the while prattling off Rei's Miranda warnings.

When I materialize in the backseat of the cruiser next to Rei, he won't look at me. I reach out and touch his shoulder, but he just shakes his head to acknowledge me.

My heart crumbles for him. I honestly think Rei believed that his good intentions would protect him from this, and the reality of how an arrest will look on his college applications is probably starting to dawn on him. I brush my hand against his cheek, hoping to get his attention. His eyes are leaden when they finally meet mine, but I try to convey everything I want to say to him. *I'm sorry. This sucks. This is my fault. If I hadn't talked you out of going to the falls, none of this would have happened.*

He closes his eyes, leans his head against the back of the seat, and sighs. Okay, I can take a hint. I fade away and give him his space.

After Seth is stuffed into the back of the cruiser, the cops congregate. They congratulate themselves. They congratulate the dog. Apparently, the arrest of the notorious Seth Murphy, murderer-at-large, is a very big deal. They seem a little too excited about capturing Rei as well, which makes me wonder if they work on commission. Part of me realizes they are just doing their job, but the rest of me is not feeling all that benevolent toward them. I take a moment to indulge my darker side's suggestions.

I bide my time until Officer Tall starts driving back to the police station. At the exact moment Officer Short raises his paper coffee cup to his mouth, I turn on the FM radio as loud as it will go. The sudden blast of music startles Officer Short enough that he squeezes his cup and the lid pops off, spilling lukewarm coffee all over his lap. "Son of a *bitch!*"

Officer Tall jabs at the button to turn the radio off.

I just turn it back on. Again and again and again (hey, I could do this all day!), until both cops are yelling for the other to "fix that damn thing," and I see the corners of Rei's mouth curve up ever so slightly. I slip back beside him, still invisible, and listen to the hammering of his heart.

At the police station, they take fingerprints and mug shots of both Rei and Seth, then they search them both for God knows what and lead them, minus their shoelaces and belts, into separate cells. I am convinced there is a psychological game that's played out during an arrest. It seems that the police officers slam the metal cell doors much harder than necessary to make that *CLANK* reverberate as loudly as possible. Seth jumps a mile, but Rei doesn't even flinch. Officer Short seems disappointed. The thin mattress on the cot is stained, and I know Rei—he'd rather sleep on the floor than on something that skeevy. He leans his back against the wall and slowly slides down until he's sitting on the floor. He closes his eyes and after a few minutes, his breathing becomes slow and deep. Apparently, he's just going to float through this ordeal in a higher state of consciousness.

"You get to make a phone call," Officer Tall informs Rei a short time later. Rei doesn't look particularly pleased with this information, but he reluctantly calls home. He keeps his eyes closed during the entire conversation, his thumb pressed into that spot on his forehead, and at times he holds the phone a few inches away from his ear while Yumi vents. As soon as she's finished raking Rei over the coals, she wants to talk to the arresting officer. Rei looks at Officer Tall with a trace of sympathy as he hands the phone back.

I am having a fan-freaking-tastic time at the station—there are so many things to spill and drop in this place! Maybe it's blasphemous, but I feel like God bringing a plague of locusts on the Egyptians, and I even holler *Let my people go!* at Officer Short for dramatic effect. Of course they can't hear me, but the increased tension is duly noted and the happy high everyone felt after the arrests has been significantly reduced, one toppled coffee cup at a time.

Officer Tall drops a prepackaged sandwich and a bottle of water onto the cot in Rei's cell. What's for lunch? Sodium nitrates, bovine growth hormones, and saturated fat, all nestled between four triangles of squishy bread—or to the nutritionally unenlightened, ham and cheese on white. Rei hands the sandwich back with instructions to please give it to Seth.

Rei can't hear them talking at the front desk, but I can. According to them, Seth is wanted in Vermont for first-degree murder, so as soon as the paperwork is complete, he'll be extradited back there. They are not quite sure what to do with Rei, though. There's a discrepancy about what exactly he's being charged with, if anything. Rei and Seth both told the police that Rei was there to talk Seth into turning himself in. The police got hold of Matt and he confirmed this, and apparently, Yumi pointed this out several times in her conversation with Officer Tall. Officer Short still wants to book him as an accessory, but Officer Tall wants to release him. I leave Officer Tall's coffee standing in a gesture of goodwill.

Rei's dad, Robert, arrives at about two in the afternoon with Seth's dad. They both look a lot more concerned than angry, and Robert looks positively sympathetic. When Robert and Officer Short approach the cell, Rei watches them impassively from his spot on the floor, as if pulling himself up from the rock-bottom depths of despair requires too damn much effort.

Once his cell door swings open, he asks his father one thing: "Did you bail out Seth?"

Officer Short has a hearty chuckle over this and claps Robert on the shoulder as though they are old friends. Idiot! It takes me all of three seconds to locate his latest cup of coffee and knock it over.

"There is no bail set for Seth," Robert explains as gently as possible. "Jack drove me here. He's talking to Seth now. They'll bring him back to Vermont as soon as the paperwork is settled. There was no bail set for you, either. No charges were filed."

Okay, well, I must have been busy wreaking havoc with someone's coffee when they made that decision. This is good!

Rei doesn't look quite as happy as I would have hoped. He presses his back against the wall, pushes himself up to a stand, and gives Officer Short a raw look as he leaves the cell.

"You know," Robert continues, "you were very lucky they didn't press charges. In the state of New York, you're old enough to be charged as an adult."

"Yeah," Rei agrees, "lucky me. So why did they keep me locked up if they weren't pressing charges? Why didn't they just let me go?"

"Talk to your mother," Robert says without looking at him. "I had nothing to do with that."

CHAPTER 23

The Highlander was towed to the police station just in case they needed it for evidence, but apparently nothing of interest was found because Robert is free to take it. I hang out in the backseat to hear if Robert interrogates Rei on the ride home, but the sound of the wind rushing past the windows is punctuated only by occasional fatherly concerns. "Are you hungry?" "Are you thirsty?" "Do you want to stop at the rest area?" Rei shakes his head at the appropriate times, but otherwise, he leans back against the headrest and stares out the passenger window. His eyes are reflected in the side mirror, looking lost in thought.

It's quiet when Rei gets home, too, because Yumi chooses to inflict the silent treatment on him. I resist the wicked urge I have to topple her teacup. It doesn't take long for Yumi's resounding silence to split straight through Rei's armor.

"*Look*! I'm *sorry*! Do you think I *planned* for this to happen?"

"I *told* you to leave this alone! What do you think your chances of getting into M.I.T. would have been if they decided to press charges?" Yumi shoots back.

"Is that all you care about? What about Seth? What about Anna?"

"What *about* Anna? What does she have to do with this?"

Rei shuts his mouth. "I'm going upstairs."

"We are *not* finished with this conversation!"

"Maybe you're not, but I am."

He tosses his duffel bag onto his bed and heads directly into the weight room. Even though the door is closed, I hear the sound of windows closing and shades falling shut. He wants to be alone.

I just hover around the swing chair and try to form a rational thought. I know he's devastated. Even though Rei is only half Japanese, Yumi has drilled into him the cultural philosophy that honor is a coveted virtue . . . a coveted virtue that has now been defiled. It doesn't matter that no charges were filed. Just the fact that he was detained and spent the morning in a jail cell was a violation in itself. Plus I'm sure he did not enjoy that pat down search. By a guy. Rei's funny about stuff like that; in fact, I'm surprised he didn't head straight for the shower, but it seems he needs to clear his mind first.

He's been in there for close to an hour when I hear the sound of an engine gunning, and the passing sound of squealing laughter. I follow the noise to a cloud of dust as Cori's car pulls into my driveway and slams on the brakes.

When Taylor climbs out of the front seat, the first thing I notice is the large square of white gauze taped to my upper arm.

"I hope your arm doesn't hurt too much tonight!" Cori yells as she throws her car into reverse.

"It's fine! Don't you love it?"

"WE LOVE IT!" comes a chorus from the car as the four giggling girls peal out of the driveway.

Taylor pulls on her hoodie before she walks into the house, bumping several shopping bags against her thigh. Neither my father nor Taylor acknowledges the other. My mom hurries out of her bedroom, though, and Taylor invites her into my room to see her "goodies."

Goodies? *Goodies?* That can't be good.

My mom ooohs and aaahs over every item that appears from each bag, and she even giggles when she sees the red thong underwear from Victoria's Secret. It's not until Taylor swishes her hair back over her shoulder that my mom stops and stares at the sparkly studs now decorating my earlobes and cartilage.

"Oh!" my mom says stiffly. "You've decided to pierce your ears!"

"Yeah, I didn't think you'd mind since you thought the nose piercing was a cute idea. And look at what else I did!" Taylor's eyes light up as she takes off her hoodie and presents her gauze-wrapped arm to my mom.

My mom and I both gape when she peels the tape off to reveal a black-ink drawing of Taylor Gleason's face neatly tattooed onto my upper arm.

I offer up the mother of all swear words into the universe!

"I was trying to think of some way to commemorate Taylor Gleason. And it only cost $250! Don't you love it?"

Rawr! She told me she'd found my money stash, but I never thought she'd blow half of it on a tattoo! My mom nods mutely, then walks out of my bedroom and directly into the kitchen where she pours herself a glass of wine.

Whatever Rei was doing in his weight room didn't help him feel any better. I come storming back to Google "tattoo removal" on his computer, and I find him lying prone across his mattress with a pillow over his head. He's scaring me. Rei has always been my rock, the one security I could rely on in an otherwise unstable world. This is not my Rei, though, this person spiraling out of control.

I'm at a loss here. Do I try to cajole him out of this depression? Attempt to shake some sense into him? Would pulling him through this narrow space just push him further from me? I have no experience when it comes to fixing people. I've always been the one in need of repairs, and Rei has always been my mechanic.

I hover next to him and pull enough energy to get his attention.

Are you okay? That's such a stupid question, because of course he's not okay, but I don't know how else to broach the subject of what happened this morning.

Rei looks out from under the pillow as soon as he hears the click of the keyboard. He makes a face. "I'm fine. I'm just . . . mad at myself. I can't believe I didn't see that coming."

You were just trying to help Seth.

"Yeah, a lot of help I was. Now he's in jail."

They would have caught him anyway. This wasn't your fault.

Because it's *my* fault, of course.

I'm sorry. I should have gone ahead of you and checked to make sure there were no cops. I should have known they'd find your car.

What I *really* should have done was listen to Rei and stay in my body in the first place, but it's too late for that.

Rei sits up slowly. He still hasn't showered or even changed his clothes, and now there's dried mud on his comforter.

"It's not your fault, Anna, it's my fault."

Stop saying that! We just need to come up with a better plan since the sage didn't work, and then I'll be the only witness. I'll testify he tried to save her when she slipped. They'll drop the charges and we can all move on with our lives. Except for Taylor. She can just be dead.

"Yeah, well there's our next dilemma. How're you doing with that? Did you check up on her at all or did you just hang out with me in jail the whole time?"

I just hung out with you in jail the whole time.

"I know." He sighs and brushes at the dirt on his comforter with his fingers. "So," he clears his throat, "how'd you like jail?"

It sucked. I felt like a gerbil.

He looks up at me with an unexpected grin. "Was it my imagination or were those guys a little klutzy with their coffee?"

Extremely klutzy—they should learn to drink more responsibly.

"Yeah." He sighs and lies back down.

Guess what Taylor got for me.

He lifts his head to read what I've typed. "What?" he asks suspiciously.

A bunch of piercings and a tattoo.

It's like he's been catapulted to a sitting position. "A . . . *tattoo?* You're kidding me, right?"

Wrong. And it's not even something good. It's a portrait of Taylor. Is there a way to get rid of tattoos or will I just have to amputate my arm if I ever get my body back?

Rei groans and lies back down, the heels of both hands pressed against his forehead. "I'm sorry. I should have skipped that class! None of this would have happened!"

I float over and tug at his hands. When he finally uncovers his eyes and looks up at me, I shake my head at him.

It's not your fault.

I realize something else.

It's not my fault, and it's not Seth's fault, either. It's Taylor who is screwing everything up, and she's got to go.

CHAPTER 24

Rei sits up and presses his thumb against that space between his eyes. "Okay, I'm going back online to see if I can figure out a Plan B. Can you just check on Seth and see if he made it back to Vermont?"

I track Seth easily to the Byers jail where he's lying on a cot, staring up at the cracks in the ceiling. At least he's had a shower, and his wrist is wrapped in clean gauze, but other than that, he has that empty look of someone who has given up hope.

What will he think when he learns that Anna Rogan is the only eyewitness? Will he notice the huge difference in my personality now that Taylor is in control of my body? He saw me in the woods, trying to warn them about the police . . . what must he think about that? Will he ever forgive me if I can't get my body back and he goes to jail for a crime he didn't commit?

Just out of earshot, two male police officers and the lady who answers the phones are sitting around a desk talking and drinking coffee. Okay, so she's drinking iced coffee, and it looks very unappealingly watered down by melted ice cubes and milk. Yuck. I float over to a nearby filing cabinet because in the thirty or so seconds I've been here, I've heard Rei's name mentioned, so I'm going to eavesdrop.

". . . don't think so. I know Yumi from the store, and she wouldn't tolerate that kind of behavior. I think they were right to drop the charges." This is coming from the woman. The other officers are the short, bald guy who came to Rei's house before, and a guy with thinning hair the color of a cheese puff that's been lost too long under the fridge.

Bald Guy: "Yeah, well he *seemed* like a nice kid, but I gave him specific instructions to call us if he heard from the Murphy kid. What was he doing in New York unless he heard from him? He should have called us. The guys in New York found them coming out of the woods together, but everyone they talked to said the Ellis kid went looking for Murphy to talk him into turning himself in. Who knows? I think the kid got lucky they didn't make that accessory charge stick."

Cheese Puff: "Well, the Murphy kid's arraignment is tomorrow morning. I don't care what he pleads—he's as good as convicted. All of the deceased's girlfriends say he asked her to meet him at the waterfall."

What??!!

Bald Guy: "See? Now the Ellis kid said Murphy's phone was stolen and there was a note telling him to come get his phone at the falls. You don't know who to trust! These kids lie so much they start to believe themselves."

Cheese Puff: "Didn't that little Rogan girl say she saw the whole thing."

Bald Guy: "She said she was taking a walk, but she was too far away to hear what they said. She knew just what the girl was wearing, though, and she said she saw him rip her shirt open and drag her over to the edge and push her in. Did you see his wrist? She must have put up a damn good fight!"

Cheese Puff: "I was there when they found the body, poor kid. That Murphy kid's an animal! You should've seen her shirt—all the buttons, gone! I don't blame them for going with murder one."

Dispatch Lady: "The kid just turned seventeen about a month ago, you know."

Cheese Puff: "Doesn't matter. They want to prosecute him as an adult."

It's right about this time when Dispatch Lady gets a very odd look on her face and looks straight at me.

Not through me.

At me.

I don't care. I've been quiet long enough. It's time to shake things up.

I drift down from the file cabinet and glide slowly and deliberately over to the desk where they are gathered, their mouths and eyes now shocked into little frozen circles. I make sure to give them enough time to see me really, *really* well, because if I'm going to do this, I may as well do it big. I type on Dispatch Lady's keyboard and I make sure they all read the message.

Seth is innocent and Rei doesn't lie. Look in Seth's locker and you'll find that note.

I can tell from their auras that these are not bad people; they are just misguided, uninformed people who see only what's before their eyes. The Little Prince's fennec fox warns us about people like these. The police think Taylor was murdered, so they feel obliged to catch a bad guy, and Seth is the easiest choice. They need to open their minds to the possibility that things are not always what they appear to be. *Look at me, people,* I want to say to them. *See that anything is possible*. I stare each person in the eye, and then I let myself fade slowly from sight.

When I get back to Rei's bedroom, his computer is hibernating. Behind the closed door to his weight room, I hear him strumming his electric guitar. He's not playing anything I can name, just random, melancholy chords that wrap around my heart and squeeze.

I jiggle the mouse and a screen pops up showing Rei's last search. For a second, I think it says *exercise*, but then I realize it says *exorcism*, the exact word I've been avoiding, and I understand why Rei's in there playing dirge metal music. I scroll through any links that don't have to do with horror movies and read this . . . *oushikuso*. This is complete and total bull, and it's not going to work. Maybe a crucifix and some holy water would scare off your run-of-the-mill demon, but it won't faze Taylor Gleason.

Exorcism. I feel like we're scraping the bottom of the barrel now. We've tried shoving her out, smoking her out, asking her nicely to leave. What else is left? And it's not like I don't already feel like my body is a fire hydrant, the way she's marked her territory with tattoos and piercings.

We snickered at that first Google hit we found that suggested we convince her she's dead and her loved ones are waiting for her on the other side. But what if the simplest way is the best? What if she has grandparents or a favorite aunt who passed? Surely there is someone over there she loves so much that she'd want to pass over. Tonight is the family viewing at the funeral home. It would be easy enough to head over there and see if I can figure out who's missing from the family tree.

I leave Rei in his weight room and head over to the funeral home. Taylor's second viewing for her Long Island extended family is in full swing when I get there. The place is packed with people again tonight, including what looks like business associates of her father. Okay, well, that plan fails—all four grandparents are present and accounted for, sitting on padded armchairs in the receiving line. Taylor isn't here tonight, but judging by how she spent her day, she doesn't *want* to be here with her extended family. Who am I fooling? She cares about herself more than anyone else, and I don't know who she could possibly love enough to leave my body and cross over for.

Pfffft.

I go back to check on Rei. The music has morphed into a song I recognize, a U2 song I downloaded onto my iPod right after my father smacked me into the counter. I looped that song for weeks after, but Rei never called my overplaying foul, no matter how many times he shared my earbuds with me. He did mention once that it was a song about heroin addiction, but I pointed out that music is art, and art is subjective, which means it's open to interpretation. To me, the song is really about dislocating from the problems in your life, and heroin is just a tool people use. Alcohol is a tool. Astral projection—that's a tool, too. Rei sings along, and each word is smooth as honey, sharp as a stinger.

I toggle back to a blank screen and leave Rei a message on the computer: *Seth is back in Vermont—his arraignment is tomorrow. I'll see you in the morning.*

The Little Prince lived on a planet so small, he could watch a sunset whenever he wanted. I can watch the sunset whenever I want, too . . . from the Serengeti, the banks of the Seine, even from the rings of Saturn.

I contemplate where I should start my sunset marathon. It's about 8:30 here in Vermont, so adjusting for the time difference, I can start in Belize, zip on down to the Galápagos Islands, and then make my way up the coast of Central America. I've kept a scrapbook of all the places I astrally project to because these are the places I want to physically travel to someday. How cool would it be to hike through the Andes, scuba dive in the Great Barrier Reef, feel the cold stone steps of the *Basilique du Sacré Cœur* beneath me while I actually *eat* a chunk of that fragrant French bread I've been drooling over for so many years?

But what if I don't get my body back? I have to accept the possibility that Taylor won't come out and I will be stuck out here forever. Maybe I could be one of those bohemian spirits that haunt the cafés along the Champs-Élysées. Maybe I could go off to college with Rei and become one of those legendary campus ghosts. But eventually Rei is going to meet a girl and get married, and then what? How lonely would I be with no body, no voice, no friends or family? What would I do then? Could I summon the light again and just go off to wherever it takes me? I wander over to the willow outside Rei's window, drawn in by its comforting blue aura. Rei has stopped playing his guitar and his lights are off. I hope he's asleep, and I hope his dreams are happy. I don't get the benefit of sleep in this dimension, but it's peaceful here, just me and the willow, the stars and the moon. Somehow our vibrations blend together into something harmonious and hopeful.

Could I summon the light right now if I wanted to?

I want to.

The stars twinkle through the tangled foliage and I ask the universe to send the light to me. I try to think of good things, only good things, and it's Rei who comes to mind most often. I think of how safe and connected I feel when I'm around him, how in all the years I've known him, he's forgiven me for every stupid thing I've done.

Even though Seth is in jail and my carelessness could be the one thing that keeps him there for life, Rei does not blame me. And that's when it hits me, that Rei Ellis will probably never fall in love with me romantically, but I don't believe anyone in my life truly *loves* me as much as he does. And even though I'm not a religious person, I recognize this is a blessing. Above me, it seems as though the stars are merging into one enormous beam of light that reaches down from above. The willow reverently parts its branches for the light to enter and I'm awestruck. I can do this! I can summon the light.

But now I feel like I've prank-called a divine power. Because I don't want to go off into the light. Not yet, anyway. *I'm sorry,* I tell the light. I thank it for coming to me and to everyone else who wants and needs it, and it retracts graciously into itself and disappears, leaving me in the dark.

But I've had enough darkness this week. Enough darkness, enough sadness, enough *oushikuso*.

I set off in search of a sunrise.

CHAPTER 25

I don't plan to discuss last night's appearance at the police station with Rei. I should, I know, but if I do, I'll have to break the news to him that they are planning to charge Seth with first-degree murder, as an adult. That won't go over well at all.

I'm also a little shocked at myself. It's one thing to materialize intentionally in front of a bunch of wasted coeds who have never seen me and will never see me again, but these cops know me, if only as The Little Rogan Girl. After I disappeared, I stuck around long enough to watch them stare at each other in disbelief, then stare into their drinks as if maybe their coffees were laced with some sort of hallucinogenic drug. Cheese Puff spoke up first and said, "I didn't see anything!" Then Bald Guy's eyebrows went straight up and he said the same thing. "I didn't see anything. Pat, you see anything?"

Dispatch Lady read her computer screen and frowned. "I don't know what I just saw, but I know I'm not stupid enough to tell anyone about it. I need this job." She takes a sip of her watery coffee. "So is anyone going to get a search warrant to check out that kid's locker?"

We also haven't discussed if Rei would attend Taylor's funeral, which starts in less than an hour. I think he is since it's past eight o'clock and if Rei were going to school, he'd be long gone by now. He's still in the shower, though, and I'm hanging out near his bed waiting for him. At some point during the week, I've become somewhat of a fixture in his room, and he greets me casually when he walks in trailing the scent of oranges and cinnamon, wearing nothing but a pair of gym shorts and a towel around his neck. He roots through his drawer looking for a clean T-shirt. I may as well ask.

Are you going to the funeral?

"Yeah," he says as he rubs his hair with the towel. "Are you?"

I nod.

"I think I'll skip the church, though. How about . . ." something outside catches his eye and he leans toward the window, a curious expression growing on his face. "What the hell?"

I float over to see what's got his attention, and we turn to look at each other in surprise.

"What's up with that?" Rei asks me.

Even if I had a voice, I'm laughing way too hard to respond.

Taylor reminds me of a circus clown riding on one of those itty-bitty tricycles, except she looks even sillier. She's carefully pedaling away on my mountain bike in her megaheels, wearing a black leather miniskirt, a gray tank top, and a tight black sweater. Over this stylish ensemble, she's sporting my backpack, which looks kind of empty.

Rei just stands there with a surprised grin glued on his face. "You know, I keep thinking she can't sink any lower, but yet, she does. Are you going to follow her?"

Of course I'm going to follow her! I wave and leave through the window.

Taylor makes it all the way to Main Street pedaling so slowly, I'm anticipating the bike will tip over any second now. I expect her to take a left onto Main Street toward McGregor & Sons Funeral Home, but no, she takes a right, and it takes me a minute to realize where she's heading. . . .

She's going home.

She walks my bike up her driveway and parks it around the back of her house. Of course nobody is home right now; they are all at the church for their dearly departed's funeral service.

She finds a key under the doormat. "Bingo," she gloats. What is she up to? She lets herself into her house, and I follow her to the alarm system, where she uses the tips of those acrylic nails to key in the code to disarm it. She takes off her shoes and makes her way upstairs.

As far as I can see, her mother hasn't touched her room. There's an empty frappuccino bottle sitting on the nightstand and a silky tank top and sleep shorts lying at the foot of the bed. Taylor looks around for a moment, and her eyes are glassy. There is a long second where I feel something—empathy maybe? How difficult must this be for her? This is not just material stuff; this is her world, and it's gone. As much as I hate her for all the grief and aggravation she's put us through this week, I see everything she's lost, and I feel sad for her.

She sniffs hard, unzips the backpack, and begins to fill it with items from her dresser top and drawers. Makeup, perfume, jewelry, photos, her iPod and charger, a box of condoms . . . wait a minute, a box of *what?*

I stick my head into the backpack for a second look, and sure enough, there is a twelve-pack of glow-in-the-dark, lubricated-for-her-pleasure condoms. The package had been torn open at some point in time, and it appears that a few are missing. It's hard to read the package in the dimness of the backpack, especially since Taylor continues to shove things on top of me, but there's a date clearly labeled on the box and it tells me these condoms expired over a year ago.

I retreat to the corner of the room and take inventory. So far she's had my ears and nose pierced, my arm tattooed with a hideous drawing, and she appears to be planning the demise of my virginity. I wonder who the lucky guy is.

As soon as she's done pilfering her room, she heads into the bathroom and takes her toothbrush (eww!), a box of super-absorbent tampons (good luck with those!) and some very expensive-looking hair conditioner. The backpack is nearly full.

Downstairs, she opens a cabinet door to reveal several rows of liquor bottles. She helps herself to a half-empty bottle of vodka, takes a long swallow and sighs. "Damn, I missed you," she tells the bottle. She adds that to my backpack, along with another bottle of vodka, this one unopened.

She is careful to reset the alarm and lock up after herself. I watch her long enough to know she is heading to the church. I hurry back to Rei's house.

I arrive to find Rei at his computer, wearing his beige chinos and white polo shirt. He is surfing the internet for *exorcism* again, but as soon as he sees me point to the keyboard, he pushes back in his chair.

She went to her house to get stuff.

He raises one eyebrow as he reads this. "What kind of stuff?"

2 bottles of vodka, I type.

"That's not good."

And condoms

Rei just looks at the screen blankly for a minute, and then he squeezes his eyes shut and rubs that spot on his forehead again. When he opens his eyes, he leans over and squints at the screen for a few seconds more. "Yep, that's what I thought you said." He sees my anxious expression. "Anna, don't worry," he consoles me. "I'll make sure she doesn't get the chance to use them. Where is she now?"

At church

"At church with a backpack full of vodka and condoms," he smirks. "I'm sorry, that's just . . ." he shakes his head. "Never mind."

I frown at him. *The arraignment starts in about ten minutes. I'm going to check on Seth and I'll meet you at the cemetery after.*

"Okay, see you then."

The sight of Seth, all trussed up in handcuffs and ankle shackles, would break Rei's heart. It looks like Seth has borrowed his father's clothes, black dress pants that are too short and a matching suit jacket that's too tight in the shoulders. The lawyer next to him wears a suit that fits him perfectly and probably cost more than Seth's dad earns in a month.

The arraignment is very boring. The judge is a dumpling of a man, with wire-rimmed glasses sliding perpetually down his nose. I wonder if he pushes them up with his middle finger to send a message to the court. Seth shows no surprise when they read the charge of first-degree murder, and the judge shows no surprise when Seth responds with, "Not guilty, your honor."

The judge tilts his head back a bit so he can read without taking off his glasses. "In light of the vicious nature of this crime, the district attorney has requested the date of the trial be expedited."

There is much whispering and scribbling among the attorneys

when this Friday is announced as the date of the trial. The consensus among the defense is this does not give them much time to prepare, but nobody argues with the judge. Seth gets up stiffly from the wooden chair when directed by the bailiff and shuffles out of the courtroom.

It is just too depressing to follow him to his cell. Instead, I float around, trying to make sense of their strange terms. I understand there is no bail for Seth because he ran once already. I understand they think he killed Taylor in cold blood, so they want to try him as an adult, even though he's still seventeen. But now the lawyers are rattling off terms like "percipient witnesses" and "deposition" and "burden of proof" and "Annaliese Rogan." Apparently, I am the only eyewitness, and Taylor will be required to appear at a deposition with the attorneys this Wednesday morning at nine o'clock. I make a mental note not to miss that.

I find Rei leaning against an ancient oak tree on the edge of the cemetery, watching the crowd gathered around the white coffin. When I rest my hand on Rei's shoulder, he must feel the vibration because he immediately reaches for my hand, managing only to pat his own shoulder instead. "Hi," he greets me. I trace the letters H-I on his back. His mouth doesn't smile, but his eyes do, so I know he felt it.

Taylor stands with her parents beside the coffin. The funeral home has provided lawn chairs for her grandparents, but everyone else stands, clutching a long-stem red rose. So many nice things are said about Taylor during the service, it makes me wonder where this pastor guy is getting his information. Once he concludes the service, he invites everyone to lay their rose on the coffin, which is already buried under a heap of lilies, carnations, chrysanthemums, daisies, and several excited wasps. Taylor watches everyone as they approach the coffin, and she smiles at anyone who is crying.

Of course, she's invited back to the Gleason's house for the mercy meal, and so are all of her girlfriends. I jostle the phone in Rei's pocket to get his attention and he pulls it out, flips it open and holds it steady.

I'll stay with her.

"Okay. I'm heading to school. Let me know if you need me." He pockets the phone and walks off toward the school.

Taylor arrives at the Gleason's house and makes herself at home. Mr. and Mrs. Gleason have hired a caterer to set up a hot and cold buffet, and everything looks amazing, especially that steaming tray of lasagna, which I sniff longingly. Taylor offers to help pour soda at the bar, and I see her help herself to a few splashes of vodka in her Diet Coke. Before Taylor took up residence in my body, I had never had anything with alcohol to drink, not even a sip of wine. Okay, I drank some vanilla extract once because it smelled really good, but I didn't know it had alcohol in it and it tasted so bad, I threw up, so I don't think it counts. I wonder how much vodka will get me embarrassingly drunk. Or worse.

Taylor takes her drink and sits on the plushy sofa next to Jason Trent, the same jock/jerk who nearly caused me to drop my lunch tray last week. He's a few inches taller than Rei, but bulky, with platinum blond hair, a ruddy complexion, and arctic blue eyes that stand out against his blond eyebrows and lashes. Maybe I'm prejudiced, but I consider Rei's shoulders and arms to be well sculpted. Jason Trent just looks like he's been abusing steroids. I watched Jason hit on Taylor when she was pouring drinks, and now they are engaged in some sort of verbal foreplay. By the time dessert is set on the table, Jason's beefy hand is on her thigh. *My* thigh! I want to slap his hand right off his arm!

Taylor's cell phone rings at about three o'clock, and she pats Jason's hand twice before she has to take hold of it and manually lift it off her thigh to stand. She smiles at him in a way that looks ridiculous on my face as she sashays to the door to take the call outside. When I get close enough, I can hear it's Rei, calling to see if Taylor wants a ride to school with him in the morning. She looks amused by the call, but no, she's all set. Thanks, anyway. Maybe another time.

I'm in Rei's room less than a second later, and he still has the phone in his hand. He doesn't look all that surprised Taylor turned down his offer.

She's flirting with Jason Trent.

"Jason Trent?" Rei wrinkles his nose. "You're kidding!"

I wish I was. I desperately want to type *Please don't let me lose my virginity to Jason Trent*, but somehow that seems like too pathetic a plea to share with Rei right now.

He drums his fingers on top of his desk, thinking. "One of us has to stay with her, Anna, and she doesn't seem to want me anywhere near her or her friends."

Why? They think you're cute.

He shudders. "Okay, *now* you're scaring me."

Jason Trent is scaring me. He's touching my leg. Will you go beat him up for me?

I was hoping to get a smile out of that request, but now Rei just looks ticked off again. "Anna, if it looks like she's getting you into a bad situation, how can you let me know where they are?"

Jason has a white Jeep.

"Yeah, I know."

I'll know where she is. If you leave the computer, just keep your phone close by.

"Anna, you need to let me know *before* things get out of control. I'll need time to get to wherever she is, and I don't have the car. Maybe I should just go over now and make sure he leaves you alone."

As much as I wish Rei would go defend my honor and kick the stuffing out of Jason, it would not be a good thing. He's spent enough time in jail this week.

Not yet. I'll let you know if they leave together.

CHAPTER 26

Jason has to be at work by five, which is a big plus for my virginity. Taylor and her friends pile into Cori's car to go someplace, but they can't decide *which* place. Taylor produces the half empty bottle of vodka from her backpack, which earns her a rowdy cheer from the girls. They drive around aimlessly for a while, drinking and arguing the merits of The House of Ting versus the food court at the mall.

Hey! How ironic would it be if they got pulled over and they *ALL* got arrested for underage drinking! I bet that would cheer up Rei considerably.

No such luck. Taylor and her friends end up at the mall where they clickety-clack around in their high heels, complain about their lack of spending money, and gossip. Until now, the gossip has been benign, mostly stuff like who said what about who, but there is the distinct sound of something splattering against the proverbial fan when they bump into Kyle Rupert, whose mom works at the only doughnut shop in Byers.

"Hey, how's Rei doing?" Kyle asks Taylor. "He must be *pissed!*"

"He's fine. Why would he be pissed?" Taylor asks suspiciously. Kyle is sort of a dork, and I'm surprised Taylor's group is tolerating him long enough to have a conversation with him.

Kyle looks baffled. "Oh, come on. You of all people should know; you're, like, his best friend." He leans in and whispers loud enough for the entire group to hear. "Because he got arrested? In New York? With Seth?"

Taylor and her girlfriends exchange a voracious look.

"I was with Taylor's family most of the day, and I haven't had a chance to talk to him. What exactly did you hear?" Taylor asks.

Kyle puffs up. "My mom heard from one of the cops that they arrested Seth in New York yesterday. His arraignment was this morning, and they're pushing the trial up to this Friday. And I heard that Rei was arrested with him in New York, but they didn't press any charges." Kyle looks a little confused. "You know, I really thought you'd know that, Anna. Hasn't the district attorney talked to you yet? Isn't Rei, like, really pissed that you're testifying against Seth?"

Taylor's face is pinched. "We haven't discussed it," she says tightly. "What else happened in New York?"

Kyle shrugs. "That's pretty much what I know. I was kind of hoping you'd know more," he admits.

"No," Taylor glowers, "but I will know more soon."

She pushes the speed dial number on her cell phone so fast, I don't have time to warn Rei. I surge into view just as he checks the caller ID and picks it up. He looks right at me, but he's talking to the caller—two birds with one stone. "Hey, Anna."

The force of her voice drives the phone away from his ear. I get a look that clearly says, *Thanks for the warning!*

"Calm down!" he says into the receiver. "If you'd stop yelling at me, I'll be happy to explain." He squeezes his eyes shut and pinches the bridge of his nose. "That's better. I was planning to tell you as soon as I saw you alone. Getting arrested isn't something I'm bragging about. Nobody knows except my family and now you." He rolls his eyes. "Okay, and now Kyle, Cori, Mandy, Olivia, and Vienna. So much for damage control."

I don't know how Rei can stand that shrill voice so close to his eardrum.

"Yes, Seth's arraignment was today. Why didn't I tell you? Because it's an arraignment; it has nothing to do with you. They just read him the charges and he tells the judge he's not guilty . . . Yes, I know you think he's guilty," he drums his fingers on the desk with a little more urgency. "Well, if they wanted you there, I'm sure they would have sent you a subpoena or something . . . I don't know—I'm not a lawyer . . . No, you can't come over right now—I'm in the middle of a project for school . . . Tomorrow. Yeah, tomorrow."

He hangs up the phone and leans back in his desk chair, groaning. "And what really sucks is I know I should spend more time with her, but the girl just makes my brain hurt."

I know what he means. I had planned to learn more about her so I could figure out her weak spots, but we've been too busy with Seth's situation. But now there's nothing more we can do for Seth until Friday, so I have no excuse.

It's time to know my enemy.

Rei smiles like a proud father. "So you do listen to me sometimes."

I listen to you a lot. I just don't always follow your suggestions.

Rei almost laughs. "No . . . really?"

I have a suggestion of my own for him, but I don't want him to take it the wrong way. I just think he needs to spend more time with her, too, and there's only one way for him to do that.

Maybe it's time you bit the bullet and went on a date with her.

Rei hoots at this idea. "Me? On a date with Taylor Gleason? What, are you nuts?"

I look down my nose at him before I turn back to the keyboard. *I'm allergic to nuts, remember?*

"I was afraid it might come to this," Rei sighs. "Oh, well. Sun Tzu did say war is based on deception."

I never actually read *The Art of War,* so I'll take his word for it. I am sorry he feels so put out by the idea of dating Taylor, only because it's hard to feel that he's not rejecting part of me as well. I mean, it's still my physical body, even though it's infested with Taylor. On the other hand, I can't say I blame him. After what she's rumored to have done to the guy in New York and what she's actually done to Seth, who in their right mind *would* want to date her? I may as well just hand Rei a rope and a chair rather than suggest he go on a date with Taylor.

Never mind. I'm sorry I suggested it.

"But you're right. It's the only way I can keep an eye on her," he rationalizes. "Okay, you go hang out with her and learn what you can. I'm going to finish this project. And tomorrow, I'll play nice and ask her out."

Military strategy at its finest. I give him a thumbs-up and go off in search of the enemy.

Taylor has three messages waiting for her when she finally gets home from the mall. The first is from the district attorney. He wants to talk to her. The second is from Seth's attorney. He wants to talk to her. The third is from Jason Trent. I don't even want to guess what he wants.

• • •

The next morning, I tag along while Taylor rides to school with Cori. Taylor was the third-smartest girl in our junior class, but now that she's in my body, I can't figure out if she's hampered by my less-than-brilliant brain or if she just can't be bothered to extend any effort on my behalf. Watching Taylor's academic inertia is boring. I can't take notes and I won't remember what Ms. Bannister is talking about anyway, so I hang around the back of the class and look for ways to amuse myself. Just out of my reach, I see a pencil hanging halfway off a desk, and it makes me wonder if I'm confined to the shape of a body I no longer own. I stretch my invisible arm, farther and farther, until I reach the pencil and it drops to the ground.

Cool!

Sheets of paper, pens, anything I find light enough to maneuver, sail effortlessly off desks around the room while I hang out in the back corner orchestrating these shenanigans. Finally, Ms. Bannister walks over to the window and closes it.

I want to show Rei what I've learned. As soon as class is over, I find him at his locker and watch him swap out notebooks and textbooks. He organizes everything just so in his backpack, then he heads for the cafeteria. Once he's settled at our table with his lunch and chemistry notes, I jiggle the phone in his pocket, and he nonchalantly takes it out and sets it on the table.

Ohai

Ohai, he texts back. *I thought you were bonding with her.*

I'm taking a break.

Summoning just enough energy to text but not so much that I materialize in front of everyone else in the cafeteria is tricky. I also realize it's no fun to show him my new trick unless he can actually see me and judge the distance between me and my target.

So where is she now?

Probably in the bathroom putting on more lipstick.

Probably?

Fine. BRB

I latch onto Taylor's vibration and follow it to . . .

Holy *crap!* The windows of Jason Trent's white Jeep are open on this warm day, and the sounds coming from it are obscenely graphic. I bolt back to Rei's phone and punch in *white jeep now.*

The instant Rei reads these words, he abandons his stuff and sprints for the door. I beat him to the white Jeep, but not by a very wide margin. Rei reaches into the open window and unsnaps the convertible roof, then moves quickly to the other side and does the same. He yanks the canvas roof back in one fluid motion.

"Get off her *now!*" His voice is fierce.

Taylor and Jason both look up at him in astonishment. Jason pushes himself up on his hands so he can gawk at Rei from a better angle, and now . . .

Uh . . . you know . . . I would feel a whole lot better about this entire situation if that halter top was still tied around my neck and not all tangled up around my waist. Rei doesn't even seem to notice.

"I said *NOW!*" He punctuates this with a fist slam against the hood of the Jeep, and the resounding *thunk* makes Taylor flinch. Jason is still stuck in neutral, so Rei reaches in and grabs him by the front of his neck.

"Son of a . . ." But Jason's air is cut off and his eyes bulge nearly out of his head as Rei applies more pressure.

Taylor grabs the straps of her halter and struggles to untangle them and sit up at the same time.

"If you're smart, you will get out of there on your own," Rei tells him in a deadly calm voice before he lets go of his neck with a little shove.

Jason rubs his neck as he climbs out of the backseat. "What's your problem, Ellis? She says she doesn't go out with you." He hacks and spits something chunky on the ground.

"She has a concussion, Jason. It affects her memory. And you will respect that and leave her alone. Do you understand?"

Rei doesn't take his eyes off Jason, but he nods curtly toward Taylor. "Fix your shirt and let's go," he says in a brittle voice.

Okay. So he noticed. I wonder if this cancels out the shower invasion.

It looks like Jason is getting his second wind. I imagine he understood exactly what Rei said to him; I just don't think he cares. He seems to be calculating his height and weight advantage. When his right hand balls into a fist by his side and he draws his elbow back, I yell out to warn Rei, but he can't hear me, of course.

It doesn't matter. Rei turns just in time to catch Jason's fist squarely in his right hand. He yanks him off balance and squeezes, twisting in rapid succession Jason's hand, arm, and shoulder until Jason lies crumpled faceup in a heap on the ground.

Rei looks down at him contemptuously. "*Now* do you understand?"

He turns to Taylor, who is still stunned but at least she's fully dressed now. "Put your shoes on," he orders. As soon as she fumbles her feet into the high heels, he puts his hands around her waist, lifts her out of the Jeep, and deposits her on the pavement. "Let's go."

Wow! I've never seen this badass side of Rei before.

He marches her back to the courtyard a step ahead of him the entire way, his fingers gripping the top of her arm, right over the tattoo. He doesn't say a word until he sits her firmly down on a bench.

His face is a block of ice. "What the hell was that about?" he demands in a low voice.

Taylor finally seems to be coming out of her stupor. "What the . . . what the hell was *that* about! How *dare* you!"

"Oh, come on! Jason *Trent?* You can't have hit your head *that* hard."

"Well, at least he doesn't treat me like a little sister!" she shoots back.

"That was pretty obvious."

Taylor flushes and stands up. "Yeah, and it was pretty obvious you weren't interested, Rei. What did you expect?"

"Not Jason Trent." Rei sighs, and his voice softens. "You were going to come over today."

"What?"

"Yesterday, when I talked to you on the phone, you wanted to come over and I said I had homework. I said for you to come over tomorrow instead. And . . . it's tomorrow."

Taylor plants her hands on her hips. "I don't get you, Rei. The last time I came to your house, you couldn't wait to get rid of me."

"I know. And I'm sorry." He smiles hesitantly, and then he reaches over and slowly slides his hand underneath her hair to that spot on the back of her neck and gives her his signature squeeze. I close my eyes and replay the sensation from memory.

He sighs and lets his hand slide down to her shoulder. "And it's not that I'm not interested. I just thought it might be a little weird." He brushes the back of his fingers against the side of her neck, and she looks every bit as flustered by that simple gesture as I feel. "I miss you, Anna. I'll be home all afternoon if you want to come over."

He squeezes her shoulder gently and walks away.

CHAPTER 27

"I was wrong back there," Rei confesses when he gets home from school. He drops his backpack by the side of his desk and steps on the power strip button to turn the computer on. "I told Taylor this might be a little weird. It actually will be very weird."

I agree: it will be weird, and sandwiched in with all that weirdness is my knowledge that even though Rei has a great poker face, he's a terrible actor. How much of that performance was the art of deception and how much was fueled by real emotion? When he looks at Taylor, does he see me at all? When I look at Taylor, I barely recognize myself.

"So I know this was your idea, but are you sure you're okay with this?" he asks as the computer finishes powering up. "The good news is I guarantee you we won't be using those condoms."

Are YOU okay with this?

He shrugs and nods indifferently.

I roll my eyes at him. *Remember when we were about eight and Seth dared us to touch tongues?*

Rei smirks. "Yeah, and then you got mad because you dared Seth and me to touch tongues, too, and we wouldn't."

No, I got mad because you and Seth have double standards, but that's not my point. You thought I had cooties and you couldn't get upstairs to brush your teeth fast enough. What if she wants you to kiss her? Are you sure you want to do this?

Rei considers this. "If I have to kiss her, I'll just pretend it's you. I can handle your cooties," he jokes.

Rei has a hard time handling his *own* cooties.

I roll my eyes at him some more. *Rei, it IS me.*

"Anna, you can fill a snail shell with mud, but it doesn't make it escargot."

The doorbell rings at three thirty, and Taylor is waiting expectantly at the door when Rei opens it.

"Okay," she says as she steps into the house, "let's try this again."

What to do, what to *do*? She doesn't want to go for a walk; she doesn't want to work on homework; she doesn't even want to go to the mall. She wants to talk about Seth's trial. Nope, Rei doesn't want to talk about that.

"We're just going to have to agree to disagree on that," he says diplomatically.

Then she wants Rei to play his guitar for her. She wants to sit next to him on the porch swing while he plays and tickle his bare feet with hers. He stretches his legs out in front of him so her feet no longer reach his.

Rei plays a few of his acoustic stock songs, some of the classical and new age music he plays whenever his mom has company over and pesters him to play for them. There are no words to any of these songs, but he plays them so beautifully, I could listen for hours. After about fifteen minutes, Taylor starts to fidget. Five minutes later, she asks if he knows any other songs. Anything with words. He strums up and down fast a few times, as if clearing the music away, and then holds his hand over the strings to stop the vibration.

"I know a lot of songs," Rei says. "I just don't think you'll like any of them."

"Okay," Taylor stands up, takes the guitar away from him and leans it up against the front door. "Then let's do something different."

She comes at him like a barracuda.

I'm kind of torn. Part of me wants to stay here and spy to make sure Taylor doesn't end up accusing Rei of doing anything worse than trying to survive his first kiss, and part of me wants to go upstairs and let him suffer this humiliation privately.

I decide I'd better stay. Considering what I *do* know about Taylor, he may need witnesses.

Rei is right. It is so very weird watching him kiss me or more specifically, to watch him being kissed by me. I'm not sure what they're doing even qualifies as a kiss, really; it's more like she's attached my mouth to his face and she's slowly sucking out his soul. Well, he hasn't gagged or anything, so she must have at least brushed my teeth.

What must he be thinking right now? He must feel her rise up on one leg and throw her other leg over him like she's mounting a pony. Yeah, he definitely felt her tush land on his lap and now he looks a little panicky as she inches her way forward. He shifts uncomfortably on the hard wooden swing. God! I feel like such a perverted Peeping Tom!

"Ow!" Rei jerks his head to the side, and her lips trail over to his cheek. "What was . . . did you pierce your *tongue?*" He sounds horrified.

Great! What does this make now, eight holes she's put into my head?

Taylor sticks her tongue out and waggles it playfully to display her new hardware. She makes sexy eyes at him. "I did. Like it?"

"Can you try not to chip my teeth, please?"

She giggles and latches on to his mouth again.

This is just too painful to watch. There are four eggs in the finch's nest up in the planter hanging from the farmer's porch. There's a nearly symmetrical orb spider's web just under the west side of the porch by the spigot, and there is a neatly wrapped bug, maybe a fly, waiting to be consumed by said spider. There's a . . .

"Stop it," Rei says against her lips.

Now what is she doing? She's trying to place Rei's hand in a location that would be convenient should he decide he wants to feel up that relatively flat chest of mine, which he does not. Rei pulls his hand out of her grip and settles it safely on her back.

So, where was I? Oh, yes, there's a chipmunk living under the porch. Saya and I have been secretly feeding it sunflower seeds, even though . . .

"*Stop it!*" Rei says, louder this time, and he pulls his hand back for the umpteenth time.

"Rei, you are *so* no fun." She pouts at him while she reaches back and unties the top of the halter, holding the ties together in one hand. While Rei is still recovering from the shock of that, she giggles and with one swift tug, she has Rei's jeans unbuttoned.

"STOP IT, TAYLOR!"

CHAPTER 28

"*What did you just call me?*" She is off the swing in an instant, her fingers fumbling with the halter ties. She backs away from him like he's covered in anthrax.

Rei takes a few seconds to reconfigure his pants before he answers, stalling for time. "I said stop it."

Taylor shakes her head as she reties her halter. "You son of a bitch," she hisses. "How long have you known?"

"Anna, I don't know what you're . . ."

"Cut the crap, Rei. What, did you ask me over here just to keep Jason away from your little friend? Nice try." She spins around and stomps down the steps.

"Wait!" Rei goes after her and puts his hand on her shoulder.

"Don't you *touch* me," she swats his hand away. "Unless you want to end up in jail with your buddy, Seth."

"Taylor, look, I'm sorry. And I'm sorry you fell, but . . ."

"I didn't fall, Rei. I was pushed. By *your* friend."

"He didn't push you, Taylor, and . . ."

"You don't know that. You weren't there."

"He tried to pull you up."

"Is that what Anna told you? Or is that what Seth told you? They don't care that I'm dead. None of you ever cared about *me*. You all treated me like a leper in this town."

Rei stops short and stares at her. "Nobody meant to treat you like a leper, Taylor. You and Seth just had nothing in common. But you know he didn't push you."

"Oh, he pushed me, all right!"

"Why? What do you gain by putting him in jail for something he didn't do?"

"He should have given me a chance! If he had just gotten to know me, maybe he would have liked me. Maybe *you* would have liked me. But you know what? Jason likes me."

"Well, if you like Jason so much, why didn't you just go out with him before and leave Seth alone?"

The message in her silence is as clear to me as if she had spoken the words. Jason wouldn't give Taylor a chance, either. Despite the impression that he's been hit on the head by a few too many footballs, even he was smart enough to see that Taylor had the potential to ruin a guy's life. But he was giving Anna a chance, and Taylor would take what she could get.

Her tone is frigid. "If you bother Jason and me again like you did today, I will have you arrested. Again. And if you follow me around, I'll get a restraining order against you for stalking me. See, Rei, you've got another chance to join Seth in jail."

"Taylor, I don't care what you do to me. But Anna did nothing to you. Just give her back," he pleads.

"You want Anna back?" She turns to him with a chilling smile. "Be careful what you wish for, Rei, because I only know one way to leave this body, and you won't like what's left of Anna if she goes into that waterfall like I did."

Rei freezes as her threat sinks in.

"*Sayonara*, Rei. I'll give your regards to Jason."

I don't know if he wants to be alone or not, but I follow him, making up the rules as I go along. If he wants to be alone, I rationalize he'll go into his weight room. If he wants to talk to me, he'll stay in his bedroom. If he rushes into the bathroom to brush his teeth, well, that's an entirely different issue.

He lies on his bed and I notice the tears pooling in his eyes just before he closes them. I haven't seen Rei cry since he was eight years old and he broke his leg skiing. Well, falling, actually. Even then, he didn't cry in fear or pain; in fact, he didn't cry until Yumi broke the bad news to him that he couldn't ski for the rest of the winter. He cried in frustration.

I need the good stuff right now. I pull my energy from deep within the universe, and when I'm vibrating at full capacity, I appear and touch his arm so he knows I'm here.

"I'm sorry." He swallows hard.

We must be the two sorriest people in the universe.

He reads my message and nods.

I'm sick of apologizing for other people, and I'm sick of listening to you apologize for stuff that's not your fault.

"It *is* my fault. I screwed up and now she knows I know she's not you. Did you hear what she said?"

I nod. I heard what she said.

Tissues are light. I stretch to pull one up out of the box and let it ride a current of air over to where Rei sits.

"Thanks."

Did she at least brush my teeth before she shoved my tongue down your throat?

"Yeah. You were all minty fresh." He rubs his thumb absently over his front teeth. "She pierced your tongue, you know."

I heard. How are your teeth?

"Fine." His sigh could rival a Category 5 hurricane. "I have to keep her away from Jason. She'll probably do it with him just to get even with me." He looks about as miserable as I feel with that prospect. "Maybe if I talk to your mom, she'll tell Taylor she can't see him anymore."

Something tells me that would only make Taylor more determined to see him. No, I think Jason should meet the real Anna Rogan if he's planning to devirginize me in the near future.

I think I should pay our friend Jason a little visit. Can you help me find some good music to play for him?

"What? Why?"

Because I want to scare the crap out of him.

This thought cheers up Rei considerably. "Seriously? What's more important, music or lyrics?"

Big guitars. Lots of bass. And dark and disturbing lyrics would be helpful.

"Come on," he says. "I keep all my lyrics in here." He rolls off his bed and opens the door to (*gasp!*) The Weight Room!

The only time I've been in this room, it was dark. The view from outside the window is different once I'm actually in here. It's a room. After all the mystery, I'm almost disappointed. It's big: the size of the two-car garage downstairs. It's tastefully decorated with oatmeal-colored carpet, off-white walls, and bamboo shades over the windows. There are his weights and weight bench near the door. There's a black canvas futon, and his favorite toy, his sleek and shiny black Ibanez electric guitar, sitting on a stand next to a rather impressive-looking amplifier that I know for a fact can be heard all the way across our yards and into my bedroom if he is so inclined.

The computer is back in Rei's bedroom, so I just mouth *Wow!* and raise my eyebrows like this is the coolest room I've ever seen.

In the corner by the window where the sunlight divides into shadows cast by the willow's lacy foliage, there's a low table where several partially melted white candles sit on a tray and a pillow that's shaped like a mushroom cap is pushed to the side of the wall. I put two and two together and decide this must be where Rei meditates. I flit over and point.

"Yeah, I figured you'd have some wiseass comment about that. Why do you think I never let you in here before?"

I frown. I thought it was because I told him he looked constipated when he lifted weights. But then again, I do have a hard time picturing Rei sitting cross-legged on this pillow chanting "om." I readjust my vision: get rid of his shirt, lose the "om," the mushroom pillow has to go, too. Much better.

"My mom got that pillow for me—I never use it. And no," he says defensively, "I don't say 'om' either, just so you know."

I wish I had the computer here so I could tell him I love that he meditates. I love the serenity that flows from him, and I miss it this week. He's disappeared in here a few times, but I don't think he's spent much time charging up his positive vibes. It makes me sad to know he feels self-conscious about meditating.

"Okay, so what are you looking for . . . power metal, thrash metal, speed metal, Goth metal, punk metal, black metal, death metal . . ."

I nod vigorously.

"Death metal?"

Yes, that sounds perfect.

"Sure." He pulls a plastic file bin out from under an end table and riffles through until he comes up with a file marked *Death Metal*. Okay, that type of organizational attentiveness is scary in itself.

"What looks good?" he asks as he spreads the papers all over the floor.

I find a band whose lyrics are all equally disturbing, and Rei assures me the guitars are plenty big enough to get my point across to Jason. "Right this way," he says as he leads me back to his bedroom where he pulls up YouTube on his computer.

"You want dark and disturbing?" Rei asks. "Here you go."

I smile at him as the room begins to vibrate. Perfect.

Five minutes later, I'm in Jason Trent's bedroom, which is just as disgusting as he is, especially the stained sheets on his unmade bed. Is Rei the only guy who ever washes his sheets? There's a vaguely disagreeable odor hanging in the room, like a combination of sweaty socks and sour milk. He does have a very nice desktop computer he's left online, so it's just a matter of pulling up YouTube and searching for my dark and disturbing music video. I turn up the volume as loud as it will go, so when he runs into his room with a puzzled look on his face to see why his speakers are about to detonate, he gets a nice surprise.

Me!

Parked here next to his computer, I look as solid as any flesh-and-blood girl. For a moment, his little blue button eyes register confusion, and I can almost see the thought bubble float out of his head with the word "huh?" printed across it. He looks at the window for a second as though he's trying to figure out how I got into his room. What a dolt! Maybe if I float toward him and let myself fade a bit. . . .

He screams bloody murder and bolts out of the door, tripping down the last few stairs in his hurry.

I leave the video playing and bounce back to Rei's.

"That was fast!"

He screamed and ran away. Am I really that scary?

Rei laughs for the first time in a while. "I'm afraid to answer that."

CHAPTER 29

There are strange people in and out of school all day on Wednesday. The police search Seth's locker and they find the crumpled note, which they carefully place in a plastic evidence bag and label. While they are in there, they look through the rest of his possessions, which are mostly schoolbooks, tattered spiral notebooks, pencil stubs, and a plastic bag containing a moldy sandwich featuring some unidentifiable meat and a rancid odor which is much more noticeable now that it's been unearthed from the pile of stuff.

Someone decided it would be easier for the attorneys to come to the high school to talk with any students they want statements from rather than the other way around. There are a few empty classrooms set aside, and parents are required to be present during questioning. Annaliese Rogan is excused from her P.E. class so the district attorney can question her. My mom meets her at the classroom and listens while Taylor gives her version of events, complete with hand gestures, gasps, and dramatic facial expressions. She is amazingly consistent with her story, and the district attorney grins like the village idiot as he jots down notes.

He looks entirely too happy.

I decide my presence is required. I drift to the top of the file cabinet behind her and my mom, and surge into view. He stops smiling abruptly.

"What? Did I say something wrong?" Taylor asks as soon as she notices his frozen stare.

"No, no, nothing is wrong. So, um, you were saying something about her shirt?"

"Yes!" Taylor says. "He *grabbed* it with both of his hands and *ripped* it wide open! It looked like he was planning to rape her!"

I roll my eyes and shake my head no.

The district attorney looks at me, then at Taylor, and marks something down on his paper.

"And when she resisted him, he grabbed her by the wrist and *dragged* her over to the edge!"

I shake my head again, and the district attorney looks from Taylor to me. Taylor spins around to look behind her, but I vanish before she can see me. My mother seems to realize that if she stays very quiet and doesn't turn around, she'll get back to work sooner.

"I see. And, um, you said something about his wrist?"

"Yes! She tried so hard to fight him off, she clawed at his wrist, but he was just too strong."

I materialize again and shake my head. He has a phony little smile glued onto his face as he makes more notes.

I drift up to the chalkboard which, like most chalkboards, has a layer of chalk dust on it. My letters are so faint, you would have to know I was writing to notice them.

She lies.

I look back to make sure the district attorney sees what I've written. He does. He looks me straight in the eyes and I see question marks where his pupils should be. I let myself dissolve slowly, leaving the ghostly letters on the chalkboard as the only proof I was there.

Rei gets pulled out of his fourth period chemistry class to talk to the attorneys, and his story never wavers. He takes the opportunity to enlighten Seth's attorney about the memory issues "Anna" has been having since her bump on the head and her out-of-character behavior, including her tattoo. He also mentions the note the police found in Seth's locker, since the rumor about the police visit has circulated through the school as fast as the rancid odor from Seth's sandwich.

Seth's attorney gets a whack at Taylor, too, but I decide not to mess with him. He asks about her tattoo, but she refuses to acknowledge it.

The attorneys talk to Taylor's friends and to some of the teachers and other school staff. I overhear a teacher in the hallway tell another the upcoming trial was mentioned on the six o'clock news the night before. All we need now are some elephants and ponies, and we'd have ourselves a real circus.

Taylor trolls the area around Jason's locker from time to time, waiting for him. He shows up just before sixth period.

"Hi, Jason," she smiles up at him.

"Hi," he stutters and fumbles with his books.

"Are you busy after school today?"

"Um, yeah," he slams his locker and backs away a few steps before he turns and literally runs down the hallway.

"Rei ruined everything," she complains to her friends on the way to her next class. "Jason won't even look at me now! How can he be afraid of Rei? He's, like, an amoeba compared to Jason."

"God, Anna," Vienna huffs, "you really did mess up your

memory when you fell. Rei has, like, a second-degree black belt in karate and now he takes something else—alido? Akudo? I don't know—something. Jason would be an idiot to pick a fight with him."

"Well, I'm not going to let Rei Ellis ruin this for me!" Taylor declares.

"So if you're not going out with Rei anymore, is it fair to say he's back on the market?" Cori asks.

"Sure. Whatever."

Taylor has the tenacity of a terrier. As soon as Jason slams his locker door at the end of the day and sees Taylor standing there, he jumps a mile.

"Did I scare you?"

"Uh, kinda." He shoulders his backpack and starts to back away from her.

"Jason, if you're worried about Rei Ellis, he won't be bothering us again. If he does, I'll just have a restraining order issued."

Jason looks confused. "Rei Ellis? Why would I be worried about Rei Ellis?"

"Because he was such a jerk yesterday. I just thought maybe you . . ."

"You thought I was afraid of Rei Ellis?" Apparently this threat to his male ego trumps all fear of me. "I am *not* afraid of Rei Ellis. I just remembered I am free today. What do you want to do?"

Well, first she wants to parade Jason right in front of Rei, who takes a deep breath and starts to follow them out of the school.

"I wouldn't do that if I were you, Rei," Taylor calls over her shoulder. "That's, like, creepy stalker behavior."

"What is with him?" Jason asks as he watches Rei suspiciously over his shoulder.

"He thinks I'm his little sister," Taylor sighs.

"But you're not, right?" Jason is confused.

Even Taylor smirks. "No, Jason. I'm not."

As soon as they're out of sight, I materialize just long enough to let Rei know I'll follow her. Three people do a double take in Rei's direction.

Jason takes her to the nearest McDonald's, which is seven miles away. They sit next to each other in a booth, and he practically inhales a large order of everything while Taylor picks at his fries and sips a small diet soda. He does nothing to discourage her foot from roaming up and down his leg.

He seems to be forgetting how terrifying I truly am.

Thanks to a large root beer, nature calls. "I'll be right back," he says, and he leans in and gives her a sloppy, double cheesy kiss right on the lips. Ack!

I'm waiting for him when he comes through the door of the men's room, his hand on his fly, ready for action. I swear all I did was smile at him, and damn! I wish I had a camera! The look on his face when he sees me is priceless, and then I crack up laughing because now Seth and Jason have something in common! Wetness blooms around the front of his pants.

He doesn't even let her know he's leaving; he just bolts out the side door. After about five minutes, Taylor asks one of the staff to check the men's room. When she realizes his car is missing from the parking lot, her face turns a shade of magenta I didn't realize I was capable of.

She dials her cell phone fast and her words fly like bullets. "Cori? It's Anna. Can you pick me up? Jason Trent is the biggest . . ."

For once, I agree with Taylor Gleason completely.

CHAPTER 30

Rei is stressed out. In addition to everything that's going on, he's got a research paper due tomorrow. There are books spread out all over his bed, but when I materialize in his room, I find him pacing back and forth instead of reading.

As soon as he sees me, he practically pounces. "Are you okay? Where are they? I've been kicking myself for not following them!"

She's fine. He took her to McDonald's. I surprised him in the men's room and I scared him so bad, he wet his pants. He left without her and Cori had to pick her up.

Rei's shoulders relax. "Okay. Well that's one good thing that happened today."

It's Wednesday. Aren't you supposed to be at your aikido class?

"Yeah, but I have to get this paper in by tomorrow since I'll be in court on Friday. Want to help me?"

Sure.

"Will you search history of the U.S. election process and print out a few that look good?"

While they're printing, I give him the highlights of Taylor's deposition, and Rei looks up from reading and nods from time to time. I conveniently leave out the part when I materialized in front of the district attorney. He's stressed enough as it is.

His headache is back. As soon as I see him knead the center of his forehead with his thumb while he reads the printouts, I reach out and let whatever energy I have transfer from my fingertips to his temples.

He smiles without taking his eyes off the paper he's reading. "Do you know what you're doing?"

I'm trying to help you get rid of your headache.

"You did. It's gone." He looks up at me and his smile is sweet, but weary. "It went away as soon as you touched me. You did it a few other times before today, but I wasn't sure if you were doing it on purpose." He holds his hand up toward me, palm out like he wants to high-five me and I match my hand to his, each of my fingers mirroring his. He considers our hands. "You feel like you're purring. Do I feel like that to you?"

I nod.

"You know, my mom had to take classes to learn how to do Reiki. How did you figure this out?"

I shrug.

"I think my mom should let you work on some of her clients."

I stretch one hand out to reach the keyboard from the bed. *Your mom won't even let me teach a kids' yoga class.*

"Hey . . ." Rei looks from me to the keyboard, then back to me. "I didn't know you could reach that far. Is that something new you can do?"

In all the excitement yesterday, I forgot to show Rei my new trick. I nod.

"Cool. And she didn't let you teach the kids' class because she's obsessive about yoga fundamentals and she knew you'd focus on fun stuff. But this is different. Trust me, you can get rid of a headache a lot faster than my mom does," he admits.

I raise my eyebrows, but this confession pleases me more than he could ever know.

"It's true," he insists. "I know I tease you about being magical, mystical, Auracle girl, but so much of this metaphysical stuff just comes naturally to you, Anna. It's like a gift."

I wish I had a camera, because Rei has this look of tender admiration on his face, and I want to remember it forever. I look at our hands, flesh and spirit, still touching. I don't want to disappoint him, but I think he should know the truth.

I don't know if I'll be able to do any of this when I get my body back.

I don't even know if I'll get my body back.

I don't type that, but Rei must know what I'm thinking. "We'll get her out of you," he promises. "Whatever it takes, we will get her out of you, Anna. And when you're back where you belong, I'm going to give my mother one hell of a headache so you can show her what you've got."

I have to laugh at that. Rei has already given Yumi more headaches this week than he has in his entire life. And as much as I would like to hang out and listen to Rei say nice things about me, he still has to finish this stupid project, so I offer to help. Two hours later and I'm still confused about why the electoral vote trumps the popular vote and what the founding fathers were drinking when they came up with the idea for the Electoral College. Finally, I make an excuse that I need to check on Taylor. Considering I have a project due in history that's similar to Rei's, maybe I'll get lucky and find Taylor doing something useful, like my homework.

• • •

Things are quiet at my house. My mom is out for a real estate banquet tonight, and my father slumps in his chair, the blue glow from the television reflecting an eerie green off the whites of his eyes. He raises the glass to his mouth and drinks, swallows, scratches places best left unmentioned, and returns the glass to the watermark etched onto the cheap wooden table over the course of hundreds of days and nights just like this one.

My bedroom is no longer familiar. Everything on my bureau is gone, replaced with Taylor's stuff. The big yellow Pikachu pillow Rei gave me for my tenth birthday is nowhere to be found, and there's a new comforter on my bed that's a sorry shade of lavender. She looks so at home sitting on my bed, reading an article from a fashion magazine, an open bag of chips and a nearly empty bottle of vodka beside her.

That is not helping me in my quest to avoid becoming an alcoholic. I hover in the corner, invisible, and watch her flip pages languidly and suck down vodka. When she drains the last mouthful, the f-word flies out of her mouth along with a huff of annoyance.

She contemplates the door for a while before she reluctantly stands. The selection of clothes in my closet is alien to me, but she immediately reaches for a short, silky leopard print robe. She slides her arms into the sleeves, ties the belt loosely around her waist, and flips her hair out of the collar before she opens the bedroom door and slithers out toward the kitchen.

My father acknowledges nothing but his glass and the television. Taylor steals into the kitchen, watching him suspiciously as she tiptoes past. Under the kitchen sink, there are cleaning supplies and extra bottles of my father's liquor, courtesy of Mom, the Enabler. She decided years ago that life was much easier in the Rogan home if there were always a few extra bottles of "daddy's juice," so she buys it by the case. Taylor opens the cabinet below the sink quietly, but glass clinks against glass as she lifts out a bottle of whiskey.

There is nothing in this world my father is responsible for, except those bottles. I've heard a mother will wake up instantly from a deep sleep at the sound of her baby's whimper, so maybe my father does have some paternal instinct after all, just not where I'm concerned. He snaps to attention and turns slowly toward Taylor, but there is no place to hide in my tiny house.

I watch her shoulders droop as she carefully closes the cabinet door and hides the bottle behind her. Now my father struggles to his feet, holding the arm of the recliner for support as he squints into the kitchen.

"Wha's tha' in your han'?" Under the fluorescent kitchen light, his skin is the color of an overripe banana and his nose looks like a strawberry. All the blond in his hair has faded and thinned, so it looks like a fine layer of greasy mold covering his head.

He staggers toward Taylor, scrutinizing her. When was the last time he really looked at me? When I was born? When I was a toddler? Just before he knocked me into the counter? He's all but ignored me for so long, and now that I finally have his attention, it breaks my heart that it's Taylor he sees.

"You can't have tha'." His jaw is slack; his breathing is shallow. "Gimme tha'." He grasps for her arm, his fist closing on air.

Taylor's back and the bottle are flush against the cabinet, as if she could push herself through them and escape. She is surrounded by murky blue. Until now, my father has been nothing more than a passive, pathetic object that lives in a chair. I don't think she's ever seen him in a standing position. There's a scream building somewhere in that open mouth of hers.

Run! I silently will her. RUN! I know from experience he won't chase her; he *can't* chase her, but she just stands there, paralyzed.

"I sh'aid, gimme tha'!" My father makes one more lunge toward the arm holding the bottle, but he stumbles against the counter and falls onto his knees. He grabs a handful of her slippery robe to pull himself up.

The bottle comes up much too fast, and my father's reflexes are much too slow. Along with a shrill scream, there come the sounds of smashing glass, a muffled yelp, and finally, a dull thud as my father hits the floor. The acrid smell of alcohol fills the room, and blood spreads quickly from my father's head into the pool of amber liquid in long, red ribbons. Taylor and I both shoot out of the kitchen like cannonballs.

I'm faster.

Rei is still working on his paper when I slam against the chair and type frantically on the keyboard.

Call 911: Taylor broke a bottle over my father's head and he's bleeding badly.

Rei swears softly, grabs the phone, and starts pressing buttons.

Downstairs, the doorbell rings incessantly, until Robert emerges from the master bedroom to answer it. Taylor is crying and babbling something that Robert can't make any sense of. Behind her, a trail of red smears lead up the walkway and onto the porch. As soon as she hears my voice, Yumi hurries out of their bedroom, still pulling on her bathrobe.

"Anna? What happened?" She wraps one arm around Taylor, pries the broken bottle neck out of her hand, and hands it to Robert with a knowing look.

Rei is up and out of his bedroom door. The commotion woke Saya, and Rei corrals her with one arm as she wanders out of her bedroom, rubbing her eyes with her fists. He whispers something to her and lifts her up, and she clings to him like a tired little monkey as he carries her back to her room, rubbing her back.

Yumi steers Taylor over to the couch. "Anna, honey, your foot is bleeding. Let me take a look at it. Robert, get me some paper towels and the first aid kit, please."

I swoop back to my house to find my father still crumpled on the floor, moaning. It's hard to tell just how much blood he's lost since it's mixed with the whiskey, but blood still seems to be oozing from a deep ragged gash down his forehead, through his eyebrow and dangerously close to his left eye.

A siren wails in the distance, then pulses of blinding red and white light burst through the living room window. The door was left wide open in Taylor's hasty departure, and warm night air and mosquitoes meander through it. Rei appears at the door like a shadow as the paramedics hoist my father onto the stretcher. He follows them out and watches them load the stretcher into the ambulance, then talks to one of the paramedics briefly before they slam the doors shut and pull out of the driveway. The lights and siren slash through darkness and then it's silent once again.

Once they're gone, I follow Rei back into the house. Everything around us feels sticky and thick, and it has nothing to do with the humid night air. It's my father and Taylor, all the anger and drama of tonight, so much negativity has sucked away most of the existing light and left only this dark density. I'm not strong enough to reach through this heaviness to pull the energy I need to materialize, and Rei can't feel me beside him, even when I touch his hand. He's busy surveying the mess in the kitchen—broken glass, blood, and booze. I wish I could tell him to go home and leave the mess, but he wouldn't listen anyway. He picks up the bigger pieces of glass carefully, drops them into the trash can by the back door, and uses almost an entire roll of paper towels to blot up the liquid mess. In the garage, he finds a bucket. He mops quickly and methodically, leaving behind the telltale chlorine fumes that tell you he is eliminating something far too foul for regular floor cleaner to handle. He locks the door as he leaves.

At Rei's house, Taylor wears a Hello Kitty Band-Aid on the bottom of her foot, and a sliver of glass sits on a bloody paper towel on the side table. She has curled herself into a ball in the corner of the couch, and she's still crying softly. Robert went back to bed, but Yumi is on the couch beside her, trying unsuccessfully to find out what happened. Rei comes through the door hesitantly and turns off the light over the kitchen table before he turns the chair halfway around and straddles it, resting his arms on the back of the chair, facing the couch.

"Is Steve okay?" Yumi asks at once.

"I don't know," Rei says truthfully. "It looks like he lost a lot of blood. They're taking him to Burlington Memorial."

"She won't tell me a thing." Yumi pats Taylor's shoulder and stands up. "Anna, honey, Rei's here now. Why don't you tell him what happened while I call your mother."

Taylor only sniffs and curls up tighter.

As soon as Yumi is out of earshot, Rei sits next to Taylor on the couch. "Are you okay?"

"What do you care?" she mumbles.

"I care." He lowers his voice. "Just because I don't want you to unbutton my pants doesn't mean I don't care."

"You just want *her* back."

"It's her body; of course I want her to get it back. But that doesn't mean I don't care what happens to you."

Taylor peeks up with tear-drenched eyes. "If I leave here, I'll be dead, and so will she. I've already told you, I don't know how to get out."

"Well, maybe I can help you."

"How can you possibly help me?"

"I don't know yet, but I can figure something out if you're willing to try."

She takes a deep, shaky breath. "I have another idea."

"What's that?"

"I stay where I am, and you give me another chance."

"What kind of chance?" Rei asks suspiciously.

"A chance to . . . I don't know, try again." She uncurls herself a little and turns toward Rei, and the blues surrounding her lighten. "You said Seth and I had nothing in common, but you and I *do*, Rei. We both know how it feels when parents push, when all they care about is grades and what looks good on our college applications. They don't care what we have to give up." She wipes a fresh tear away on the sleeve of her robe. "I *know* your mom rides you hard, Rei. Kids hear her talking about you at the store. Everyone knows what colleges you're applying to and what you plan to major in."

Well, no, not everyone. Rei still hasn't told *me* where he wants to go to college. I'm not sure he knows himself.

"That coffin was just a formality." Taylor leans closer to him. "My parents stuck me in a box a long time ago. I was expected to get into Yale, graduate with honors, and go to law school. My father used to hint around that I could be a Supreme Court justice, if I wanted to. But not if I had a baby." She wipes her eyes with the heels of her hands. "As if I actually wanted to be on the Supreme Court."

"I'm sorry," Rei says.

"I'm sorry, too." Her voice drops to a whisper. "I just want someone to . . . understand me, you know?"

Rei nods dutifully. He looks like he just wants this night to be over.

"If you gave me another chance, I could prove to you I'm not this terrible person you think I am. I wouldn't rush you this time." Rei shifts away from her slightly. "And I wouldn't testify against Seth," she adds quickly.

"So what are you saying?" he asks. "Seth will go free, but Anna's stuck where she is."

"Rei, I'm scared," she whispers. "That light people claim to see when they die? There was no light. Not for me." Two more tears drop. "If I leave here, I don't know where I'll end up. Please?" She laces her fingers through his, almost shyly, and looks up into his eyes. "At least think about it."

Rei looks down at their hands linked together.

"Ahem." Both Rei and Taylor jump a little, and even I didn't hear Yumi's quiet feet walk down the hall. "Rei, can I talk to you?"

"Sure," Rei disengages his hand from Taylor's and follows Yumi down the hall into the office. She closes the door quietly.

"Did she tell you what happened?"

"She just said he came after her, and she hit him with the bottle."

Yumi looks perplexed. "So what was all that whispering and hand-holding about?" she asks.

Rei assumes his poker face. "She's just nervous. She thinks her mom will be mad at her. When's Lydie coming, anyway?"

Yumi looks unconvinced. "She's leaving now, but she wants to stop at the hospital for a few minutes to check on Steve. She should be here in an hour or so. Rei," Yumi pauses, "you know you don't have time to get involved with girls right now."

This seems to catch Rei completely by surprise. "Huh?"

"Rei, think about it. You have all the pressure of keeping your

GPA at school, aikido class, work, college applications, and things will only get busier next year. When would you have time to date? And I know you're very fond of Anna, but dating your best friend is just asking for trouble. Trust your mother on that one," she smiles and reaches up to pat his cheek.

"That's not something you have to worry about," Rei tells her in a wintry voice.

Suddenly, I have this overwhelming urge to topple a teacup.

CHAPTER 31

Taylor pretends to sleep. I know it. Rei knows it. I think Yumi knows it, too. When my mom gets to Rei's house and tries to wake her, Taylor feigns sleep like she's the living dead. Oh, how silly of me. She *is* the living dead. Rei ends up scooping her up into his arms and carries her across the dark path back to my house.

My mom opens the door for them, and Rei deposits her on top of the lavender comforter in my bedroom. As soon as he slides his arms out from beneath her, she is suddenly wide awake.

"Rei?" She catches his hand in hers.

"What."

"Will you just think about what I said?"

"Yes." He gently slides his hand out of hers and leans over her to take the empty vodka bottle off the bookshelf.

"Rei?"

"What."

"Don't you ever want to break out of the box they put *you* in?"

He hesitates. "Yes," he admits. "You should get some sleep." He shuts the door on his way out, leaving her in the dark.

My mom stands at the kitchen sink surrounded by an army of bottles lined up on the counter, and she pours the contents of them, one by one, down the drain. I'm feeling a little tipsy just breathing in the fumes.

"Any more?" Rei asks.

"There should be a box in the garage," she sniffs.

Rei comes back with four bottles full of whiskey and the empty vodka bottle in a cardboard box and sets it on the counter. As soon as my mom empties each bottle and rinses it, he fits it into the box between the cardboard slots. When they are done, there are ten empty bottles in the box. My mom opens the refrigerator door and pulls out a half empty bottle of Chardonnay. She looks at it wistfully, then uncorks it and pours that down the drain, too. Rei adds that bottle to the box, locks the cardboard flaps under, and shoulders it.

"I'll bring it to the store and recycle them for you."

"Thanks, hon." My mom sighs and blows her nose on a paper towel. "Did she tell you why she hit him?"

Rei shakes his head. "She hasn't really been herself since she hit her head."

"No, she hasn't." My mom rips another paper towel off the roll and wipes a few random drops of whiskey and water off the countertop. "He's not a bad person, Rei. I don't know if you remember what he was like before the accident, you were so young. I know Anna doesn't remember."

"She will. She'll get her memory back, and who knows, maybe this was good. Maybe he'll stop drinking." Rei shifts the box over to his other shoulder.

My mom sighs. "She didn't remember anything good about him even before she hit her head. She just . . . I don't know. I don't think she wants to remember. She doesn't understand this isn't his fault. And what's really frustrating is we were getting along so well this week. I felt like we were finally connecting."

"Um, yeah, I've got to go. I'm in court on Friday and I still have some homework to finish up tonight."

"Oh, that's right. How did your deposition go today?"

Rei shrugs. "I don't know. There are a lot of different versions of what happened."

"Is that why you two haven't been talking as much as usual?"

I'm surprised she noticed that. I thought she was pretty oblivious to my social life.

"That and other stuff. There's a lot going on."

"She had to tell them the truth. You know that, right?"

"Maybe she thinks she's telling them the truth, but I know Seth. He would never kill anyone. I'm surprised they even believe her after she hit her head."

My mom looks uncertain. "I wasn't there at the falls, Rei, but why would she lie? She doesn't know this girl. I can't believe she would jeopardize her friendship with you and testify against Seth unless she was absolutely positive."

Rei looks too tired to argue with her. "I have to go," he repeats and pushes through the screen door into the darkness.

I'm waiting for him in his room when he gets home.

I'm sorry, I type on the keyboard even though I really want to type *YOUR MOTHER HATES ME!* He looks too wiped out for me to bring that up now, though.

"Aren't you the one who said we must be the two sorriest people in the world and that you were sick of apologizing?" he asks.

Yes, but I'm still sorry. If I had just listened to Rei and stayed in my body, well, maybe Taylor would still be dead, but there would be no eyewitness. What was the term I heard on *Law & Order?* Burden of proof? Unless some of Seth's DNA survived underneath her fingernails during her extended bath in the river, they couldn't prove anything.

Rei rolls onto his bed and lies on his side, his elbow angled under his head. "She said if I go out with her again, she won't testify against Seth."

Wow. What a deal.

"I can't do that."

I know I'm going to hate myself for saying this, but I can't resist. *That's right. Your mom doesn't want you to date.*

"Oh. You heard that," he says flatly.

I nod solemnly. *Especially your best friend.*

"It's not just you, it's anyone," he points out. "She thinks I don't have time. The only reason she said that stuff about you is because if it didn't work, she's afraid it would ruin our friendship, that's all."

Of course. We've been friends for almost seventeen years. Why rock the boat?

What do you think about Taylor?

Rei rolls onto his back and stares up at the ceiling. "She's scared. She thinks she'll wind up in hell or something." He closes his eyes, and he's quiet for so long, I decide he must be asleep. I pull enough energy to flip the switch on the table lamp next to his bed, leaving only the glow of the computer screen to light the room.

"She said dying is the only way she knows to get out of you," he says out of the blue.

She doesn't know what she's talking about. I don't bother to type it, but now she's got me thinking.

She doesn't need to be dead to get out of me, but she doesn't know how to disengage herself and slip out like I do. There's no way I could talk her out, not unless she wanted to leave, but . . .

What if we found a way to weaken her or disable her somehow? Maybe that would loosen her grip enough to let me pull her out.

He rolls back onto his side to read the computer screen. "How would we do that?"

I don't know. How hard do you have to hit someone on the head to knock them out?

Rei looks at me funny. "It depends," he says carefully. "I don't think we want to be hitting her in the head, though. That's your head, too." He pauses, thinking. "Besides, she already hit her head when she fell out of the desk chair. Didn't you try to get back in then?"

Yes, but she was still conscious. Maybe she needs to be unconscious.

"Why can't you just go back in when she's sleeping?"

I tried that; it didn't work.

Rei rubs his top lip with his knuckle as he thinks. "You know about pressure points, right?"

Like acupuncture?

"Kind of, but acupuncture is meant to heal. If one of those pressure points was hit too hard or squeezed too long, that's dangerous. We learned about them in aikido so we can avoid getting hit there." Rei sits up, cross-legged, and pats the bed in front of him. "Come here."

As soon as I am mirroring him, he points to the top of my head.

"This is the *tendo* point. You don't want to get hit hard here."

That sounds logical to me.

He moves his index finger down to the middle of my forehead, right at the hairline. "This is the *tento* point." Now down slightly to the middle of my forehead, about an inch above my eyebrows. "This is the *uto* point." Yes, the familiar point where all of Rei's tension seems to congregate.

He moves from here to a spot between my upper lip and my nose, then just below my lower lip, over to my temple, and then to the spot just behind my ear, telling me the Japanese name of each pressure point as he points to it.

I know I feel like nothing more than a gentle vibration beneath his fingers, but I can feel him, so gloriously solid.

I feel like a dream sitting next to reality.

I try to forget the other reality—the nightmare of knowing this may be the closest we can ever come to touching each other. I am eye level with his mouth, watching his lips move as he talks. I don't know why, after so many years, I find his lips so irresistible. Because Taylor's kissed him? If Taylor used my mouth to kiss Rei, did I get cheated out of my first kiss?

"Anna? You with me?"

I look up into those indefinable eyes of his and nod. Using the vibration as a guide, he slides his hand slowly to that familiar spot at the back of my neck, his fingers on one side and his thumb on the other. He clears his throat. "This is the *shofu* point." He moves his hand to the front of my neck and runs his fingers lightly over where my pulse should be. "And these are your carotid arteries. Thirty seconds of pressure here should knock you unconscious."

Does he know? Can he tell I'm just floating here wondering how it would feel to kiss him? It's pretty obvious to me. Every breath he takes echoes through me, slow and even, and when he slides his hand from around my neck, his energy swells through me like a gentle caress.

"Anna?" he whispers.

Even if I had vocal chords, I couldn't speak. I'm infinitely grateful that I don't need oxygen because I couldn't breathe if my life depended on it. All I can do is nod once.

He leans in toward me and his sigh is sweet cinnamon. "It's too bad we can't just give her a peanut butter cup."

CHAPTER 32

Rei doesn't notice I'm deflating like a balloon with a slow leak.

"You know, it was stupid of me to tell her she's allergic to peanuts." He leans to the side and flips the light back on. "That might have worked, you know. Why do you look all mad?"

Why? Because I do *not* want to talk about peanut butter cups right now! I want him to turn out that light and continue his guided tour of my pressure points, but I can't tell him that, so I come up with another reason, and it's a good reason, too.

Because if you got caught handing her a peanut butter cup, you could get arrested. Again!

"Well, then, the challenge would be not to get caught."

You really liked jail, didn't you?

"No, but think about it. The first time you ate something with peanuts, you had a reaction and you just bounced right out of there, didn't you. Maybe the same thing would happen to Taylor."

Maybe. You'd have to make sure you had my epi with you.

"How long?"

How long what?

"If I can figure out a way to sneak her something with peanuts, how long do I wait until I use the epi? Do I wait until you're unconscious? I mean, we'd need to maximize your chances." He's actually considering this dangerously stupid idea!

Rei, that's not something they teach you when you learn how to use an epi. You're taught to act quickly, that every second counts. You are NOT taught to play chicken and see how long you can go before you die. How am I supposed to know how long to wait?

"Why are you still mad? I think this might work."

Well, I think you and Seth will end up in neighboring cells in a maximum security prison. It's too risky for you.

Rei scoffs in the face of danger. "I'm more worried about you. As long as I use the epi in time, you'll be okay, won't you?"

Not necessarily.

"What do you mean, 'not necessarily,' " he asks warily. "I thought the epi was your safety net."

I mean, not necessarily. I need to get to a hospital in case I have a second reaction. Plus I've only ever had that one reaction. I have no idea if another one will be more or less severe. It's a gamble for both of us. I vote we just clock her on the head.

"Can I use the keyboard?"

Sure. Just make sure you hold it with both hands when you hit her with it.

"Very funny."

I glide away, and he sits and Googles "anaphylaxis." I give him a sour look and wave.

"Why are you leaving? Are you still mad?"

I have no idea what I feel right now. Mad? Confused? Frustrated? Scared? All of the above? Yeah, that sounds about right.

I'm going to check on my father. I'll see you later.

Despite the many stitches in his head, my father is not in nearly as much pain right now as he will be when he learns my mom has poured his entire stash down the drain. His head is bandaged like a mummy's, and there's an IV taped firmly to the back of his hand. He is probably heavily sedated, although I suspect he's still quite drunk, as well.

I've always known him to have a dense gray aura, but now it's nearly black. I've spent so many years trying not to look at him, hoping that maybe if I ignore him he'll just go away. Well, now he's gone, for a little while, anyway. I suppose if I vacuum out the deepest crevices of my brain, there are memories of the man who supposedly kissed my toes and blew raspberries on my belly. But what's the point of remembering? Then I'll just have to mourn the loss of what's gone. It's easier this way.

But I can't help feeling a tiny bit of compassion for this broken man. I can't gather any energy in here, it's too heavy, so I go out under the starry sky and soak up what I can. I carry it back to him and release it, bit by bit, until the black fades to gray and the gray fades to blue.

Even though helping my father made me feel a little better, I'm not quite ready to go back to Rei's right now. He's overwhelming me with his obsessive need to save me and Seth, and a small, hopeless part of me wonders . . . what if? What if Rei is wrong? What if I never get back into my body? What if Rei does something stupid, tries to pass off a candy bar to Taylor and she survives, only to point a finger at Rei as the culprit who tried to kill her? What if Seth is convicted of Taylor's murder and spends the rest of his life in prison? Even if we do get Taylor out of me, how do we keep her from haunting us for the rest of our lives? How did this one twisted girl get so much power over us?

And what the hell am I going to do about it?

CHAPTER 33

Rei is still sleeping when I cruise in at seven the next morning. Is he sick? I poke at him for a minute, which does nothing, so I bombard him with energy until he opens his eyes and stares at me.

"What?" he asks groggily.

The computer is still on. I have a feeling he stayed up late into the night surfing the internet.

You're late for school.

He lifts his head up to read my message, and then he lies back down and closes his eyes. "I'm not going to school today. I'm going to finish my paper. Then, I don't know, maybe I'll hike up to Red Rocks or something. I need to get away from everything for a while to think."

Hiking? There's one day left until the trial and he's going *hiking?*

Okay, bye.

He opens his eyes once he hears the click of the keys and reads. "Where are you going?"

You need to get away from everything.

"Not from you!"

Oh. I watch him yawn and stretch. His hair is all tousled; his eyes are still soft and sleepy; and he does look very adorable, even though I'm still kind of mad at him. He sits up and the sheet slides down to his waist. Okay, I forgive him.

"What did you do for the rest of the night?" he asks as he pulls his shorts on over the green plaid boxers he slept in.

Same thing I've done just about every other night since I got locked out. I watch Taylor sleep and hope she slips out during a dream. Do I snore?

"Well, as boring as that sounds, it's good thinking on your part. And no, you don't snore. Why?"

Because Taylor snores, so I wonder if I snore, too.

"I've never noticed you snoring. And even if you do snore, so what? I'll be right back."

This truancy is very un-Rei-like. I hear the toilet flush, the water run, and Rei's quiet footsteps coming back down the hall.

Are you skipping school because you want to avoid Taylor?

He sits on the bed and combs his hair back with his fingers as he reads my message. "That's part of it. I just don't want to talk to anyone at school about the trial, and I know people will ask me questions. Plus things were so hectic last night, I never finished this paper," he admits.

He doesn't have much left to finish on his paper, and then he invites me to go hiking with him. It's a relatively short drive to South Burlington, and from the parking lot, it's only about two and a half miles until we reach the top of Red Rocks. He's quiet on the way up the trail. I'm not sure if this is because he doesn't want to look like a crazy person, talking to himself, or if he feels the difference in vibration now that we are so close to the lake.

Water is a good conductor, not just for electricity, but for other kinds of energy, too. I've spent a lot of time on the beaches of

Indonesia and Australia, where day is parallel to our night, because I love the erratic vibration of the ocean. The quiet hum of the lake is soothing after this crazy week. Even the trees are at peace, surrounded by a shimmery blue.

The view is incredible from the top, eighty feet high overlooking Lake Champlain. Kids come here all the time to cliff jump into the deep water below—in fact Rei and Seth were here last summer, but Rei didn't tell me until after they got back. You have to wear old sneakers when you jump unless you either want to swim all the way up to the sandy beach or risk shredding your feet on freshwater mussels that live on the rocks along the shore. Rei is wearing his good hiking boots today.

He sits on the edge of the cliff, one leg dangling over. Except for a few boats motoring around the lake, no one is around, so I materialize beside him and we sit in companionable silence. Every now and then he tells me something random, like how the red quartzite rocks below us got their color from thousands of years of underwater oxidation during the Cambria period, and that he once dreamed he fell into an ice-covered lake and how the sun looked shining through the ice and water above him as he ran out of oxygen.

He puts his hand out toward mine and when I line up my fingertips with his, he finally confesses he's afraid Taylor will keep me forever. He's sitting six inches away from an eighty foot drop, and Taylor is what he fears.

I would have loved to stay and watch the sunset with Rei, but he has to pick up his parents and Saya from the store when it closes. I get to Rei's house before he does, and I can see the day was for nothing. Taylor sits on her front steps, wearing a pale blue cotton sundress I've never seen before. Her eyes are trained on Rei's driveway.

As soon as they park and his family walks into the house, she runs barefoot through the path between our houses. She looks so different from me. With her hair down and only a touch of makeup, she looks like a delicate fairy skimming over the grass, and for a moment, I'm jealous that she looks better in my body than I do. It must be the dress.

"Hi, Rei."

"Hey, Taylor." Rei has the hatchback open and he's reaching for his backpack.

"You weren't in school today."

"Nope." He shrugs the nearly empty backpack onto one shoulder and slams the hatch.

"Where were you?"

"Hiking."

"Oh. You were gone all day. You must be exhausted."

"Not so much."

"Did you think about what we talked about last night?"

"Yes, I did," Rei says very seriously. "I thought about it all day, Taylor."

She steps up closer and stands on tiptoes so she can look into his eyes. "And?" Rei doesn't say anything for a minute. He just looks at her with a torn look on his face. Just when I think I may have to poke him to get him moving again, he lets the backpack slide off his shoulder and he leans down to kiss her.

Okay, that was unexpected.

It's a good kiss, though, much better than the one on the porch. I stare at him in shock and awe for a moment and then it hits me: an unexpected wave of jealousy crashes into me. This was *his* idea. He *wants* to kiss her! His color blushes pink, a few shades lighter than Taylor's. Ugh! I should give him some privacy and leave, I know, but

I can't seem to tear myself away. It's like I'm experiencing this vicariously, imagining his hands come up and brush gently around my neck instead of hers, his fingers slide up into my hair, his thumbs circle the soft spot where her pulse counts out what were once my heartbeats, one by one.

And then something else hits me. . . .

What was the name of that pressure point?

She's all into the kiss, up on her toes like a ballerina, her hands making their way up his arms and around his shoulders, and she's breathing so heavily, I doubt she'd notice the lack of oxygen if he were to . . .

Squeeze.

Thirty seconds. That's all he said it should take. Part of me wants him to do this, to press down on that soft, vulnerable pulse point until she passes out from the lack of oxygen to her brain, and then maybe, just maybe, I can yank her out while she is unconscious. The other part of me, the part of me that wants no harm to come to Rei, wants him to stop. What if she accuses him of trying to strangle her? What if he *likes* kissing her? What if he likes kissing *her?*

I'm so close to them I can see her tongue slide past his lips and the creases on the joints of his thumbs grow more pronounced as he presses slowly into the soft flesh of her neck.

Just a little longer.

Suddenly, he stops. He stops pressing. He stops kissing her. He lets go of her and reaches down to pick up the backpack.

"I can't do it," he says, almost apologetically.

Her breath is ragged and I can see the vibration of her heartbeat pounding through the thin dress.

"What? *Why?*"

He pauses. "How can I sell out one friend for another, Taylor? I couldn't live with that."

"*What?* So you'll just let Seth down?"

Rei shrugs. "He's already down. They'll get up together or I'll go down with them."

That's not why he stopped. I'm sure what he told her is true, but I can tell he's hiding something else behind that poker face of his.

As she absently rubs her neck, her expression morphs from disbelief into something sad and wistful and wanting.

"Rei?"

Rei swings the backpack over one shoulder and shrugs as if he didn't hear her. "I'll see you tomorrow," he says, and he heads toward the house without looking back.

As I watch her watch him slip away from her, one more thing hits me: whatever Taylor is feeling for Rei has gone beyond lust, beyond need, beyond her desire to own a man like others would own a pet. She is not chasing after him with threats or ultimatums, she just watches him walk away with tears in her eyes. She sincerely likes him.

Only when he shuts his front door behind him do the tears finally spill over, and she turns and slowly makes her way back to my house.

I'm waiting for her in my room, and the computer is powered up and ready to go when she gets there.

Hello, Taylor, I materialize as I type and the click of the keyboard startles her.

"Oh. It's you." She bites her bottom lip. "I suppose you've come to gloat because Rei wants nothing to do with me."

It's not you. It's his mother. She doesn't think I'm good enough for Rei.

"Well, no offense, but . . . never mind." Taylor pulls out the new desk chair my mom bought for her and sits down. "Why doesn't she think you're good enough for Rei?"

Look around you. Alcoholism can be hereditary. And I'm not exactly the brightest star in the sky when it comes to school. I don't think these are traits she wants passed down to her grandchildren.

This seems to make her melancholy, and the colors around her deepen. "But I looked through all your photo albums. You and Rei have this whole history together. How can his mother just throw you under the bus like that?"

Because Rei is her baby boy and I'm just the girl next door. And it's not like she's thrown me under a bus—she's been really good to me all my life. You know what it's like to live here with my father. Can you imagine what my life would have been like if I hadn't had Rei and his family next door?

"Your father scares the shit out of me!"

I know. He scares me, too. But you didn't have to hit him with that bottle. You could have easily outrun him. And you shouldn't be drinking unless you want to end up like him someday.

She gives me a dirty look. "What do you want, Anna? I found all your travel brochures and stuff you downloaded. Why don't you go someplace exotic and leave me alone?"

What do YOU want, Taylor?

"What difference does it make what I want? I never get what I want." She takes a deep breath and unleashes her frustrations. "I wanted to go out with Dylan, and he dumped me as soon as he found out I was pregnant. I wanted to have my baby, but my parents wouldn't let me. I did not want to move to Vermont, that's for sure. I don't want to go to Yale. I don't want to become a lawyer. I wanted to go out with Seth, but we all know how that worked out. Jason Trent is a total ass. And who knows what's up with Rei. What difference does it make what I want? I never get what I want."

Well, you wanted my body and you have that.

"Anna, no offense, but I did not *want* this body. I needed a body. It was here, and now I'm stuck in it."

I can talk you out.

"I knew it! I knew you had to have an agenda. Save it, Anna. I have nowhere else to go."

It's hard to stay positive in the face of so much negativity. It's hard to feel love for this girl who has so much hate within her. It's hard to see her as a victim when she seems so intent on hurting others. It's hard to forgive her, but that's exactly what I have to do. If I can't replace her negativity with something positive, I'll never be able to summon the light.

You do have somewhere to go, I type, and then I think back to the cradle of the willow, to the feeling of harmony and peace. I apologize to the light for bothering it yet again for another false alarm, because I know she's not ready to cross over yet, but I want her to know it's there. We're taking baby steps here, Light, I tell it. Please work with me.

"Anna, what are you doing? You look . . . weird."

And then I hear her gasp and I know even before I open my eyes that it's worked, that she sees the light and when I open my eyes, there it is, illuminating the room in all its glory.

You do have somewhere to go, Taylor, and this is how you get there.

CHAPTER 34

Think this looks okay to wear to court? I stand in front of Rei, smoothing out imaginary wrinkles on the puddle bunny T-shirt I've worn since Taylor pirated my body. The big plus in this dimension is you never get dirty and you never sweat, so there's no need to shower. What would Rei do with all that free time?

Rei has on his trusty beige chinos and white polo shirt. I swear, if I ever get my body back, I am taking that boy shopping.

"Who's going to see you besides me?"

You never know.

Rei looks at me. "What are you up to?" he asks suspiciously.

Nothing.

"Really!"

I smile innocently at him. *I'll see you in court.*

"Hey, Anna?"

I look up at him.

"Stay close to Taylor today." His voice is a little too casual. Something is up.

What are YOU up to?

He doesn't smile back at me. "Maybe nothing. Maybe something. I haven't decided yet. Just try to stay close to her, okay?"

I nod. After she saw the light last night, she sort of freaked out on me and told me to get out of her room and take that light with me. I'm not sure what her mood will be like today, so I was planning to shadow her all day, anyway.

"Anna?"

The seriousness of his expression scares me. "It's *your* body. Don't forget that. Okay?"

I nod.

"Promise me," he insists.

I nod again. I feel like a bobblehead.

There are so many people here for the trial, the police have actually blocked off the street. Yumi and Robert closed the store for the day so they could be in court with Rei, and they end up parking in a garage two blocks away. There are television reporters snooping around the crowd and inside the courtroom people have to squeeze together on the long wooden benches in the gallery to make room. Yumi may be tiny, but she has sharp elbows and she's not afraid to use them. I float around the judge's chair and watch everyone assemble and wait.

Wait.

Wait.

Yawn. There are official court procedures that must be followed. I notice Taylor sitting between my mom and her parents. She looks very . . . grown up. She's wearing a modest navy skirt and jacket, with a scoop neck white shirt underneath it. Even her shoes are conservative, navy pumps with a two-inch heel. Her hair is down and hides the hardware in her ears, although even if they saw it, it would in no way make her any less credible as a witness. I wish I could wiggle the jacket off her so they could see that tattoo, though, because only a psycho would permanently ink their arm with the portrait of a dead girl she barely knew.

Keys rattle and a door cranks open. At first I think, *Yay! It's the judge*, but then I see, *Boo! It's Seth with his ankles and wrists shackled*. He's accompanied by two police officers with really big guns in their holsters. What's left of Seth's aura is the color of cement, and it clings to him in a thin layer. I make the mistake of checking to see if Rei saw Seth come in, and of course he did. Seth makes eye contact briefly with Rei, and their shared misery takes on the same gray hue. The two armed police officers direct Seth to a table where his lawyer is already seated, and once he's settled, the officers stay nearby.

"All rise!" The bailiff sounds the same as the one on *Law & Order*. They must all sound the same, like sports announcers and the ladies on the phone who tell you to press one for English.

The crowd stands mechanically. The judge comes in dressed in his solemn black robe. I scoot away from his seat before he sits on me and swoop to the back of the room. I wonder if he can see way back here with those glasses sliding down his nose.

He is making a speech about the grave nature of this trial when I decide to put this question to the test. When I materialize, it would appear I'm actually standing on the back of one of the bench seats while leaning against the back wall, all suitably attired in my gym shorts and T-shirt.

He sees me. He's panning the audience as he makes his speech, and when his eyes reach mine, he slides his glasses up his nose which, intentionally or not, gives me the finger, and his mouth sinks into an intimidating frown. "Would the young lady in the . . ." I vanish. He stares at the space where I was, where I still *am* floating, invisibly, and his jaw goes slack. "Er, never mind." He notices Taylor sitting between the mothers, and his frown reaches epic proportions. He takes one more quick look at the back of the room before he removes his glasses and polishes them on the baggy sleeve of his robe.

"All right, then, Defense, you may call your first witness."

That would be Rei.

They make Rei swear to tell the truth, the whole truth, and nothing but the truth, so help him God, and he does just that, despite the district attorney's best efforts to trip him up by asking the same question phrased just a little differently every time. Rei is a rock, and he refuses to get tangled in the district attorney's web of obscure questions.

Taylor's friends are less successful with Seth's attorney.

"She didn't really *steal* it," Vienna testifies. "She just borrowed it as a joke. She was planning to give it back to him."

"Just answer the question, yes or no. Did Taylor Gleason take Seth Murphy's cell phone without his permission?"

"Well, yes, but . . ."

"That's all."

"But . . ."

"I *said*, that's *all*." Seth's attorney picks up the wrinkled note and shows it to the jury, then reads it out loud before he holds it in front of Vienna. "And did she ask you or one of your friends to tape this note to Seth Murphy's locker?"

Vienna bursts into tears. "She's *dead*! *God*! Can't you just be *nice* to her?"

They take a break mid-morning. Everyone stretches, shuffles to the end of the benches, and goes off in search of bladder relief, caffeine, a quick smoke, whatever.

Rei appears to have something else in mind.

Taylor stands with her friends, who are busy vilifying Seth's attorney for making Vienna cry. As Rei approaches them, the conversation stalls, and all eyes are on Rei. He does look very handsome with his hair neatly combed away from his face, and nobody seems to notice this is the third time he's worn the same outfit this week. As he passes them, he smiles directly at Taylor and says hi, and this simple word somehow floats off his lips surrounded by tiny hearts and flowers. There is a collective sigh as he pushes through a metal door that leads to the first floor.

Rei makes his way down the stairs and into a hallway where there are restrooms and an alcove with soda and snack machines. Several coins later, he is now the owner of his first package of peanut butter cups.

What the *hell* is that boy doing? He already ate a bowl of oatmeal and a banana for breakfast, and it's not like Rei to eat candy. I can only surmise he plans to give them to Taylor, but I desperately hope he's not planning to hand those to her in this crowded courthouse with all these television cameras. That would be like, Go To Jail. Go *Directly* To Jail.

He peels off the wrapper, stacks the peanut butter cups and shoves them both into his mouth at once.

Holy crap! Where's my camera when I need it? I surge into view to show him my astonished expression as he drops the wrapper into the trash.

He holds up one finger to tell me *hold on a second* while he chews them slowly, and I start to laugh at his chipmunk cheeks, but he isn't laughing with me, so I stop. I can't remember Rei ever eating peanut butter; it's just one of those things Yumi never had in the house to keep things safer for me.

"Stay close and stay invisible, okay?"

I nod and fade out of view as footsteps come click-clacking down the stairs.

"Rei?" I didn't realize my voice could sound so sexy.

He swallows hard. "Hey, Taylor."

"I'm up next, to testify."

"I know."

She wilts against the wall. "I don't know what to do, Rei. I just . . . I would get up on the witness stand and tell them this was all a big mistake if I thought maybe you and I could . . ." She touches his arms, and her fingers crawl toward his shoulders like spiders.

I know that expression on Rei's face, the one he has when he doesn't want to do something he knows he has to do. He takes a deep breath . . .

. . . and he kisses her.

Again!

Somewhere upstairs I hear the bailiff's loud voice telling people court is ready to resume, but neither Taylor nor Rei show any sign that they heard him. Rei slides his arms around Taylor and pulls her closer to him.

This time, it's Rei who's all into the kiss, *his* mouth forcing her lips apart, *his* tongue sliding deep into her mouth. *Really* deep! Okay, a little too much tongue there, buddy! She certainly seems to like it, though. She lets out a little moan and her back arches as her arms come up around his neck. Ack! Aren't there laws against inappropriate public displays of affection in a federal building?

She moans again, but this time it sounds different, not pleasure, but . . . something else. Her bright pink aura sallows. She tries to twist her head away from Rei's, but his hand cups the back of her head and he holds her mouth tight to his until she pushes hard against his chest.

"Rei, stop. Something's wrong, I . . ." She can't seem to catch her breath. Now she looks scared and she holds on to Rei because she has to, not because she wants to. "I can't . . . breathe! What's wrong with . . . me?"

Rei sits on the floor and pulls her down onto his lap. "Where's the epi?" he asks while tugging her purse strap off her shoulder.

"The . . . what?"

"The epi! Remember I told you to keep that with you all the time? Where is it?"

"I think it's in . . . my backpack."

Oh, I wonder if she means the backpack that's at home sitting on my bedroom floor.

"*What?*" He yanks open the zipper of her purse and searches unsuccessfully for the familiar cylinder case. "Taylor, you were supposed to keep that with you all the time!" He wrestles his cell phone out of his pocket and dials 911, adjusting his arm to catch her head as it lolls back and she starts to gag. "Come on! Come on!" he urges the dispatcher to pick up. He talks fast, and as soon as he flips his phone shut and pockets it, he lifts her up in his arms and takes the stairs three at a time.

The police officer in the hallway takes one look at Rei and pulls out his radio.

"I've already called 911," Rei tells him. "See if you can find Lydie Rogan in the courtroom. Tell her that her daughter is having an allergic reaction and she doesn't have her epi with her."

The cop doesn't argue; he just hustles away.

Taylor's face is inflating into a big, blotchy mess, and her lips look like sausages. Rei looks around him wildly for I don't know what—my mother, the paramedics, me? All of the above?

I surge into view right in front of him.

"Is this disabled enough?" he asks me.

Taylor writhes in his arms as she tries to breathe.

"I'm sorry!" Rei looks down at Taylor, then back up to me with an anguished look on his face. "I couldn't think of any other way."

I nod, but I don't have time to listen to his apologies right now. If I don't make this happen now, it will all be for nothing. Sirens scream in the distance, but anything can happen in the time it takes for that ambulance to get here, especially since my insurance policy is sitting at home in my backpack.

I don't need a deep breath, but I go through the motions of taking one anyway. I feel like I'm standing at the top of Red Rocks preparing to leap eighty feet down and plunge into the icy waters of Lake Champlain. Taylor is clearly suffering from the histamine that's flooding her body right now. Her breath rattles in her chest since it's hampered by her swollen esophagus. For over a week, I've wanted nothing more than to get Taylor Gleason out of my body and reclaim what's rightfully mine. Now that moment has come, and I'm wishing I was anywhere but here, poised to pull Taylor out of that mess that is my body and dive in myself.

The first thing I do is make sure I have enough energy to finish what I start. I close my eyes and pull, from beyond me, out into the farthest depths of the universe, until I'm sure I can do this, I can just reach in and . . .

. . . pull.

She is so weak and disoriented from the allergic reaction that she pops right out of my body. She responds with a panicky howl.

"No! NO!"

Rei sucks in his breath when my body goes limp in his arms and the slits that are my eyes turn white. This is probably happening because nobody's in there right now, but someone better find that epi and find it *fast!*

"Anna! *Anna!*" My mother is running on her sturdy legs, followed by the policeman, who shouts into his radio. Some idiot with a television camera has followed them into the hallway, and a few other people have come out to gawk, as well. Great . . . an audience. I close my eyes and psyche myself up to dive in anyway.

Right . . . now!

Something grabs my wrist.

"No, Anna, please! You have to let me back in! Please!"

The word *please* only works in certain situations and this isn't one of them. She's weak, I can feel it. We scuffle to get back in, but she's now molded to fit into my body, and I no longer am, so she claims my body once again.

"Anna! Honey, can you hear me?" My mother kneels beside me, crying, and tries to pull me out of Rei's arms, but he won't let go.

"Check your purse," Rei orders my mom. "She needs an epi."

I reach out, and the boundaries of my body are permeable to me now. It's as simple as pulling someone's hand out of a mitten.

"No!" she wails as she pops out for the second time. "Anna, please! *Please* don't do this to me!"

The echo of Rei's voice reminds me what is mine.

"Sorry!" I apologize for the last time as I scramble in and . . .

Oh! *Oh!* I don't remember the first allergic reaction I had when I was four because I left fast, and I didn't come back until it was over, but this is . . .

. . . agony!

I desperately want to duck back out of here and tell her she can have my body. I've been free for so long that being stuffed back inside my body feels like I'm trapped in a sarcophagus and buried alive. There is no air in here, something I've taken for granted not needing for the past week, but I need it now, need it *badly*, and there is none. The itching from the hives is excruciating, and there's so much chaos within my body, it's nearly impossible to get the vibrations to merge. I feel her clawing at me, trying to get a grip on me to yank me out, and I stretch out fast, latch my discarnate fingers into my flesh fingers as best as I can and try to hold on, but all I want is to let go and fly away from all this pain.

I feel myself losing consciousness. Somewhere above me there's a loud buzz and spinning lights and voices sound so very . . . very far away. Rei's voice is a mantra, begging me to "holdonholdonholdon. . . ."

The pain is sudden and sweet in my thigh, and a rush of chemical energy floods through my body, giving me just enough strength to . . .

. . . vomit. Except my esophagus is still swollen and it feels like I've inhaled some of it. I'm wasting all my precious oxygen trying to cough it out, but there's nowhere for it to go.

There's a commotion around me involving people who hold my head and force my mouth open, then they shove something down my throat and I panic and fight against it because it *hurts*, but everyone is stronger than I am right now. Rei's voice is there somewhere begging me to hold still and it sounds like he's crying.

And then there is air, sweet beautiful wonderful air.

I try to open my eyes, but they feel puffy and through thin slits I see the ceiling above me is filled with unfamiliar faces. It occurs to me that everyone from the courtroom has probably filled the hallways to rubberneck as I'm loaded onto the stretcher and carried out to the ambulance. I hear Rei say he's coming with me in the ambulance and some guy tells him, no, he's not, and then Rei's voice gets that same dangerous tone he used with Jason Trent and he says, "Yes. I. Am."

And then I hear someone with that polished television kind of voice asking questions that are nobody's business, and my mother's voice says, "Her name is Annaliese Rogan, and she is the only eyewitness."

CHAPTER 35

In the emergency room, they won't let Rei in to see me right away, not until they evaluate my risk for a biphasic reaction, which is, in plain English, a second reaction that's even worse than the first. This is when I know my sense of humor is back because I laugh in the doctor's face with my floppy lips and tell him nothing could possibly be worse than throwing up on the six o'clock news.

They let my mom in, though, and she is full of nervous energy, fluttering all around and driving me batty. She's completely worked up about my reaction, which was probably even scarier than the first time this happened since this time we had an audience of about a hundred people and a television camera.

After a while, they decide to admit me for one night. They wheel me down the hall in plain view of the normal people who are just visiting and can't help staring, so I pull the sheet up over my head and let everyone on the elevator wonder if I'm dead. My mom comes into my hospital room long enough to get me settled, then she leaves to get some lunch and check messages from work.

It takes a long while to settle back into my body after so much time away. It feels squishy and uncomfortable now, and heavy, like

I'm made out of lard. I keep wondering why my arm is so sore until I remember, oh yeah, hideous tattoo. I'm still really itchy and puffy and my throat hurts from the stupid tube they shoved down there. I entertain myself by trying unsuccessfully to get the assorted studs out of my ears, tongue, and nose, but even if I didn't have these stupid acrylic nails on my fingers, my manual dexterity is still way off since I haven't worked all the way back into my fingers. I work on the tongue stud first, which is a royal pain because it has some sort of screw-on backing to it, and I feel like I have lobster claws instead of fingers. I have about half the studs out of my ears when I hear a knock at the open door.

"Anna?" Rei's voice sounds so tentative.

When I look up, he *looks* so tentative, as if maybe he's intruding or he thinks I might be mad at him. Even though I can no longer fly, I launch myself off the bed and three steps later, I feel his arms around my waist and my feet swing out from under me as he spins me halfway around.

I promised myself I wouldn't cry when I saw him, but that's a lost cause now. It sounds like he's crying, too, so it's okay. At some point during all these tears, he lifts me up, just like he did Taylor and carries me over to the bed. I'm dreading the moment he'll plunk me down, just like he did Taylor, but he doesn't. Instead, he sits and leans back against the pillows, holding me in his lap. "I'm sorry," he says over and over into my hair. "I am so sorry!"

"Stop it!" I cry into his damp shoulder. "No more sorries!"

He leans back so we are eye to teary eye and whispers, "You said it was risky, but I thought you were exaggerating because you were scared I'd get caught. God, Anna," he chokes back a sob, "they were pulling out the defibrillator in the ambulance. They didn't think you were going to make it."

"But I did make it. And you couldn't have known how bad it would be. Even I didn't know for sure what would happen this time." I look him straight in the eyes so he knows I am fine. We are fine. Everything is fine now.

"I should have listened to you," Rei persists. "Yesterday when I kissed her, I thought I could knock her unconscious by pressing on her carotid artery, but it was taking too long and I was afraid she'd figure out what I was doing. I thought the peanut butter cups would be . . ."

"Shhh," I hug him tightly. "It's over, Rei; it all worked out. Don't second-guess it."

He hugs me back and his shaky sigh of relief seems to blow away the top layer of his sorrow. We sit like this for I don't know how long, and all I can think is how good it feels to be touched again. His neck smells sweet and his breath warms my cheek. Every now and then, he rubs slow circles on my back or brushes his chin against my hair, as if he wants to make sure I'm really here.

Even before I was trapped outside my body, the only person who really touched me was Saya. My father never touched me unless it was to grab my arm and squeeze. My mom always seemed to have fresh lipstick on when she was leaving, so I didn't even get a goodbye kiss from her most of the time. Rei limited himself mostly to those affectionate squeezes around the back of my neck.

But when Rei and I were much younger, we were all over each other the way kids are, totally unconcerned with boundaries. We used to wrestle, tickle each other mercilessly, use each other as a pillow or a footstool. Before Saya was born, Yumi used to give Rei back rubs to get him to sleep, so of course, we used to give each other back rubs, too. Rei taught me games: with our fingers we would draw treasure maps on each other's backs with an X to mark the spot, or he'd draw giant concentric circles on my back that gradually got smaller and smaller until he would pretend to pull a string from the center of the circle and it would feel as though the very core was being pulled from my body. One day when we were about eleven, Yumi walked into Rei's bedroom and found us both shirtless, me straddling Rei's backside with a handful of lotion. To say she was not very happy is an understatement. The two of us got a long lecture about how we were getting older now and what constitutes appropriate behavior between young men and women, and that her Boswellian Body Butter was very expensive and not to be played with. After that, it was as though Yumi put a fence between us.

I realize now how much I've missed him, not just during the past week but for the past five years. Even though he was right next door, it felt like some part of me was missing. Rei is the yang to my yin, not my opposite, but a complimentary force that balances me out. Right now, I just want to align myself with him, to stretch out on the bed and pull him over me like a blanket. Right now, there is no other place I want to be.

But nothing lasts forever. Eventually Rei runs his hand up and down my bare calf, which I hope Taylor took the time to shave this morning. "Are you cold?" he asks, and he squeezes my bare foot. "You are—your feet are freezing! Didn't they give you any socks?"

"Socks? What socks?" I say and hope he doesn't see the plastic bag containing one pair of fuzzy but hideous gray no-skid socks I tossed on the vent underneath the window. I change the subject. "Want to help me take out the rest of these studs?"

"Sure. As soon as you get under the covers and warm up your feet. And yes, you do need socks. You don't want to walk on the hospital floor with bare feet. Who knows what you'll catch."

What would I do without Rei to point out all the dangers I

overlook? "I missed you," I confess as I slide off his lap and under the blanket.

"I missed you, too. Did you get that tongue stud out?"

"Yes, that took forever with these stupid nails." I wiggle my fingers.

"I bet. Let me see . . ." Rei tucks my hair behind my ear and gently pries the back off the first stud. "Well, at least she didn't put gauges in."

"No, but she pierced my belly button. I discovered that when I went to the bathroom."

Rei grins. "Do you need me to get that out, too?"

"Um, no. Actually, I thought I'd leave that one in."

Rei stops mid-earring. "Really?"

I grin at him. "Kidding."

"Oh. Not that you couldn't leave it. I mean . . ."

"Too late. It's out."

"Oh." Rei pries the back off another earring. "So . . . not to get you worried or anything, but do you think Taylor's still around somewhere?"

Okay, so everything is not fine. I don't answer him right away because I'd like just a few more seconds of blissful denial, but Rei is right. I was a little too busy to notice, but I doubt the light appeared this time because I didn't die and Taylor was already dead. She's obviously still stuck in this dimension and she could be hovering in the corner of the room right this minute for all we know.

"Anna?"

"Yeah, I heard you. Even if she's not here now, I'm sure she'll show up at some point." I tell him as he pulls the last earring out of my ear. Oh! It feels so good to scratch without all that hardware in there.

"Careful, you don't want to make it bleed." Rei takes both of my hands and sandwiches them between his. I try to wriggle my hands free, but he's got me in one of his ninja finger locks. "So I know you sometimes pop out during dreams, but is there any way you can control that? I mean, what if she gets back into you?"

"Those are two very good questions. And I wish I had . . ."

My mom hurries in without knocking, twinkling with cheeriness. As soon as Rei stands up to greet her, I scratch my ear quick. My mom looks surprised to see the pile of earrings sitting on the tray.

"What are you doing?" she looks from me to Rei.

I have about four seconds to figure out how I'm going to spin this past week. The only logical thing that comes to mind is to just pretend I remember nothing after I fell off my desk chair.

"I'm trying to figure out why I'm in the hospital," I blurt out. "The last thing I remember is falling off my desk chair and now I'm in the hospital with my ears all pierced. What happened?" Rei grins at me behind my mother's back.

"Oh, honey," she hurries over to the bed to hug me. "I missed you!" This revelation surprises me after all the fun my mom had at the mall with Taylor and everything they have in common. "I was so worried about you, sweetheart. You were not at all yourself. You don't remember piercing your ears?"

"No."

"Do you remember getting a tattoo?"

"Tattoo! When did I get a tattoo!" I don't dare glance at Rei because I won't be able to keep a straight face.

"Oh, baby," my mom hesitates. "Do you remember hitting Daddy with a bottle?"

"I did *what*? Why would I do that? Is he okay?"

"Well," her eyes fill with tears. "They ran some tests on him when they first brought him in, and it's probably a good thing you . . . did what you did, honey, because they found out his liver is badly damaged. If he kept drinking at the rate he was going, the doctor says he might not have lived much longer."

Oh. I might not be crazy about the guy, but I don't wish him dead. "But he'll be okay now?"

She sniffles. "Well, it's strange. When they changed his bandage this morning, they noticed the gash on his head is healing much faster than they expected. They took more blood this morning, so we'll have to wait for the results to come back to see if his liver counts show any improvement."

I think of last night and the energy I shared with my father. This is the same energy I use to get rid of Rei's headaches, but even though Rei claims I'm better than aspirin, it's not something I can see or measure. Could I have had something to do with my father's surprisingly fast healing? While my brain considers this possibility, my mouth goes on autopilot. "So when can he come home?"

"He's got a long road ahead of him, honey. It will be a while before they let him come home, but when he does, we need to be supportive."

I hate to suggest this, because the thought of a big kumbaya with my parents and a therapist just makes me cringe, but I think it's time to admit my family has some serious issues to deal with. "Maybe we all should go in for some family counseling."

"I think that's a good idea, honey."

At about six thirty, after Rei has all but played airplane with me to get me to eat my dinner, Yumi, Robert, and Saya show up. As soon as hellos are exchanged, my mom makes an excuse to go visit my father, but something was off in the way my mother and Yumi greeted each other. There's some underlying tension there I can feel, but I can't quite figure it out. I look at Rei, but he doesn't seem to notice it.

Saya bounces on the bed and plays with the buttons that make the bed go up and down while Yumi and Robert murmur little sympathies about my allergic reaction. When she thinks I'm not looking, I notice Yumi looks at me suspiciously, which makes me wonder how much she knows, whether or not she saw Rei and Taylor kissing in the driveway. Eventually, Robert redirects Saya over to the box of rubber gloves attached to the wall. He shows her how to blow them up and release them so they make a loud obnoxious noise as they sail around the room . . . and out into the hallway. Saya, Robert, and I find this much more entertaining than Yumi, Rei, or the nurse who marches in and tells everyone that visiting hours are over, even though it's only quarter to eight.

As the nurse hustles them out, Rei reaches over and tickles my bare foot. "Remember what I said about popping out."

Well, that just ruined any chance I might have to sleep tonight. The doctor admitted me for a night of observation, but what if Taylor spends more time watching me than the nurses? If I slip out during a dream and Taylor gets back into me, not only will she testify against Seth, but I'm sure she'll blame Rei for her allergic reaction. I can't let that happen. Fortunately, it's easy to stay awake in this strange bed with all the quiet beeps and dings I hear coming from the hall, and every few hours, a perky nurse comes in to stick a thermometer in my mouth.

By the time my mom and Rei take me home the next morning, the swelling in my face has gone down almost completely. I cannot wait to get these acrylic nails off, but first I want to change my clothes because my mom brought me one of Taylor's shirts and those stupid red thong underwear to wear home from the hospital.

Inside my closet and my dresser drawers, all I can find is Taylor's stuff.

"Mom!" I holler. "Where are all my clothes?" Especially my normal underwear and my favorite hiking boots that cost me six weeks' worth of pay.

"You packed them up in trash bags and told me to get rid of them," my mom calls back from the linen closet where she's looking for nail polish remover with acetone in it.

"No, no, no! Please tell me you didn't throw them out!"

"They're still in the garage."

"Yes!"

Rei squeezes the back of my neck. "I'll get them," he offers.

While he's doing that, I use my arm to sweep all of Taylor's makeup off my dresser and into the trash. Her expensive iPod Touch is sitting there, too, along with a bunch of her jewelry, and I wonder what I'm going to do with that now. Oh, crap! And where's that box of condoms? I need to get rid of those before my mom finds them!

"Here you go," Rei plunks two bulging plastic trash bags on the floor.

"Bless you!" I rip open a bag and hug an armful of my clothes, even though they smell like garage.

After I've changed into white cotton bikini underwear, jeans, a T-shirt, and one of Rei's hand-me-down hoodies, Rei and I sit at the kitchen table while I soak my fingers in a bowl filled with nail polish remover. I want to talk to Rei about Seth and what I'll tell the district attorney, because as far as I know, I still have to testify, but my mom parks herself at the table with us, so we limit the conversation to how much acetone stinks and the headaches we are both getting from it.

"So, Rei," my mom says in the same aspartame voice she uses when she's trying to sell someone a house with a radon mitigation system, "your mom and I were talking and she's a little concerned that you and Anna might be . . . dating."

I would scrape his chin up off the table, except both my hands are busy right now.

"Not that I have a problem with you two dating because *I've* always thought you two would make a cute couple," she points out.

"Mom!"

"I wasn't sure if you'd remember or not, honey, so I thought I'd bring it up."

"Mom!"

"Because Rei, your mom saw you two kissing in the driveway the other . . ."

"MOM!" How do I make this woman stop talking? "Don't worry about it! We're not dating."

"Anna, honey, Yumi is just concerned about Rei's hectic schedule and she wants to make sure he's not distracted while he's applying to colleges. I'm sure you understand that."

I turn to Rei. "Am I distracting you?"

"No."

"Okay, then. Let's declaw me and go for a walk."

It's a sunny, warm day and everything is green. I love green. It's my favorite color.

"How's your head?" I ask as we walk down the path between our houses toward the woods.

"It's fine."

"Still hurts, huh?"

"A little," he admits.

"Okay, let's see if I can still do this." I close my eyes and stand very still, pulling energy from around me. The trees seem happy to share with me; I tap into the sunlight and I discover I can still access the good stuff from space. It's not as easy to absorb it with this wall of flesh around me, but soon, I feel it tingling all over. I concentrate the tingle to my fingers. With both hands, I reach up and feel around Rei's face for his temples. I feel him smile under my fingertips.

I purge a little at a time, until he says, "You did it."

I open my eyes. "Is your headache gone?"

"Gone. I'm telling you, Anna. We have to tell my mom you figured this out."

"I don't want to think about your mom right now," I start walking again. "Where shall we go?"

"Where else?" Rei asks. "The falls."

The falls is the last place I want to go right now, and I think Rei knows that, but Rei is a face your fears kind of guy, and he's right. I can't start avoiding the falls just because of what happened. I can't let Taylor have that kind of power over me.

"We need to figure out what you're going to tell the district attorney now that Taylor's gone," Rei points out as we walk down the path. Oddly, I can still see a faint blue glow around the trees, and when Rei moves into the sunlight, I can make out a soft orange hue surrounding him, too.

"How about I just tell him the truth?" I'm only half kidding. If nothing else, they'd just think I was bonkers, and I don't think they put crazy people on the witness stand.

"How about we just lock you up now and throw away the key?"

"Hey, other people astrally project and write books about it and nobody locks *them* up. So did I tell you I let the district attorney see me when he was questioning Taylor?"

Three seconds to impact . . . two . . . one . . .

I love that face Rei makes when his eyes get all big and his mouth gapes like a fish. It's so adorable. "You *what?*"

"You heard me."

"Anna. Why? *Why?*"

"Look at it this way. It's not like he can tell anyone; they'd think *he* was crazy. And if I tell him the truth, he just may believe me now that he's seen me. Either way, they've lost their star witness, so they have no choice but to let Seth go."

"Yeah, well, in theory that should work, but you know nothing is ever simple."

"Oh, ye of little faith."

"Anna," he reaches over and takes my hand. "We really need to decide this before you do anything . . . impulsive."

"Impulsive?" I squeeze his hand before I let it go. "You mean, like, stupid."

"No, I mean impulsive. We have to think about Seth."

"I *am* thinking about Seth."

By the time we reach the ledge, the rush of water is loud in my ears. I step up and close my eyes. I need to return to the falls one sense at a time.

"You okay?" Rei asks as he steps up behind me. His hand gravitates to that place at the back of my neck reserved only for him.

I nod. I'm fine. I just need to do this slowly. When I open my eyes, the first thing I notice is the graffiti. Some of our local juvenile delinquents have decided to pay their condolences to Taylor by spray painting huge red letters on the boulders that border the falls. "You know . . ." I begin in exasperation. "What jerks!" I walk toward the edge to see just how much damage they've done, and Rei is on my heels. When I still have three steps to go before I run out of rock, he hooks his arm around my waist.

"Close enough."

"Rei, I just want to . . ."

"Close enough," he says firmly. He wraps his other arm around my waist, pulls me right up against him and rests his chin on top of my head. "So what do you think?"

Think? How does he expect me to think with him holding me so close? I feel like I'm caramelizing here.

"Anna?"

"Hmm? Oh. Why are we here again?"

"To see if you can think of anything to tell the district attorney."

"Oh, right."

I look around, reliving the events of last week. I give Rei a play-by-play of what happened where, and the closer I get to the part when Taylor falls over the edge, the tighter Rei holds me to him. I think he's afraid some small part of me will slip over the edge, too, now that I'm back here to face what's happened.

My lack of sleep is beginning to catch up with me, so I lean my head back against his shoulder and point to a spot on my right. "And this is where Seth was standing when Taylor slipped."

Rei says something so quietly, I can't hear him over the thundering of the falls.

"What?" I twist my head to look up at him and he leans down like he's about to repeat himself, but now that he's moved his head, the sun is right in my eyes so I squeeze them shut to block the light just as something soft brushes against my lips.

Um . . . not that I have anything to compare it to, but that felt suspiciously like a kiss.

I let the sensation linger for a moment before I open my eyes. He's staring at me with an intensity that turns my knees to jelly.

"Did you just . . . was that . . ." I stumble over this simple question because what if I'm wrong? What if he was just brushing away a mosquito or something? How stupid would I feel if I asked if he kissed me and the answer was no?

"I'm sorry," he's quick to apologize. "I just . . . I didn't mean . . ."

I turn within the circle of Rei's arms to face him, but what startles me is the sight of another face, murky and menacing, hovering right behind him.

Taylor.

CHAPTER 36

It makes sense that without a human body to contain our energy, size is no longer relevant. I had only recently figured out I could stretch my energy far enough to knock pencils off desks or type on Rei's keyboard, but it never occurred to me I could stretch twenty feet tall when I was out of my body. It looks like a cool trick that I'd love to try if I ever *do* leave my body again, but now that Taylor's towering over Rei, it's just plain scary.

"What the . . ." Rei looks up in alarm and wraps me like a burrito in his arms just as a whirlwind of grit and leaves spins up around us.

"You're the one who killed me this time!" she yells. "I hope you rot in hell, Rei Ellis!" Her voice sounds like she's talking through a paper towel tube, but I'm surprised I can hear her at all since Rei could never hear me when I was out of my body.

Rei braces himself to keep us from blowing over. How is she this strong? She is spawning some serious wind here, and the sand stings my skin and buries itself in my hair. Just as quickly as it started, it stops. I look up cautiously, but she's gone.

"Could you hear her?" I ask Rei, who is carefully brushing sand away from his eyes.

"No, could you?"

"Her voice was distorted, but yes. That's strange."

"So what?" He is starting to recover from the shock of a supersized Taylor and he's understandably pissed off. "Is she going to haunt us for the rest of our lives?"

"Not if I can help it. Come on, let's go back."

My mom waves a pink sticky note at me when we get back to my house. "The district attorney called to see how you're feeling."

I would find that very considerate if I didn't know what a hurry he was in to prosecute Seth. "Okay. Does he want me to call him back or something? I mean, it's Saturday. Don't these people have a life?" I take the paper from my mom.

"Yes, I told him you'd call him when you get back."

Rei and I never decided what I would say, except that the truth was not an option. Now we have to make a decision quickly.

"You don't remember anything that happened," Rei points out for my mother's benefit. "It seems like you lost your memory when you hit your head the first time and the allergic reaction triggered your memory to come back. How would you even remember what you were going to testify?"

"I don't know."

"So maybe your mom can ask your doctor for a note or something."

"Oh, I can do that," my mom assures us.

I call the district attorney at what turns out to be his cell phone, and he is less than pleased with this information. "What do you mean, you can't remember anything about last week?" he asks.

I repeat my spiel about my many medical woes from the past

week, but he's not letting me off the hook so easily. "All right," he says, "bring your doctor's note to the judge on Monday morning before nine. I will meet you there, and I want a statement from you right after."

No pressure there.

Not more than five minutes after I hang up my phone, Rei's mom calls *his* phone to remind him he's helping with inventory at the store all day tomorrow, plus he still has to do his laundry and other fun stuff tonight. I'm actually glad because I am tired, that curl-up-right-where-you-are-and-nap kind of tired. I'm still afraid I might pop out during a dream, but I know I get grouchy when I'm overtired and Rei's taken enough abuse today.

"Come on, I'll walk you out." I want to say goodbye away from my mom, just in case he may want to try that kiss again.

"I'm not comfortable leaving you alone with Taylor on the loose," he says as we make our way slowly across my barren yard.

"I'll be fine," I assure him. Plus I hate to point out to Rei that despite his years of martial arts training, there's not much he could do to stop a metaphysical attack.

"But what if she comes back? Who knows what she'll do next?" he worries out loud.

"How about I watch TV with my mom tonight. I doubt she'd show herself when my mom's around. And then I can try to convince my subconscious not to pop out when I'm dreaming."

"Do you know how to do that?"

"No, but I thought it might be like meditating. I was hoping you could teach me."

Rei cracks a small smile. "It's a lot like meditating. When you go to bed, relax and get yourself comfortable, then clear your mind of everything except that one thing you need to know."

"Okay." It sounds easy enough. "So I just chill out and repeat

'I will not pop out during a dream. I will not pop out during a dream.' "

"Exactly." His phone vibrates in his pocket. He pulls it out, checks the caller ID, silences it and shoves it back into his pocket. "I don't know how long it will take to finish inventory, but if I can come over when I'm through, I will. And I'm planning to take the day off from school on Monday to go to the courthouse with you."

"Won't your mom get mad if you miss another day of school?"

Rei shrugs. "So she gets mad. What else is new?"

"I don't want her mad at me. She made it crystal clear she doesn't want me distracting you."

"Yeah, well," Rei keeps his eyes on the ground as he walks, "distracting me isn't on your agenda, anyway."

I stop short. "What's that supposed to mean?"

Rei shrugs. "Nothing. Forget it."

I bet the entire neighborhood can hear Yumi's irate voice echo across the yard. "Rei!! Let's go!"

I can't tell if he's annoyed or relieved. "Call me if she shows up."

I hang out with my mom for the rest of the evening. We microwave frozen dinners, then we watch some show about badass women detectives who chase down sexy bad guys while wearing stilettos. It's amazing how fast these women can run in those shoes. At eleven o'clock, my mom yawns, which makes me yawn, too.

"You ready for bed, sweetie?"

"I don't know." I surf over to Animal Planet where there's a show about adorable kittens. "I think I'll watch this. Maybe dad will want to buy me a kitten when he gets home."

"Oh, honey." She laughs half-heartedly. "It's good to have dreams."

Ha. No it's not, at least not while Taylor's around.

"Sleep tight," she says and closes her bedroom door.

By the time I brush my teeth and get into bed, I can already hear my mother's light snores through the thin wall separating our bedroom. Through my open window, I hear the faintest music, and it sounds like Rei is up late playing his guitar. Even though it's getting cold out, I leave the window open and pull the ugly lavender comforter Taylor bought up over my bare legs instead. Just as I'm relaxing in preparation for a good, long chat with my subconscious . . .

Snap!

The comforter goes flying off me. I shriek out of sheer surprise. Somewhere in the shadows, I hear Taylor snicker.

My hairbrush, my pink magnifying mirror, my Cherry Chapstick all shoot off my dresser like machine gun ammunition. I scramble to get my pillow up as a shield. "Stop it!" I whisper urgently at her. "You're going to wake up my mother!" Books drop off my bookshelf, one by one, then the closet door wrenches open and clothes start falling into a heap.

I thought positive energy was stronger than negative energy, but with the damage Taylor is inflicting right now, she's totally blowing that theory of mine.

"How do you like it?" she asks in that mutant voice of hers. "Every night until you die, I will haunt you, Anna. Unless I'm next door haunting Rei. Or at the jail haunting Seth."

I was afraid of her at the falls today, but now, I'm just mad. I turn the lamp on and she immediately turns it off.

"Fine!" I huff at her. "Be that way."

Newton's law of motion dictates that for every action, there is an equal and opposite reaction. So if she wants to be negative, I'll be positive. If she wants to stay in the dark, I'll surround myself with light. It's harder to concentrate since I'm so tired, but before too long, I manage to summon the light.

"Enough with that damn light!" Taylor yells before she bolts, snapping my window shade up so hard on her way out that it falls off the bracket. I look around at the mess I'll have to clean up before my mother sees it and decide it can wait until morning. I have just enough energy to reach down and pull the comforter back over me.

"Thank you," I whisper.

When I was about twelve, my mom decided I needed some religion in my life. Every Sunday morning for about a month, she would cart me off to church where I'd spend an hour admiring how pretty the sun looked shining through the stained glass windows and trying to figure out why people got up so early on a Sunday morning to mumble the same canned prayers they mumbled last week. "Faith," Rei told me when I asked him. "Some people feel closer to God in a church or temple or wherever their religion tells them to go."

Rei likes to learn about different religions, but for the most part, I find them convoluted and confusing. I *know* that an afterlife exists, so I'm not bound by the fear that death is eternal sleep. And if I want to feel closer to God, I just go outside and look up at the starry sky. To me, faith is about trusting my instinct when logic tells me I'm an idiot. Tonight, it's faith that tells me to close my eyes, that it's safe to sleep because the light will keep Taylor away, and I am grateful.

The next thing I know, there is sunlight streaming in through my unshaded windows.

Schmoozing is an important skill I need to learn, and my mom is a seasoned pro. I tag along to the hospital with my mom who schmoozes with the hospital staff until they track down the doctors who treated me. Both doctors write notes to the judge, saying it appears my concussion resulted in severe memory loss and perhaps even in dissociative amnesia (whatever that is), but apparently the stress from my allergic reaction triggered the full restoration of my memory.

In plain English? In the doctors' professional opinion, I am not a reliable witness.

After we secure the notes, I sit downstairs in the waiting room trying to stay awake while my mom goes up to see my father. I am not allowed to see him yet. Apparently, my mom was right. Detox is not a comfortable thing unless you enjoy sweating, shaking, and hallucinating that little people are crawling all over the walls. My mother doesn't want me to see him like that, as if this will somehow diminish my opinion of him. I don't argue, though. She's promised to take me to KFC when we leave, and I'm beside myself with anticipation of a two-piece extra crispy meal with a double side of mashed potatoes and gravy, followed by a visit to see my good friends, Ben and Jerry. I haven't tasted anything really delicious for so long, although the thought of Taylor out there watching me makes me more than a little queasy.

Fortunately, Taylor stays out of sight all day. Unfortunately, so does Rei as Yumi keeps him busy at the store. It's hard to imagine there's so much inventory that it takes him until after six o'clock to count it all, but apparently, there is. He stops over at my house on his way home, apologizing for not showering first, and I can tell by the dark circles under his eyes that he's wiped out. It's the end of a long week, and there's still tomorrow to go.

"I would love for you to stay," I tell him, and I can't resist reaching out to trace one of those dark circles with my thumb, "but you need to sleep."

"Who can sleep?" he asks. "Taylor showed up after midnight and trashed my room. I spent the rest of the night cleaning up and waiting for her to show up again."

"I'm sorry. She did the same to mine."

He just stands there, unshaven and exhausted, his jaw slack with disbelief. "So you didn't sleep all night either?"

"No, I did. I, um . . ." I've never tried to explain the light to Rei. "Don't freak out if you see a light in your room later tonight."

"What kind of light," Rei asks suspiciously.

"Well, it's the same light that comes when people die, so . . . "

"Oh, *that* light." Rei very nearly smiles. "Sure, no problem."

"I know it sounds strange, but when we were in New York, I figured out I could call the light," I explain. "I've been trying to convince Taylor to go into it, but whenever she sees it, she runs away. So I asked the light to stay in my room last night, and it did. So maybe it will come to your room tonight."

"But what about you?"

"I'm pretty sure this light can be in more than one place at a time."

After Rei leaves, I can't face another night of mindless television with my mother, so I hang out in my room. I try texting Rei, but he's not answering, so I hope he's finally asleep. I torture myself by checking online concert schedules, but since I can't astrally project with Taylor on the loose, it looks like I'm going to miss some amazing summer concerts.

Sadness.

But maybe I could astrally project just a piece of myself outside my body while the rest of me stays put. That can't be dangerous, can it? Hmmm . . . It takes me over an hour, but I figure out how to project my hand. Just my hand. And once I get my hand out, I stretch the energy and I can move stuff, even stuff that's across the room. I sit here on my bed and move stuff around my dresser, turn the light on and off, scatter the dust bunnies under my bed. I'm still not as strong as Taylor, but how cool is this?

My mom sweeps into the courthouse first thing on Monday morning with the doctors' notes in hand and schmoozes with the judge. He reads the notes, which are written on official doctor letterhead and signed in illegible scrawl. I stand there looking utterly confused, and he agrees it would be unethical to put me on the witness stand. That's all well and fine, but it's the district attorney who scares me. He meets me by an office and directs Rei to wait outside on a bench in the lobby. My mom stays while he questions me, and he has someone in the room, too, a rotund woman with peach-colored hair and a fancy beaded necklace holding her glasses around her neck. Her fingers fly over the keys of her machine as she records my statement.

"So," he says as he settles back into his seat and frowns at the doctors' notes in his hand, "you are no longer considered a reliable witness because you have memory issues."

"Yes."

"You have memory issues," he repeats.

"Yes," I confirm, and a knot twists in my stomach as I remember the way he tried to bait witnesses with his obscure questions. I debate whether my spectral appearance during Taylor's deposition has helped or hurt me.

"But you knew what Taylor Gleason was wearing when she died," he says. His eyes are power drill bits.

I fight the urge to blink. "I don't know how. Maybe I saw her before she walked down to meet him. I can't be sure; I don't remember."

He leans back in his chair and strokes his chin thoughtfully, staring at me. He looks like he wants to poke me to see if I'm real. Finally, he shakes his head and his icy stare thaws a bit.

"Well, since the police searched the Gleason home and found the magazines from which the letters were cut, and since all of the late Miss Gleason's friends are now crystal clear on exactly what the word *perjury* means *and* since our only eyewitness has had medically confirmed amnesia, it doesn't look like we have much of a case against Seth Murphy. But just out of curiosity, Miss Rogan," he parks his elbows on his desk and leans closer to me, "are you familiar with the concept of astral projection?"

If it was ever to my benefit to look stupid, now is the time. "Um," I look everywhere but at him, "isn't that when, uh, a person can project astrally?"

He smiles knowingly. "Indeed it is."

It seems like a good time to change the subject. "So what happens to Seth now?"

"The case will be dismissed due to insufficient evidence. Seth will be released into the custody of his father." He checks his watch. "And I have to be in court in ten minutes. Goodbye. Good luck. And be careful out there, Miss Rogan." He walks me and my mom to the door.

Rei pops up from his seat like toast when the door opens.

"Case dismissed due to insufficient evidence," I tell him, and I can actually feel the tension whoosh off him as he corrals me in a one-armed hug.

"That's the best news I've heard in a while," he admits.

"Yes," I lower my voice, but my mom is already busy checking her phone for messages, "but we've still got one problem left."

CHAPTER 37

My mom had to go to work, so Rei drives me home.

"Should we bother going to school since we finished so early?" he asks.

"I thought we called in absent for the entire day." I have the window down and I'm hand-surfing the waves of the wind current.

"We did. I just thought since you missed so much school, you might not want to miss any more."

I look over at him and he takes his eyes off the road for a split second to look over at me, and we both crack up laughing. He's in a happy mood now that he knows Seth will be cleared of charges. I am, too.

"Hey, want to see what I taught myself to do now?" I ask.

"Um, I don't know. Do I?" Rei asks cautiously.

"Watch this." Hopefully he doesn't think I'm showing off, but I'm going to show him anyway. I concentrate until my hand pops free and I stretch it to turn on the radio.

"Did you just turn that on?" Rei asks.

"Yup. No hands, baby." I flip around through the stations.

"So you're telling me you can do telekinesis now."

"I'm telling you I can disengage just one hand and move stuff. Just little stuff. Nothing big."

I decide to test myself and go for something a little bigger. Rei's cell phone bulges from his front pocket, and it takes considerable effort for me to wiggle it out and set it on the console.

Rei grins and shakes his head. "Magical, mystical, Auracle girl."

"Yeah, feel free to come up with a cooler nickname."

Rei laughs. "I'll get right on that. In the meantime, let's go back to my house and get some lunch."

Lunch? I like lunch.

Rei's idea of tuna salad is not the conventional mayonnaise-soaked sandwich. When we get to his house, I automatically head to the fridge and pull out red-leaf lettuce, grape tomatoes, a cucumber and red onion, then find cans of dolphin-safe tuna and black olives in the cupboard.

Rei is in charge of cutting up watermelon for dessert. "One for you," he pulls a paring knife out of the knife block and hands it to me, handle first. "And one for me," he gets the big watermelon knife out for himself.

"Watermelon is my favorite," I remind him once he starts cutting the slices up into bite-sized chunks.

He offers to hand feed me a piece with his fingers, and when I tilt my head and open my mouth to take it, our eyes meet and he blushes an adorable salmon pink. I really want to bring up that kiss at the falls, but I feel myself start to blush too, just thinking about it.

We eat our salad and our watermelon, then we let the clean up wait while we sit at the table talking about stuff that has nothing to do with the past two weeks. Random stuff. Funny stuff. It feels so good and normal, like we can pick up the pieces and keep on going and everything will be okay now that Seth is a free man.

Until Rei's water glass goes zooming off the table and shatters on the ceramic tile floor.

"Oops," Taylor's flat voice comes from my right and she materializes behind Rei. "What's for lunch? Oh, that's right. It doesn't matter to me because *dead people can't eat!*"

Rei spins around in his chair. "Crap," he mutters. "Where's that light you sent last night?"

"Oh no, you don't!" Taylor says just as everything in the room starts churning with the force of a small tornado. Plates, glasses, watermelon rind, lettuce leaves and onion peels go smashing haphazardly into the walls, the ceiling, our heads.

Rei stands up and pulls me roughly into him, shielding my head with his arms. "How the hell is she doing this? You could never move stuff this heavy." One arm leaves me for an instant and I can tell he's just blocked something big just by the force he uses to push it away.

"What was that?" My voice is muffled against his chest.

"The blender."

Rei is right, I could never move something as big as a blender, and I'm pretty sure I wasn't capable of my own personal tornado, either. At least when she was in my body, she was contained. Now it's like we've cracked open a nest of angry wasps. Rei is shouting over the bedlam, trying to reason with Taylor, when he suddenly arches his back and his chest shoves against me, jerking my head back.

Everything goes very quiet.

"Rei?" I look up cautiously, and Rei's eyes are fixed and staring at me. "Rei!"

"Oh *shit!*" Taylor swoops down beside Rei. "That was an accident!"

Why hasn't he taken a breath yet? "Rei? Are you okay? Breathe!"

He nods once without blinking and struggles to inhale.

"I swear, I didn't mean to do that!" Taylor insists.

I lean around him to see what Taylor didn't mean to do and the freakin' watermelon knife is jutting out from between Rei's shoulder blades.

"Oh God!" The blade alone must be a foot long, but only about six inches are left protruding from his back. Every little bit of me wants to panic. Rei has always been the level-headed person in a crisis, not me, but I can't fall apart now. An ambulance! We need an ambulance. Rei reaches back and fumbles for the knife handle.

"No! No! Don't pull it . . ."

Too late. His next breath is the rattle of dead leaves as he stares at the bloody knife in surprise. I try to take the knife out of his hand, but he shakes his head. "Don't touch it," he croaks. "I don't want your fingerprints on it."

"Why not?" I grab a dishtowel and press hard to stop the bleeding while I guide him into a chair. Stupid white dishtowel stains red in seconds. How do I leave him to call an ambulance with him bleeding like this?

"I swear I didn't mean for anyone to get really hurt. I just wanted to . . ."

"Then do something useful," I bark at Taylor. "Find the phone in this mess so I can call an ambulance!"

Calm down, Anna, I remind myself. I can't help Rei if I flip out.

"How bad is it?" Rei rasps.

"It's . . . I don't know. I'm going to pull your shirt up so I can see." My voice, my hands, everything shakes. I pull his blood-soaked T-shirt up and over his head, then wad it up and use it to apply more pressure.

"I think it punctured a lung." It's clearly an effort for him to talk.

"Shhh. Taylor's looking for the phone so we can call an ambulance," I tell him, then I yell, "Where's that phone, Taylor?"

"I can't find it!" She is tossing stuff helter-skelter, making an even bigger mess.

"Use mine. In my pocket." He moves to get it, but I intercept his hand. His fingers are freezing.

"I'll get it." I reach into his front pocket, and this nauseating sense of déjà vu nearly undoes me. I've already pulled Rei's phone out of his pocket once today, using no hands, and I left it on the console in the car. A sudden, brutal thought forms in my head that Rei might run out of blood before I could get it and call for help. It's a sucker punch thought. Even though I know with every certainty that life exists after death, I am not ready to lose my best friend to the hereafter.

"I left it on the console, didn't I?" Rei is way too calm.

"No, I left it on the console." I whisper this because I don't want my angry voice to be the last thing Rei hears.

"It's okay, Anna." He coughs into the crook of his elbow and stares at the blood that's now splattered there before he looks back up at me with steadfast eyes. "You know you're my best friend and I love you a lot."

We are not doing this. We are not saying goodbye. I switch the bloody shirt for a clean dishtowel. "I thought Seth was your best friend."

"Nah." He rests his head on the table and watches me. "It's always been you."

"Don't they have more than one phone in this house?" Taylor swoops past me.

"Office . . ." I point down the hall without taking my eyes off Rei.

Thinkthink*think*, Anna!

I can get rid of Rei's headaches and whatever energy I purged into my father helped heal the cut on his head. Maybe I could buy Rei a little time if I could slow the bleeding down. I just need to keep him alive until we get to the hospital and they can take it from here.

I close my eyes and shut everything out. I know the laws of physics dictate that positive attracts negative, but the positive energy I need to heal Rei is only attracted to positive. I push away my fear that Rei might be dying, bury the animosity I feel towards Taylor, squash the worry about what Yumi's reaction would be if she walked in on this fiasco right now. Think happy thoughts, Anna, I tell myself. I pull that positivity around me, into me, I imagine Rei's back healthy and whole again. Gingerly, I touch his back, wade my fingers through the rivers of blood until I feel an indentation and Rei flinches. Random thoughts pop into my head, like what if I mess something up? What if I seal off an artery or do something irreparable? No. I can't think about that now. I need that fearless faith I had the other night when I knew the light would keep Taylor away.

"Light." I can't tell if Rei means to whisper this or if that's all he's got left. I open my eyes, and there it is, the light Taylor hates so much. It's formed a cylinder a few feet away from where Rei sits. "Is that for me?" There's no fear in his voice, just a solemn curiosity.

I shake my head and close my eyes again.

"There's no phone down there, either," Taylor's voice comes down the hall and becomes teakettle shrill. "Why is that light here?"

I can't make her stay quiet, but with an enormous effort, I can tune her out just by reminding myself what's at stake here. Rei. That singular thought is enough to focus my attention on what I need to do. I purge the energy through my fingertips until I feel empty, then fill myself back up with that infinite supply of the positive energy floating around in the universe and purge again. I concentrate on Rei and the vibration I'm so familiar with, still weak but I'm vaguely aware that the scary wheeze in Rei's breathing has gone.

"Anna, what are you doing?" Taylor's voice is right in my ear, which makes it harder to tune out.

Rei takes a deep breath. "The light's gone."

"Really?" I open my eyes.

"Am I still bleeding?"

I wipe away the blood, but I can't even find where the knife went in.

Even Taylor looks impressed. "How did you do that?"

I shrug as I search Rei's back for a scar, a blemish, anything to show me where the knife went in. Underneath all that blood, there is nothing but perfectly smooth skin.

"You're really okay?" I ask him quietly.

"I am now. Are you?"

I consider all that's just happened and what I just did. Healing a headache seems like no big deal—Yumi does that all time. But healing a six inch deep knife wound is something altogether different. What else can I do if I try? Heal my father's pickled liver? Speedset a broken bone? Cure a child's cancer? Is this new ability an amazing gift or a curse? I don't know yet. "We tell no one about this," I tell him.

"Agreed."

I wet a dishtowel with warm water. "Want me to get some of that blood off your back?"

"Thanks."

Even Rei's back is solid muscle. I start by washing away the streaks of blood around his shoulders and try to remember I am on a humanitarian mission here. I have to rinse the towel clean several times before I reach the waist of his jeans, which are sticky with blood. "How do you feel?" I ask.

"Still kind of weak," he admits."Where's Taylor?"

I look around the kitchen at the blood, the garbage splattered all over the walls, the blood, the dishes and utensils all over the floor, the blood, the broken glass, and oh look . . . more blood. But no Taylor.

"I don't know where she went."

"This is out of control, Anna. We need to find her and do something."

"I know. We will, but I want to clean up before your mom gets home, and besides, I think better when I clean. You should sit."

"I'll help," Rei valiantly offers.

"You will not. You'll park yourself in that chair and push fluids before you go into shock from losing so much blood."

"Wow." Rei grins at me and sits. "Yes, ma'am."

Rei sips his juice while he watches me. I must be pumped full of my own natural adrenaline, because it doesn't take me long to put everything away and scrub the blood off the floor. I look around. "Did I miss anything?"

Rei shakes his head. "You did a great job. The only thing still a mess is me."

He's still a little pale, and even though I've washed most of the blood off his back, I know what he wants.

"Do you feel good enough to take a shower?"

"Yeah, I'm fine. I'm just afraid to leave you alone. What if she comes back?"

I shrug. "You shower fast. Although," I consider the possibilities, "maybe you should leave the door unlocked, just in case you pass out or something."

Rei laughs. "And what, you'll come rescue me?"

"Well, I can at least turn the water off so you don't drown."

Rei looks amused, but not convinced, and I finally see what he's getting at . . . he's afraid I'm going to peek at him in the shower again.

"Hey," I'm standing and he's sitting, so I have the height advantage for a change, "after you saw my chichis in Jason Trent's Jeep, I'm calling us even, my friend."

I'm surprised Rei has enough blood left to blush.

CHAPTER 38

Rei comes downstairs all clean and shiny, but he's still a little shaky. "Now how do you feel?" I pour him another glass of juice as soon as he sits down.

"Okay," he drinks half of it in one long swallow. "But not a hundred percent."

"Want to go chill out on the porch swing with me?"

"How about the hammock. Then I can lie down."

That makes sense.

"I want to get my phone out of the car before we go down. Maybe Seth called."

"I'll get it."

We head out and Rei waits for me at the door while I run to the car. The phone is sitting on the console right where I left it. I know all's well that ends well, but when I think of how I almost lost Rei because I had to show off, I feel awful.

"Here you go," I hand the phone to Rei.

"Thanks. Hey, there's a message . . . maybe it's Seth."

Rei calls his voicemail, and by the time we reach the hammock, he has Seth on the phone. He looks happier than I've seen him since the whole mess began. I want to give them some private guy time, so I indicate to Rei that I'm going to sit by the willow tree.

"I'll be right there," I whisper when Rei frowns. "You can see me."

He nods reluctantly.

Trees have to be some of the most patient living things in the universe. Year after year, they stand there rooted to one spot. I'd go insane. But beyond flowers in the spring, shade in the summer, and fruit in the fall, trees offer me a certain comfort, a stability that must be hard for some to understand.

"Hello," I greet the willow as I part its leafy veil. I step lightly over the carpet of tiny dead leaves and sit with my back against the massive trunk. The tattoo is making my arm itch like crazy, so I push up my sleeve and scratch off a crusty black layer. Okay, so now my arm still itches, but I've made myself bleed. "So how'd you like to have *this* carved in your bark for the rest of your life?" The willow's branches bob around like there is a sudden gust of wind, but I know it's just laughing at me.

I'm wondering if I can heal myself when I realize I'm not alone. Taylor hovers just above me, looking down contritely. I glance over, but Rei hasn't noticed I have company.

"Hello," I keep my voice low because I don't want Rei to worry.

"I didn't mean for him to get hurt," she's quick to point out. "I was just venting."

"But yet, he got hurt," I remind her. "You nearly killed him."

"But you healed him, Anna. How is that even possible?"

I nearly laugh. How is anything possible? For all the time I've spent in and out of my body, I still don't understand even a fraction of what's possible in this complex universe—I only know things are better when I surround myself with positive energy. Even now, I can feel Taylor's negativity oozing from her, like sludge.

"Taylor, what do you want? Seriously. I can't believe you want to spend eternity haunting us."

She looks up, down, everywhere but at me. "I don't know anymore," she admits. "I want to be alive, but that's not happening. Although you know," she smiles wishfully, "after I saw what you did for Rei, I had this crazy idea that you could dig up my body and bring me back to life."

Oh, just what I want . . . to be responsible for starting the zombie apocalypse. "Taylor, I can't do that."

"No, I realized that wouldn't work. I just . . . *want* . . . I *need* . . . I . . . I know life's not supposed to be fair, but what happened to me sucks on so many different levels. I don't know how to make peace with this, Anna."

Well, I know how she can find her peace. I close my eyes and concentrate until I hear her say, "I had a feeling you were going to do that." She surveys the light warily and reaches one finger out, as if to see how hot it is. "Where does this light even go?"

I shrug. "All I know is whenever someone dies, they have a choice to step into the light, but I don't know what's inside it."

"Take a guess, Anna. I want to know where you *think* it goes."

"Well . . . I think it will take me somewhere my grandparents are waiting for me, I won't be allergic to peanuts, and I can have as many kittens as I want," I say slowly. "Rei's been reading all this Buddhist stuff, so he thinks it goes to a place where people wait to be reincarnated."

She thinks about this for a few seconds while she reaches her hand further into the light, assessing it. "So he thinks we get another chance. That's ironic." She smiles ruefully. "But if we really are reincarnated, we should be able to learn from our mistakes so we don't repeat them in the next life. You know what I mean?"

I know exactly what she means. "Taylor, after the week we've had, who's to say anything is impossible. Maybe the light would take you to a place where there are no regrets."

"No regrets . . . that's someplace I would like to go." She pokes her toes into the light like she's testing the water at the beach. "Will you keep the tattoo? Just so I know someone will remember me?"

Oh crud. I would pacify her with a yes, but I know I will regret it every time I look at my arm. "Taylor," I search for the most delicate way of disappointing her, "what if I found another way for people to remember you, like, a scholarship or something."

She considers this for a minute while she studies the tattoo on my arm. "Was my nose really that lopsided?"

"No," and I can't help but smile, "you had a really pretty nose."

She smiles back at me. "The Taylor Gleason Scholarship? I like it." She leans a bit more into the light just as I hear Rei call my name. Taylor hears him too.

"Would you tell him I'm sorry? I really would have felt terrible if I had, you know . . . "

I nod, holding my breath, until she takes a step back and the light embraces her. In that instant, a warm breeze passes by me. Taylor looks up for one awestruck moment, then smiles as the light retracts, taking her with it.

Gone. Taylor Gleason is gone. I should feel ecstatic that finally, *finally*, she's gone but all I feel is dizzy, and I realize I am still holding my breath.

"Anna?"

I finally breath and I sweep back the willow branches and find Rei sitting up, ready to launch into ninja mode.

"Stay there, I'm coming." I run over the sun-kissed grass in my bare feet, feeling lighter than cotton candy. "Guess what?"

"What?" Rei pats the hammock beside him, so I climb on, kneeling in the empty spot. He looks so happy, I can only guess it's because Seth is a free man.

"Taylor's gone into the light."

He looks stunned for a second. "You're sure?"

"I'm positive. I just watched her go."

"Hallelujah!" He pulls me into a full-body hug and falls back into the hammock, taking me down with him. I let out a squeal, just because he's caught me by surprise, then we both realize we're lying in a rather intimate way.

"Um . . ." There's a lot of awkward shimmying on both our parts until I'm beside him and my head finds that sweet spot on his shoulder.

"Soooo," I say to break the silence, "she wanted you to know she's sorry she accidentally stabbed you."

Rei nods, then rests his chin on top of my head.

"Is Seth okay?"

"Seth is excellent! They let him out right after we left. He's coming over later this afternoon."

What must Seth think? Anna Rogan was ready to testify against him and send him to jail for a crime he didn't commit. "Is he mad at me?" I have to ask.

"No," Rei sounds surprised. "Why would he be mad at you? I told him you hit your head and your memory was a mess. Although he thinks he saw you in the woods the day we were caught in New York."

"Yeah, I figured he saw me."

"I didn't even think of it, there was so much going on. I'll have to figure out a way to talk us out of that one." Rei strums his fingers against my shoulder.

"Is it the worst thing if he knew? I mean maybe not the part about how I healed your back, but I don't want Seth to think he's crazy on top of everything else."

"I don't know. I think the worst thing would be if you left your body and someone else got in," Rei admits. "Or if you got sucked into a black hole."

I poke him in the stomach. "Why are you so paranoid about black holes?"

He laughs. "I just want you to be safe."

There cannot be a better place anywhere in the universe than right here, lying next to Rei. I rest my hand on his chest, just over his heart, and he weaves his fingers through mine. It's an almost perfect moment. But what would I do for this boy I have known my entire life? Would I give up the keys to the universe? I would. "I don't want you to worry, Rei. I can't guarantee I won't ever slip out during a dream, but if you'd feel better, I won't leave again intentionally."

He's just staring off into the trees. "I wouldn't ask you to do that, Anna. I know you love going places, and I wouldn't stick you in a box like that. It's no fun in a box. Just . . . maybe can you stay on earth?"

"I can do that." I think. But as right as it feels to cuddle up in this hammock, something still feels wrong, and I realize what I can't do is sit here in Rei's box with him and worry about Yumi. "You know if your mom comes home and sees us lying on this hammock together, she'll have a fit."

"Then she has a fit."

"But what if she's right?" That thought is so painful, but I want him to know what's making me uncomfortable here. "What happens when you go off to college? You'll meet other girls who don't have alcoholic DNA and who actually have some common sense steering their train of thought."

"Anna," Rei begins, but I lean up on my elbow and put my fingers on his lips to shush him.

"And you are brilliant and you're going to do something amazing with your life, and what am I going to do?"

Rei sighs. "You don't have defective DNA. And you don't even know where I want to go to college or what I want to do with my life."

"Of course I don't. You've never told me."

"Because I was afraid to admit it. But the one good thing Taylor did while she was here was make me realize I don't have to follow the line my mother drew for me. Just because I'm good at math and science doesn't mean I want a career in either of them. I know what I want to do, and she's not going to like it, but she has to accept that it's my decision, not hers."

"What *do* you want to do?"

"I want to go to the University of Vermont," he says. "I want to take a double major in nutrition and business, then I want to get an MBA, open up a few stores like my parents' and franchise them." He looks at me hopefully. "What do you think?"

Wow. He's obviously given this some serious thought. There is just one problem. "So if you have a degree in nutrition, will you give me grief every time I eat a cookie?"

"No."

"Then I love it! Will you hire me to teach the little kids' yoga class?"

"Is that what you really want to do?"

What do I really want to do? A week ago I would have said that I would love to teach little kids yoga, but now I feel like I've discovered this gift of healing for a reason. Maybe there is a way to channel that healing energy to do some good in a way that doesn't draw too much attention to myself.

"If I could afford to go to school to learn more about alternative medicine," I say tentatively, "maybe you would need someone to do Reiki in your stores."

"You're hired," he says immediately.

"Wait a minute." I laugh and roll onto my stomach, leaning up on my elbows so I can look at him, lying there so adorably. "Shouldn't we discuss stuff like salary, vacation time, a benefit package?"

"What kind of benefits are we talking about here?" he asks.

"Well, medical insurance . . ."

"Okay." His smile is irresistible.

". . . and dental . . ." I did brush my teeth recently, didn't I?

He leans up to meet me halfway, and the connection between us is audible, like a seat belt clicking together. Like a key opening a lock. Like the first bite of a warm cinnamon roll with melted icing, his kiss is warm and sweet and tender. I can't help it, "Mmmmm" just slips out, and I feel his lips smile against mine. He moves his hand down my back and rolls us over so I'm on the bottom, and deep inside my stomach, there's an insatiable feeling that I could just stay right here kissing Rei until . . .

. . . the bottom of the world drops out.

Okay, I admit I screamed as I fell. One of those surprised little shrieks, and the word that popped out of Rei's mouth was definitely in English. Fortunately, it wasn't too far down to the ground.

"Sorry! Are you okay?"

I start to laugh because I landed on top of him, so of course I'm fine. "Yes. Are you?" I push up on my arms to look down at him, and he looks just as amused by our tumble. "What happened?"

"Gravity happened. I guess I didn't pay enough attention to where the edge of the hammock was. Hey," he says as he slowly tilts his head back and looks around, "what's up with the willow tree?"

I look around and sure enough, everything is perfectly still except the willow's branches, which are swaying like a gale force wind is blowing through.

"That's really strange," Rei observes.

"No, it's not. And that's not a weeping willow," I inform. "It's a peeping willow."

He laughs. I let the sun fill me up with its light until I feel it glow within me, then I run my fingers from Rei's temple down his cheek to his chin.

He feels the familiar tingle, and turns his head to kiss my fingertips.

"Do you know what's even better than a supernova?" I ask him.

"What's that?"

I lean down so our foreheads are touching, so when I talk my lips barely brush against his.

"This . . ."

ACKNOWLEDGMENTS

Infinite thanks to the two people who made publishing *Auracle* possible: My agent, Andrea Somberg from Harvey Klinger, Inc. for rescuing me from the slush pile, for patiently going above and beyond the call of duty, and for finding *Auracle* the perfect home. And my editor, Katherine Jacobs from Roaring Brook Press, for saying "*Yes!*" for loving my characters as much as I do, and for paving a smooth and joyful road to publication for me.

Thanks also to the entire team at Roaring Brook Press, especially to Sarah DeCapua and Jill Freshney for copyediting with such sharp eyes, Roberta Pressel for her special design work, and Mike Yuen for the gorgeous cover.

To my early readers—Dee Avery, Victoria Cetrone, Marissa Duckworth, Becca and Deborah Mathis, Jill Mulholland, Gale and Tatiana Taylor, Ariel, Cassie and Dorothy Weithman—to my critique group, the Nashua Area Children's Authors—and to the talented authors from the Class of 2k12 and the Apocalypsies debut author groups.

To Barb Aeschliman for my webpage, Marc Nozell for my photos, Sensei Verne for martial arts advice, Holly Robinson for that first boost of confidence, Joe Annutto for answering a desperate legal question (any errors are mine), and special thanks to Peggy Annutto for sharing her thoughts about the power of positive energy.

To Marcia McNulty, Wendy Thomas, Laura Denehy, Carol Figueroa, Diane Fitzgerald, Cindy Hann, Rosemarie Rung, Paula Super, my Broadway Bound friends and everyone who cheered *Auracle* on.

To my sister, Cathy Cabral, my brother, John Cetrone, Joe Turco, Jerry and Mary Rosati, Art, Linda, Brad and Scott Everly.

Endless love and gratitude to my husband, Jerry, and my children, Jerry and Laynie—you are my sunshine!

Special thanks to my Marys, especially my mom, Mary Hurley, who is smiling down.

And to you, wonderful readers. Writing is much more fun when I'm not just talking to myself.